EXTINCTION POINT: EXODUS

Also by PAUL ANTONY JONES:

Toward Yesterday
Extinction Point: Book One
Dangerous Places (short story compilation)

EXTINCTION POINT:
EXODUS

PAUL ANTONY JONES

47N⬥RTH

Published by 47North
PO Box 400818
Las Vegas, NV 89140

ISBN-13: 9781477805060
ISBN-10: 1477805060
Library of Congress Control Number: 2012956119

For Jeff Wayne and Herbert George Wells
Thank you for fueling the fire of my imagination

PROLOGUE

Commander Fiona Mulligan had made a habit out of watching the sunrise.

Of course, when you were on board a two-hundred-and-forty-foot-long hunk of metal, hurtling along at just over seventeen thousand miles per hour in a low orbit above the earth and completing almost sixteen revolutions of the earth a day, you got to see a lot of sunrises.

The longest most crew members of the International Space Station got to sleep at any one time was about six hours; couple that with the disorienting effect of waking surrounded by darkness after one period, then sunlight the next, and it could play havoc with your biological clock. Fiona had found a simple solution, though; whenever the opportunity presented itself, she would try to time the end of each sleep period to coincide with one of those sunrises.

Dawns aboard the ISS were a very different affair from those the billions of souls on the gleaming blue planet beneath her feet experienced. Most earthbound sunrises could be obscured by clouds and smog and cityscapes, obfuscating the simple wonder of watching the birth of a new day. By contrast, the little market town of Dorking, in the UK where she had grown up, had given her an exemplary view of the heavens and fueled her love of space when she was just a child. But even those misty mornings and ebony nights of her childhood paled by comparison to the godlike perspective afforded her and the ISS crew, so many miles above the earth. Up here, they were simply glorious.

Watching from the cupola of Tranquility (Node 3), a room-size cylinder jutting out from just below (or above, depending on the station's orientation at any given moment) the US laboratory Destiny, Fiona could see the lights of cities moving slowly by through the darkness beneath her. In the distance the faint glow of the rapidly approaching morning cut a laser-sharp crescent against the arch of the earth. Slowly, it expanded into a thin band of spectral blues and yellows and began to creep from the horizon across the curvature of the earth toward the station, revealing clouds floating above a blue sea and the far-off coastlines of islands and the undulating curve of the continent of Africa.

An aurora of surging light painted broad strokes of turquoise over the South Pole as the sun emerged, rising sideways like an ancient phoenix from the blackness of space. It pushed back the shadows enveloping her world, until finally the planet's home star appeared in all its glory, welcomed by the gentle whirring vibration of the station's solar panels as they gradually oriented themselves to collect its life-giving energy.

According to the station's telemetry system, they were currently over the South Atlantic Ocean, rapidly heading toward Namibia. They would pass across that massive continent that had given birth to humanity, skirting Europe, and then onward over central Russia.

She had seen many sunrises during her two-month stay on the station. Each one was different in its own way, depending on the orientation and position of the station over the surface of the earth.

Sunrise the day the world ended was different for another reason.

At first, Commander Mulligan thought the anomaly was some kind of optical illusion; a refraction of light off the low-lying clouds that blanketed most of the view below them, or maybe it was some kind of visual artifact of the aurora borealis that still flickered and played far to the north. But as she continued to focus on the unusual phenomenon stretching out far below, Fiona realized this was something else altogether, something quite extraordinary.

Trailing behind the rapidly advancing dawn was a scintillating ribbon of red that began as a barely distinguishable needle-thin line south of her position toward Indonesia and extended over the horizon toward Finland. As she followed the ribbon north, she could see it was gradually expanding in width. By the time it passed over the equator, it had grown to a thick band of crimson. Fiona estimated it was at least thirty miles wide at its broadest point, from leading edge to trailing edge. As it passed over the Tropic of Capricorn, she could see the crimson line begin to taper off again before it became nothing but a slight thread in the distance and then disappeared completely a few miles short of the Arctic Ocean.

She had immediately reported the strange event to mission control while relaying the station's incredible images back to the agency as the ISS swept over the phenomenon, continuing along its orbit.

No one seemed to have any idea what it was she was seeing. The ribbon of red appeared to be moving in an almost regimented progression across the globe. Scientists on the ground and in the ISS postulated that it might be some kind of freak weather event, or maybe the smoke from an unobserved undersea volcanic eruption. But if either of those theories were correct, then surely there would have been some kind of disruption to the consistency of the ribbon, just as a contrail of a high-altitude aircraft will slowly lose its coherence. It stood to reason that whatever this event was, over time it should begin to dissolve, pulled away by winds and disruptive weather patterns. But there was no loss of cohesion; its edges had remained sharply defined as it swept methodically onward across the globe.

And whatever this stuff was made of, it was sufficiently dense that it was impossible to see through to the sea beyond. She watched as it completely obscured a small black dot that was probably a supertanker plying its way between countries. The tanker disappeared as the red streamer passed over it before reappearing on the opposite side and continuing on its way to wherever it was bound. It seemed unharmed, and there was no sign that it had changed course or even seen the red band that it had passed directly beneath.

It was difficult to say just how high above the surface this strange red anomaly was, but judging by the ship's unaltered course, the captain either hadn't considered it a threat or hadn't had time to make any evasive maneuvers. Not that it would have helped; the ribbon seemed to be spread almost completely across the globe.

The observation port of the cupola of Tranquility had the best view of the ongoing event, but it was too cramped to comfortably fit any more than two observers at once. Each member of the crew joined the commander in turn to watch the slowly advancing ribbon and offer up his or her opinions and theories.

It was Ivan Krikalev, the team's resident flight surgeon as well as a highly competent engineer, who finally voiced what everyone else had been thinking. "Perhaps it is some kind of alien life-form," he whispered as he floated next to Fiona, watching through the observation port next to hers.

"What?" she said, not sure she had heard him correctly.

The implacable Russian slowly rotated to face her. "I said, perhaps it is alien in origin. The theory of panspermia is an accepted possibility of how life began on earth. Maybe what we are observing is an example of that theory in action. Who knows for certain? I have no other suggestions."

Fiona vaguely remembered watching a documentary on the Discovery Channel at some point that briefly covered the theory behind the unproven hypothesis. "Isn't that the idea that life on earth originally came from outer space?"

"You are basically correct," said Krikalev. "The theory is more complex than that, of course, but it has been around since the fifth century. It is all mainly conjecture, of course—life is transferred from planet to planet by microorganisms trapped in meteors or blown on the solar winds, just like pollen travels on the wind. There are many theories, but, in the end, it boils down to life being seeded throughout the galaxy. Perhaps we are quiet witnesses to one of those very events."

As the ISS sped onward and away from the rapidly receding thread of red bisecting the horizon like a giant bloody slash across the earth, Commander Mulligan found herself pondering Krikalev's theory, wondering what it would mean for the planet speeding by beneath them and the life that called it home if he was right.

■ ■ ■

Approximately eight hours later she received her answer.

The crew of the ISS had slowly begun to lose contact with its global tracking stations and mission control centers.

First to go was the ISS mission control center in Korolev, Russia, closely followed by Moscow. Then, as the deadly effects of the rain swept indefatigably across the continent, the center in Oberpfaffenhofen, Germany, went dark; the Space Research and Technology Center in the Netherlands went down not long after that. By the time the ISS lost contact with the European Space Agency Headquarters in Paris, the crew had managed to piece together as clear a picture of what was going on down on the ground as was possible given their limited access to experiential data.

The station's final contact had been with a radio operator from the Twenty-Second Space Operations Squadron based at the Kaena Point Satellite Tracking Station on the island of Oahu in Hawaii. The young operator had tried her best to sound calm as she relayed what little news she had about the events taking place worldwide.

The girl was from Colorado originally, she had told Fiona. Her family and husband still lived there, just outside Denver. She had lost contact with them hours earlier. The woman was trying to be brave as she kept the station updated with the little information that still crossed her desk, but Fiona had heard the fear gradually creep into her voice as the inevitable deadline approached the American military base. The operator had died midsentence; Fiona had heard her scream her daughter's name before the connection had broken.

It was in that instant, as the horrified crew listened to the dying woman, that Commander Mulligan and the crew of the ISS had come to the realization that what had been their home for the last four months had, in a single instant, almost certainly become their tomb.

Of course, the station had enough fuel to maintain its orbit pretty much indefinitely, but they would all be dead long before that was exhausted. They had enough provisions to last them for the next four months or more, and the onboard oxygen-generating systems might last for at least that long, and there were also several redundancy measures built into the station that would keep them alive long past the last meal.

But what then? There was no hope of rescue, only a slow painful death as they starved.

Her crew was a pragmatic bunch, made up of the best of the best and not given to snap judgments, but there had already been calm discussion of breaking out the little red boxes the European Space Agency had considerately provided them for just such an occasion. Each box contained three pills of a derivative of tetrodotoxin, a fast-acting neurotoxin that would leave them dead—painlessly, they had been assured—within minutes of swallowing one. They had all agreed to give it as long as possible before resorting to such extreme measures, but she knew no one on board held out much in the way of hope that rescue was even the slightest of possibilities.

They had spent the next few days taking shifts on the communication systems, working their way through the military and private bands in the hope that there might be someone out there still listening or transmitting. There had to be military and government installations still left untouched by the red rain, they reasoned. Whatever the event had been, it could not have been so viciously effective at its job that it could reach out and wipe out even the secret hardened command-and-control bases they all knew existed in their home countries.

Could it?

They had picked up some minor radio chatter, fleeting and ghostlike as it crackled across the airwaves, and for a moment hope had bloomed that their situation was not as terrible as it seemed. But the transmission was in no language they recognized. "My best guess is it's probably encrypted in some way, maybe military. Who knows? Without the key there is no way to decrypt it," Bryant, the team's communication expert, had explained.

As time rolled on, from the vantage point of the ISS, Commander Mulligan and her crew had an unprecedented view of the changes that had begun to unfold across the earth. With each revolution the station made, they noticed subtle changes to their planet, changes that appeared miniscule from the distance they were watching from but that must have been massive and rapid at ground level.

There had been nothing for the first day or two. The world kept revolving, storms moved across oceans, and, at night, cities still glowed as brightly as they always had done. If they had not known better, the crew would have thought they were a part of some elaborate practical joke that had just gone on for far too long.

Krikalev was the first to point it out, a slight red bloom in the air over Kirovograd in the Ukraine.

With each orbit, the astronauts could see new blotches of red, small and barely visible at first, mainly concentrated over the most densely occupied cities across the globe. The next time their orbit passed over that area, they could see those same pinpricks of red had blossomed and grown, spreading out like drops of red dye splashed into water. By day five after the event, the sky beneath the space station and the earth had become clouded with angry alien storms. Thick tendrils of swirling red reached out across continents, carried on trade winds across oceans, spreading out and blanketing the world in a gauzy web of red that grew ever thicker and more complex with each passing hour. Huge swirling hurricane-size storms had developed off the southeast coast of the United States and had begun to move inexorably toward the East Coast.

Fiona found herself transfixed by the inexorable spread of the creeping red across her planet. There was a pattern to it, she was sure, but she simply could not put her finger on what that pattern was. It was a futile exercise, anyway, she supposed. There was nothing any of them could do but watch as, day by day, the world was slowly suffocated beneath a veil of red death.

CHAPTER ONE

Emily Baxter had a craving. She wanted a burger...bad.

Not just any burger, either. In the four days since she had escaped from her apartment in Manhattan, she had passed by plenty of abandoned McDonald's, Burger Kings, and God knew how many other fast-food restaurants. Those were all easily ignorable.

No, what she had a hankering for was a Five Guys bacon cheeseburger with grilled mushrooms, onions, mayo, pickles, and tomatoes; hold the ketchup and mustard. She would add a large order of their fries—Cajun-style, of course—and an extra-large, ice-cold Coke. Emily felt her saliva glands begin to water at the thought of sinking her teeth into that juicy burger.

There had been a Five Guys franchise over on West Thirty-Fourth Street, just a ten-minute walk from the apartment she had left behind in Manhattan. She'd stop by there at least once a month when she had the urge to add an extra couple of inches of cholesterol to her arteries. She was already bored by her diet.

Canned beans. Canned soup. Canned fruit. Canned everything. A burger would be the only thing right now that would satisfy her desire for real, honest-to-goodness all-American junk food.

Of course, that wasn't going to ever happen, seeing as how the world had come to an abrupt, and total, end.

Maybe it was all the extra exercise she was getting? She had thought herself a pretty proficient cyclist before the red rain, but these past few days of constant pedaling had helped prove her wrong. Everything ached. She had no idea how Thor did it, poor thing. The malamute padded uncomplaining alongside her bike.

Only a few days had passed, but the event that had wiped all but a handful of humanity from the face of the earth already seemed distant and vague to her now. The red rain had fallen across the world, seemingly from nowhere. Within hours everyone and everything was dead...well, apart from her, Thor, and a bunch of scientists trapped in a research station in the Stockton Islands on the far north coast of Alaska. That was where she was heading. Alaska.

Guess there's something to be said for the end of the world, she thought. It had certainly done a world of good for her cardio health. The post-apocalypse diet: guaranteed to trim inches from your waistline, or you'll die trying. She could have made millions in book sales, if there had been anyone left to sell the book to.

Thor, an Alaskan malamute, had been Emily's only companion since he had rescued her from an attack by a trio of alien creatures in an equally alien forest just outside Valhalla. In their brief time together, she had often thought he must have received some sort of training, because he responded to many of her commands and was very protective.

"So, what do you say, mutt? You hungry?"

Thor looked up at his mistress and bounced his tail back and forth enthusiastically.

"Okay, then. Let's find somewhere we can eat." Emily slowed the bike to a crawl and began looking over the street in front of her. She quickly found the building she was looking for, pulling to a stop outside a small corner convenience store and dismounting. She could feel the burning ache in her calves as she wheeled the bike toward the sidewalk. The military-style backpack strapped to her back had grown lighter as she and Thor consumed the initial stockpile of food she had brought with her. Emily had to admit, losing the bulk of the weight had been a relief, but it was time to replenish her stock.

Pausing for a second, she scanned the street ahead of her; grayscale buildings lined both sides of the empty road. It was the same everywhere she had traveled since leaving Manhattan. No sign of any other living creature except for her and Thor. No birds, no dogs, no cats—not even an insect, as far as she could tell. And no people. She had no idea what that meant for the world, but she knew it couldn't possibly be good. What would be the effect of the total destruction of most, if not all, of the earth's indigenous species?

It was no mystery what had happened to life on this little blue planet. It had been annihilated by the red rain, consumed and then reconstituted into the weird alien life-forms she had encountered in the days after everything had died.

As she continued traveling north, Emily had seen more signs of the insidious encroachment of the red forests into the earth's environment. The second day into her ride, she had noticed small pockets of the towering trees similar to what she had encountered in Central Park scattered here and there along her route, usually near a water source like a lake or a river. She had seen a couple of small clusters of trees growing on sidewalks with their roots spiraling down inlets into sewers, but these had been much smaller, almost scaled-down versions of their bigger brothers. But by day two and three, she had begun to notice larger groups and far more frequently. To her mind, there was an almost exponential growth occurring, although she had seen nothing on the scale of the forest she had traveled through in Valhalla. Not yet, at least.

She had seen little of the spider-aliens other than the occasional distant sighting, but on day three she had found one, or at least the desiccated remains of one, hanging from an iron security fence outside a block of offices. Evidently it had impaled itself on the spikes when it had leaped from the building; she could see the telltale circular escape hole in a window three stories up. She was tempted to take a closer look, but Emily had begun to recognize that her reporter's nose was more likely to get her into trouble these days. She gave the thing a wide berth and continued on her way.

The only other survivor she had spoken to was Jacob Endersby. He was part of a team of scientists on the remote Stockton Islands, just off the northern shore of Alaska. She still wasn't convinced that Jacob's hypothesis—that the farther north she traveled, the colder it would get and the less of a foothold the invading alien life-forms would have—was right, because it sure as hell didn't seem to be having much of an effect so far. Truth be told, there was little in the way of temperature difference in the hundred or so miles she had already traveled; so maybe it was going to take a much more severe drop before there was any observable decrease.

Emily slipped the backpack from her shoulders. The wounds she had sustained during the attack by the alien creatures in the forest were healing nicely; her shoulder still ached and she felt the occasional spasm of pain if she moved her arm too quickly or spent too long riding her bike.

She knew she would have to find an alternative form of transportation soon. With winter closing in, and the temperature already starting to drop, finding a vehicle that would protect her from the elements was also going to have to be a major consideration in her plan of reaching the Stockton Islands. There were thousands of cars and trucks left at the side of the road or waiting in garages for owners who would never return.

Of course, that meant she would have to learn to drive.

She'd need something easy to handle but large enough that she could stash her bike, supplies, and, of course, Thor. It was also going to have to be robust enough to cope with the bad weather she was sure to hit when she crossed over into Canada. Roads were going to be closed once the winter weather set in, with no one to clear the inevitable snowfalls that would make them all but impassable. She would give it some serious consideration over the next couple of days, she decided.

The pain in her shoulder paled into inconsequence when compared to the soreness she had experienced in the first few days of eight-hour cycling sessions. She now knew the true meaning of the old cowboy phrase *saddle sore* because her butt chafed like nobody's business after long hours parked on the saddle of the bike. She learned quickly that she needed to make frequent rest stops or suffer the consequences, that and the liberal application of cream from a tube of Desitin she had picked up from an abandoned pharmacy to her more tender areas.

She had decided to follow the Hudson as far north as she could. Keeping the river to her left gave her a sense of security; it was one direction she didn't think she'd have to worry about an attack. Staying on the east side of the river also had the added advantage of keeping the half-mile stretch of water between her and what had been, up until only a week or so ago, some of the more populated areas of New York.

That first day, as she and Thor had stood on the hill and looked back at the village where she had spent the previous night slowly succumb to fire, Emily had worried her canine companion wouldn't be able to keep up with her. But as she rode along the deserted highways and side roads, she had quickly learned how wrong she was about that. Thor was more than capable of matching her pace. In fact, he could go far longer than she could between breaks; a result, she believed, of malamutes having originally been bred as sled dogs. She found herself having to limit herself to a maximum of thirty or so miles a day for herself rather than the dog. Emily guessed that Thor would be able to easily cover twice that distance, if she gave him his head.

Thor wasn't the problem, though. It had quickly become apparent to Emily that cycling the forty-five hundred miles to reach the Stockton Islands and the group waiting for her there was going to be a next to impossible undertaking. She was utterly exhausted by the end of each day. She had been lucky so far and not had any accidents, although she had come close on a couple of occasions. But she knew her luck wouldn't hold out forever, and the odds were stacked well and truly against her traveling that kind of distance and not hitting a pothole or letting her attention slip momentarily and ending up lying in some ditch with a broken arm, leg, or worse.

And then, of course, there were the alien creatures she had encountered. Who knew what strangeness was wandering around the world ahead of her? It was like living in some crazy zoo where she was the prey.

Emily glanced down at Thor sitting patiently at her feet, his ears alert, tongue lolling from his mouth as he panted gently in the warmth of the afternoon sun.

"Coming?" she asked the dog, but he seemed quite happy to stay where he was. "All right," she said after a second. "You guard our things. I'll be right back out." She picked up the almost empty backpack from where she had set it down and walked toward the store.

The door was unlocked. Surprisingly, the shelves looked untouched and almost fully stocked, unlike the majority of shops Emily had stopped at on her trip so far. The unmistakable chaos of panic buyers and thieves marked virtually every location she had tried to look for food.

Sunlight cut through the glass window and illuminated the two middle rows of shelves. The rest of the small room was shrouded in shadow. She paused for a moment, listening for any sound of movement that might indicate that she was not alone. Motes of dust floated gently through the shaft of light; just regular dust, not the weird semi-sentient stuff she had witnessed in Manhattan.

As she walked to the nearest aisle, she began running through a mental checklist of the items she would need. Soup and fruit, maybe some cans of meat if she could find it; it would still be good. She'd also need to grab a bag of dog food for Thor. He was running low.

A shadow to Emily's left shifted. She stopped midstep, her breath catching in her throat. Instinctively, she reached for the Mossberg shotgun she kept strapped around her shoulder, but it wasn't there.

"Damn it," she cursed under her breath as she took a step backward. She could have sworn that she had brought it in with her, but she must have left it with the bike.

Emily took another slow step backward and reached behind her as she searched for the exit she knew was just a few feet away. If she could just get to the door, she could alert Thor and make a run for—

The shadow separated from the darkness surrounding it and moved into the dim light.

It was a spider-alien. Its eight articulated scimitar-clawed legs clicked across the tiled floor of the store. As she watched, first another and then two more joined it from the shadows. One climbed over the nearest set of shelving, perching on the top boxes of instant potato, its two eyestalks swaying back and forth as it focused on her.

She took another step backward. As she did so, the leading spider matched her.

A glass jar of preserves smashed against the floor to her right, the sound like a thunderclap in that enclosed space. Emily yelped. Another creature was climbing over the nearest shelf. More of the freaks were emerging from the darkness, edging toward her across the floor.

She counted seven, then eight, then twelve. Her chest felt heavy as the air she had sucked into her lungs seemed to turn into a dense fog.

Emily could hear Thor barking ferociously from the other side of the door and the frantic scrape of his claws against the glass as he tried to get to her. But the door opened outward, so there was no way he was going to be able to reach her.

She took another step back, too afraid to take her eyes from the ruin of monsters advancing on her. It was some kind of a nest; she had stumbled into a rally point where these things collected and waited to move on to become a part of one of those huge alien trees, or who knew what else.

Her encounters in Manhattan, when one of the ugly bastards had fallen into her room and she had almost been run over by another in Central Park, had taught her that the things seemed mostly harmless, unwilling to attack her while they were gripped by whatever deep motivation drove them. But these were reacting differently; they seemed pissed, and by the way the eyestalks flicked and wavered like an agitated cat's tail, she was pretty sure they weren't in a mood to share their new-found home with her.

Emily kept moving back, one slow careful step at a time, until, finally, her hand closed around the door handle. Thor was still growling and whining his frustration and anger outside, his paws batting against the door so hard that she was afraid to open it; he might slip in and go straight for the nearest creature. She was sure he could easily dispatch one or two of them, but there were at least twenty stalking her now, and he would surely be overwhelmed if he tried to take them all on.

"Thor," she hissed, "be quiet, boy."

At the sound of her voice, the gathered creatures' serrated lower jaws jittered up and down so fast she could barely see them. They sounded like dry autumn leaves blown over pavement.

Thor's agitated scratching at the door stopped, and his barking dropped to a low growl.

She chanced a glance over her shoulder; Thor had stepped back a few paces and was now sitting, staring at her, his tail moving back and forth across the flagstone pavement in either agitation or anticipation. But she could not see any new threat behind him.

When she looked back, the creatures had advanced on her again—the walls and ceiling were covered with them, and every featureless black bulbous head and eyestalk was turned and focused squarely on her. As she watched, a barely noticeable ripple of movement flowed through the creatures.

One after another the creatures launched themselves at her.

Spinning around, she pulled the door toward her and slipped through the crack, pulling the door back into place behind her. Black bodies flung themselves against the glass, smacking against it before dropping to the floor. She clung to the handle, leaning back and pulling it against the jamb as wave upon wave of the creatures tried to get to her. The weight of the mass of flailing aliens kept the door closed.

As more and more of the creatures sank to the floor, they began to form a drift of twig-like flailing legs, writhing eyestalks, and chattering jaws that soon became indistinguishable as individual creatures.

At a mental count of three, she let the door handle go and stepped away. For a second she stood and stared at the monsters as they mindlessly tried to reach her.

"Fuck you!" she yelled eventually, then flipped them the bird, grabbed her bike, and hurtled away from the swarm.

CHAPTER TWO

The next afternoon Emily found herself in the rustic town of Stockport. It had taken her almost that long to shake off the encounter at the store. Thoughts of the creatures had even invaded her sleep when she had finally pulled over for the night.

Until she had stumbled into their lair, she hadn't seen any sign of the spider-aliens for days, and to come across so many of them concentrated in one location was a disconcerting new development in an already surreal week. The more she thought about it, the more it was as if they had been congregating in the store, like troops awaiting fresh orders. Maybe that was exactly what was happening; maybe they were waiting to be given new directions by whatever was orchestrating this strange overthrow of her world.

If that was true, then it would mean that there was some kind of intelligence behind the annihilation of life on earth. And that thought was even more frightening than the idea that she might stumble on more of the creatures.

It was just more strangeness for her to think about.

And she still didn't know why she had survived the red rain when it had first fallen. Or if there were other survivors. Once she made it to the islands, she would have to convince Jacob's group it should be their primary goal to locate and rescue as many survivors as they could. Quite how that particular feat was to be accomplished was another thing altogether.

All that day, Emily had been keeping her eye on a huge bank of billowing clouds close to the horizon. It looked as though it was still many miles away, but it was hard to get a clear view of it as she traveled along the narrow, tree-lined streets of Stockport. The storm clouds were preceded by an honor guard of red sky that swept from a coral pink behind her to a deep crimson where the sky mated with the storm. There was not an inch of blue left up there.

It was a breathtakingly beautiful sight.

The red sky had become a permanent fixture. Emily guessed it was a result of the dust she had seen the alien forests releasing into the air. It didn't take much of a stretch of her imagination to draw a disturbing conclusion: the red rain had killed off the indigenous species of the earth, humanity included, then used their bodies to create their own life-forms. Those in turn had created the alien forest and whatever those creatures were that had attacked her, and the trees were now spreading the red dust across the world. Whatever plant life the dust touched began the transformation process, as it was turned to the invaders' own needs. It would not be long, Emily estimated, before what little was left of earthborn life was totally subsumed and replaced.

And then there was whatever she had seen growing in the forest. Just thinking about the strange orbs hanging from the tree in the forest gave her the creeping heebie-jeebies. She had no idea why. There was just something about them that seemed...wrong. They were all smaller parts of a much larger, much more complicated conundrum, and she didn't have the first clue as to what it meant.

Rounding a corner, Emily came to an abrupt stop.

Thor stopped beside her, panting heavily as he looked up at her. Ahead, the road was blocked.

Stretching out into the distance before them was a river of vehicles of all descriptions. They filled both lanes, even overflowing onto the grass border on either side of the road, pushing up against tree trunks and fences. Most were crushed against its neighbor, bumper-to-bumper, but here and there she saw an SUV, compact, or truck that stood on its own. All the cars Emily looked into as she wheeled her bike between the snaking alleys of metal were empty, their doors either ajar or one of the telltale perfectly round holes testifying to the occupant's fate.

That, in and of itself, was disturbing enough, but the award for weirdest experience of the day definitely went to the three-quarter-finished alien tree sprouting up from the tarmacadam of the road, its roots burrowing deep into the blacktop. Beyond the first tree, several hundred feet or so farther along the road, Emily could see the outline of another, and, beyond that, another and another.

The occupants of the vehicles had not had to travel very far to complete their part of the alien agenda, it seemed.

Emily stood below the first tree, straining her neck to look up at the black trunk. Halfway up, fracturing the almost perfect symmetry of the shiny black surface, Emily could see the back end of a silver Buick jutting out at an odd angle. She walked around the base of the tree, climbing over the thick roots that had burrowed into the road's surface, uprooting concrete and tilting cars as though they were nothing. On the other side, farther up the tree, Emily saw another car—this time it was just the front headlight of some indistinguishable make—embedded in the trunk. Unconcerned by the sea of vehicles, their newly transformed owners had simply built straight through them.

It was, Emily had to admit, an amazing feat of bioengineering. In fact, the whole subjugation of planet Earth had been an astonishingly successful process, as much as she did not want to admit it, and it hinted at an intelligence so far ahead of humanity's that it was godlike in its brutal, ruthless efficiency.

Shading her eyes from the glare, Emily scanned the road. If she had been in a car, she would have had to turn around and find some secondary road that hopefully wasn't as choked. It was one advantage the bike had over a car; obstructions like this meant she only had to walk until she found a clear route through the mess. It wasn't much of an advantage, though, and again she wished she had taken driving lessons. A nice, safe BMW or Mercedes looked more and more attractive with every aching muscle that reminded her she still had a very, very long way to go.

Still, she consoled herself, a car was one thing. Solving how and where she would find gasoline for it was another thing altogether. She'd figure it all out when she could. The important thing right now was to get past this roadblock and continue on her way.

A concrete footpath ran parallel to the road, a line of trees separating it from the crush of vehicles. The path had not been resurfaced in years. It was a lot rougher to ride on than the blacktop. But, while uncomfortable for her long-suffering butt, it was better than pushing the bike through the lanes of empty cars.

Emily stumbled across the downed airliner two miles farther along the route.

It had come back to earth in the center of the town, smashing through houses and demolishing everything for several hundred feet. Burned-out shells of homes lay on either side of the deep furrow gouged out of the earth. The blackened skeletons of trees, unaffected by the original crash but destroyed, she assumed, by the subsequent fire, extended off in all directions and had helped spread the blaze away from the crash site. The pungent odor of jet fuel still lingered in the air, mixing with the smell of burned wood and...something else...something she couldn't quite put her finger on.

The debris field stretched for at least a mile; scattered wreck-age was strewn across the road and what was left of rooftops. In the street in front of Emily lay the cowling of one of the airliner's engines. The actual engine was nowhere to be seen, though. Not far from the disemboweled cowling, Emily saw the first body. At least, she assumed it was a body. She had heard the phrase *burned beyond recognition*, and, looking at the black lump of charcoal, she understood exactly what it meant.

"Thor. Sit and stay," she told the malamute, afraid he might step on some small piece of debris or broken glass while she approached the body. There was no way to distinguish whether it had been a man or a woman as the burns extended over every inch of it. The body was curled almost into a fetal position; the arms and hands looked like claws, twisted up to the blackened chest, the legs pulled almost up to the chin. White teeth gleamed incongruously from behind fleshless charcoal lips. The body smelled of overcooked meat, like a roast that had been left too long in the oven.

"Interesting," she said, surprising herself with how simple it was for the reporter within her to still so easily disengage from what should have been a horribly disturbing sight. She glanced up from the corpse; in the wreckage of a destroyed car—it was impossible to distinguish the make or model—another body sat on the frame and springs of what had once been the driver's seat. The body's skeletal hands gripped what was left of the steering wheel. Again, the corpse was unrecognizable, but, she noted, it was still there. It had not been consumed by the red dust.

Did that mean the red rain needed live flesh to consume and use to create the creatures so intent on changing her world? Emily could not say. Maybe it had been the fire that destroyed the red rain infection? It was impossible to discern, but it was certainly interesting. Whatever the reason, it was good to know that the rain could be stopped. It might be too late for most of the earth's inhabitants, but who knew what the future held? Especially when it was measured by the yardstick of the past ten days or so.

There was no way she was going to risk taking the bike or Thor through the crash site. So she reversed direction and headed back to the previous cross street, then rode at a right angle away from the debris field for a mile or so. When she was sure she was clear of the debris, Emily turned north again and began heading back toward her original destination, trying to ignore the smell of burned meat that still lingered in her nostrils.

But, rising up above the roofs and trees, the storm that had seemed so far away just a short while ago had gained on the two travelers. The huge anvil-shaped mass of cloud now seemed to tower over Emily, a wall of red jutting high into the stratosphere, threatening to collapse on them at any moment. It extended from the eastern horizon to the far west, consuming the sky like some ancient angry dragon.

There was an electricity in the air that set the tiny hairs on the back of her head alive. A sense of dread began to beat like a drum in the pit of Emily's stomach, a dull syncopated rhythm that twisted her belly into tight knots.

She looked down at Thor keeping pace with her. The fine fur of his coat was standing almost erect.

"Come on," she called out to the dog as her legs began pumping the bike's pedals.

■ ■ ■

They reached the town of Stuyvesant before the storm finally caught up with them.

A flash of livid white lightning, followed almost instantly by a horrendous crash of thunder, made Emily leap six inches off her saddle and sent Thor scurrying sideways as the blast exploded almost directly overhead.

"Shit!" she yelled as the first heavy drops of red-tinted rain— eerily reminiscent of the blood rain that had ended the world— began to fall, splattering loudly on the pavement.

She had badly misjudged the storm's approach, and now they were caught out in the open.

They needed to find cover, and they needed to find it right now.

To Emily's left was a field surrounded by a few trees that would be no use as cover, but off to her right, a gravel driveway wound up a steep hill. She could just make out the roof of a house on the opposite side of the hill.

"Come on," she called to Thor.

Emily raced up the gravel road toward the crest of the hill, her legs pumping hard at the pedals as Thor sprinted ahead of her, understanding exactly where they were heading and apparently just as eager to get to shelter.

As she reached the crest of the hill, the gravel road turned into a concrete parking area leading up to a three-car garage. On the side of the garage was a weatherworn door, its paint peeling from the surrounding frame, and Emily rode directly for it. She jumped from her bike and rattled the door handle: it was locked. Racing back around to the garage entrance, she tried each of the roll-up garage doors in turn. The second one complained and squeaked, but after a quick tug on the handle, it started to grate and rattle along its tracks until there was a large enough space for her to slip the bike through and duck under.

Inside, there was just enough daylight for Emily to make out the shadowy outline of a silver Dodge Durango SUV parked in one of the bays. The other two bays were empty. A workbench sat off to one side, and Peg-Boards filled with tools and boxes lined two of the walls. Whoever had lived here had been an incredibly organized neat freak.

A door led from the garage into the main part of the house. Emily leaned her bike against the workbench and tried it. It swung open easily, and Emily and Thor both stepped inside. Thor's nose instantly went to the ground as he disappeared along the hallway and into the main area of the house while Emily waited patiently in the corridor. This was a routine they'd automatically fallen into since they had found each other: Thor would quickly explore the house and then come back and let her know if the coast was clear. At least that was what she thought he was doing, as they hadn't come across anything threatening in any of the other homes they'd spent time in.

A set of car keys, presumably for the Durango in the garage, hung from a hook fastened to the corridor wall on the opposite side of the door.

Another huge crash of thunder pounded Emily's eardrums. She heard Thor give a frightened yelp somewhere farther into the house, then the patter of his claws on tile before he skidded into the corridor and sprinted to join her. "It's okay, baby. I'll protect you from the nasty thunder," she cooed to the frightened dog as she stroked him gently behind his ears.

She stripped off the backpack and leaned it against the door to keep it open, then backtracked to the metal roll-up garage door, pulling it shut behind her. There was a dead bolt halfway up the door, and she threw that into place just to be on the safe side. With the area secured to her satisfaction, she picked up her backpack and moved off down the corridor into the main house. Rather than racing ahead as he usually would, Thor stayed pinned to Emily's side, his ears flat against his head and his tail down almost between his legs.

Her hand found its way to the strap of the Mossberg, and she slipped the shotgun into her hands. It would be easy to blame Thor's uneasiness on the almost constant crash of the storm, but after her encounter at the store, she couldn't be sure it wasn't because he sensed something in the house.

Emily didn't think it was anything to worry about, just the storm that was frightening him rather than any sense of a threat within the house, but her hand found its way to the strap of the Mossberg slung across her shoulder anyway.

The corridor led from the garage into a tiled mudroom, which in turn opened into a kitchen adjacent to a dining area. She moved quickly from room to room, shotgun poised and ready as she swept each new area for any possible threat. The dining room was adjacent to a large living room. A large potbellied stove sat in one corner, its chimney pipe disappearing into the rafters. One wall of the living room was nothing but windows stretching up to dark wooden beams that crisscrossed the ceiling, a good eighteen feet above her head. A set of sliding glass doors led out onto a beautiful wooden balcony.

"Wow!" said Emily as she stared out at the view beyond the wall of windows, all thoughts she might not be alone forgotten.

The house she had broken into was perched on the opposite side of the hill she had just ridden up. She was on the top floor and, as she looked down, she could see the second and third stories of the house below her, each one following the natural line and declination of the hill as it swept down into a valley filled with trees, several hundred feet below. She thought she saw the glint of a pond or a stream from within the green of the woods, but she couldn't be sure.

The view was breathtaking.

The hill the house was built on extended off to the east and west before curving north to form a horseshoe-shaped valley. Across the gap between her side of the valley—about a quarter mile or so, she approximated—Emily could see two more homes nestled in the trees. The larger of the two buildings was at almost the same height as this one, but the second, smaller one was close to the floor of the valley.

On either side of the valley, Emily could see the angry clouds of the storm eating away at the remaining sky as it moved quickly toward the opposite horizon. And yet, oddly, the sky above her little valley remained curiously clear. She could see the occasional flash of lightning deep within the clouds, and the area beyond the hill was obscured by a pinkish curtain of rain, yet on this side of the valley not a drop seemed to be falling.

"Weird," she whispered.

But then, what wasn't these days?

Another crack of thunder broke Emily from her reverie, and she suddenly realized just how deathly quiet it was in the house. Surely she should have heard the hammer of the rain on the slate roof of the house; there was no attic space above her head, after all, just the rough beams running through the open space where it would have been. She was sure the storm had been just seconds behind her when she had crested the hill. She glanced back out through the windows. The sky was overcast, but there was still no sign of the storm over the valley, and the trees remained as still as stone giants.

The sky outside her window lit up momentarily, but Emily could not see the lightning bolt. She did, however, hear the thunder that rolled in a second later; the pressure wave rattled the glass in the windows and sent poor Thor to his belly as he tried to wrap himself even tighter around her legs.

This dog was a tangle of contradictions, she was quickly learning. Here was this incredibly valiant animal that had pulled her, quite literally, from the jaws of death reduced to a quivering puppy as the thunderstorm raged on the far side of the house.

"Well, I guess we know what your Kryptonite is now, don't we, Superdog?" Thor apparently didn't see the funny side as he whined and continued to push himself against her legs.

"Come on. We might as well make the most of it. Let's eat."

■ ■ ■

Each evening since leaving Manhattan, Emily had placed a call to Jacob using the satellite phone she had picked up from the offices of the newspaper where she had worked. Ostensibly it was a nightly routine that Jacob insisted on so he knew she was safe, but Emily thought it was equal part Jacob's way of helping ensure she remained connected to reality. It would be so very easy to lose sight of her goals out here, alone except for Thor and Jacob's distant, but always welcome, voice.

The hiss of static filled her ear as she waited for him to pick up her call. The past few days had seen a slow degeneration of the quality of each call she made. Whether that was down to technical problems with the now unmonitored satellite or the red storm's interference, she could not say. It was worrisome either way.

"Hello, Emily." Jacob's voice sounded distant as it ebbed in and out.

Emily quickly filled him in on her day and the disconcertingly violent storm that had forced her to hole up for the night. "What's weird, though, is that the storm didn't seem to touch this valley," she explained.

Usually Jacob would find her revelation too fascinating to resist and offer some kind of a theory. So, when he didn't offer up his usual attempt at an explanation for the weather phenomenon, Emily asked him if everything was okay.

He paused for a second before answering. "No. Things here have been getting a little…strained," he admitted. "The shock of what happened has worn off, and we're beginning to feel the pressure. I…we all left wives and families behind, and I think I held out a little hope that maybe there would be more survivors. Knowing that they are all dead, well, let's just say it's taking its toll."

It would have been easy for Emily to offer up some kind of false hope to Jacob, but that would have been all it was. Instead, she simply said, "I'm sorry."

"Not your fault, Em," he replied. "I can handle it. After all, we are all the family we have left now."

"So, I'm thinking about trying my hand at a little grand theft auto," she said, changing the subject.

"What?"

"I'm thinking of stealing a car." She laughed. "Of course, I'm going to have to learn to drive it first."

"That's a great idea," Jacob replied, his voice becoming all but inaudible above a sudden whoosh of static. "Make sure you choose something simple and automatic. It needs to be automatic."

"It scares the living crap out of me, to be honest, but it's going to take forever by bike, and I'll probably freeze to death before I make it even halfway to you. And after my little encounter yesterday, I think I'll feel safer with four wheels beneath me rather than two."

"I have every confidence in your ability, Em. Just make sure you find some kind of open area to practice in before you hit the open road, okay?"

She promised she would take her time.

By the end of the conversation, Jacob's mood had improved.

"Ride carefully," he reiterated. "I need you here in one piece."

Emily felt a cloud descend over her after she hung up. She had not given that much thought to Jacob's plan. What would it be like to be stuck up there in that unforgiving land of perpetual winter? In fact, had either of them really thought through this plan of theirs? Were they supposed to spend the rest of their lives sequestered away in that research station?

The more Emily thought about it, the more she wondered if it was such a great idea to pin all her hopes on reaching the Stocktons. At some point she was going to have to talk with Jacob about his plan for what would happen once she got there.

But that was something she would deal with on another day.

The windows lining the far wall of the living room showed nothing but darkness now. Night had arrived as she'd talked to Jacob on the phone.

Emily caught a glimpse of her reflection in the mirrorlike surface of the glass. She stood and walked over to the windows to take a better look. Her clothes were not too bad, a little sweat stained and a bit grubby, but it was her hair and lack of makeup that really hit home. She had bags under her eyes and her blonde hair was scraggly and knotted. Half-healed scratches from her flight and fight through the forest stood out starkly against her pale skin.

"You look like shit," she told her mirror image. She surely could not deny it.

CHAPTER THREE

The storm had quieted at some point during the night, but red clouds still lurked ominously in the sky the next morning.

Emily heated a pot of water on her portable gas stove and sipped from a mug of steaming coffee as she wandered from floor to floor, room to room of the house, checking for anything that might be of use. In the master bedroom, on the large wooden mantelpiece above the fireplace, she found a framed photo of a couple, the home's owners she presumed, smiling broadly out at her from the confines of a gold frame. She guessed they were both in their midfifties; she a pretty brunette with faint signs of crow's-feet creeping in around her eyes, he with salt-and-pepper hair and a day's worth of stubble across his lower jaw. Behind them was an ocean, deep blue and stretching off to the distant horizon. They both looked so happy. Even now, there was a sense of peace in the air, as if the owners had simply stepped out for a minute. She half expected to open a door and find someone sitting on a bed crocheting.

On the ground floor, she found a set of wooden steps that led from the bottom level of the house most of the way down to the flat valley floor below. The final hundred feet or so was a well-walked path of bare earth that wound its way through an open patch of grass and then into a copse of ash trees. Emily could see no signs of any footprints in the soil of the path, but here and there was some obvious new plant growth, blades of grass pushing up through the earth. Life was quickly reclaiming the path now that there were no humans to trample the young shoots.

Thor was intent on following scent trails, tail wagging as he moved in and out of the trees and then dodged back to follow another. Occasionally, he stopped and lifted his leg against the trunk of a tree or a bush and marked his territory.

The path continued into the trees for several hundred feet, winding left and right, occasionally forking off from the main route. Emily stuck with the original path. She was sure the sparkle of water she had seen when she'd arrived had been more toward the center of the woods, and this path seemed to be heading in that direction.

A few minutes later, she heard the unmistakable sound of sloshing water, and, as she rounded a bend obscured by a growth of thick black cohosh atop an embankment, Emily saw the pond. It was fed by a stream that ran down from the opposite side of the valley, its source unknown as it disappeared between the trees. At the sight of the water, Thor gave a joyful, deep bark and took off in its direction. Launching himself from the embankment, he landed with a splash that sent a wave of water high into the air.

A flurry of shapes exploded into the air amid a panicked flapping of wings and quacking. It was ducks, four of them; they launched themselves into the air and took off flapping toward a clump of tall reeds at the opposite end of the pond, their wings clipping the surface of the water. Thor made a halfhearted attempt at grabbing them, missed, and continued to paddle his way around the pond unmoved by the astonishing sight.

"Ducks!" Emily shouted. "Fucking ducks."

Apart from Thor, these were the first earth animals Emily had seen since disaster struck. How had they survived? Were they immune like her and Thor? Emily followed the dog down to the pond's bank. Thor, who had paddled out to the center of the pond, now turned back, making a beeline for her.

"Oh no you don't," yelped Emily. She could see the mischievous glint in the dog's eyes as he headed back to her. She immediately started backpedaling away from the pond's edge, but she wasn't quick enough. Thor pulled himself out of the water, ran the last few feet to her side and immediately began shaking himself dry, sending a huge shower of water over Emily.

"Oh! Oh! Oh!" was all she could manage as the freezing water covered her. "Damn dog. You did that on purpose, didn't you?" Thor answered with another shake that sent more water her way. Dear God, it was cold. So much for the idea of taking a dip. She'd freeze to death before the water got as far as her knees.

"I swear, Thor. If you weren't the world's last remaining dog, I'd trade you in." The threat didn't seem to cause Thor much concern as he gave a final shake.

Emily brushed as much of the water as she could from herself and looked around. She could see there were several well-walked paths that snaked deeper into the trees. Well, with the early morning bath off the itinerary, she might as well take a look at the other homes she'd seen.

She took a second to orient herself, called to Thor, who had disappeared into a large bush, and headed down the path leading in the direction of where she thought the houses should be.

The earthen path led deeper into the woods. When Emily came to the next fork, she took the one leading up the hill. She couldn't see the houses through the trees, but, judging by the gradual incline, she was heading in the right direction at least. The path branched off again a few hundred feet farther along, and, sure enough, Emily spotted the first of the two houses in the distance.

It was the smallest of the three in the valley: single story, with two bedrooms, a living area, and a bare-bones kitchen, more like an apartment than a permanent residence. Emily wondered, given the lack of any kind of road or garage for a vehicle, whether it might be a guesthouse for the other home higher up on the ridge.

Other than a few pieces of crockery, the cupboards were empty. A small refrigerator sat against one wall in the kitchen. Emily had pretty quickly learned that opening up the refrigerators she inevitably found in the homes she spent the night in was a bad idea. The food was often spoiled and stank to high heaven after more than a week of no electricity. Delving around in decomposing lettuce and rancid milk looking for something edible was usually not worth the effort or the assault on her nostrils. She pulled the door on the minifridge anyway; there was nothing but a couple of ice-cube trays inside. Emily was about to check the bedrooms when Thor started barking outside.

It wasn't an aggressive bark, but something had definitely gotten his attention. Maybe the ducks had followed them up the path? She made her way back to the front door and looked out. Thor was standing on the path facing up the hill; his tail was wagging frantically, and he kept stealing glances back at Emily before snapping his head back to whatever had piqued his interest.

"What is wrong with you?" she called as she stepped outside. "There aren't any—"

Emily stopped midsentence. Standing just a few yards away, frozen to the spot by Thor's barking, was a terrified young girl.

CHAPTER FOUR

The kid didn't stay frozen long—and she could move. Ten, maybe eleven. Tall for her age, wide blue eyes, skinny, in cutoff blue jeans that terminated in tattered threads just above her scuffed knees, muddy sneakers, and a blouse. Her eyes flicked between Thor and Emily as if she was trying to decide which of them to be more afraid of.

"No! Wait!" Emily yelled.

But she was already outpacing Emily, dodging between the trees and leaping over rocks and outcrops. She obviously knew the area like the back of her hand. If not for Thor, the kid would have lost Emily in the first thirty seconds. As it was, she could barely keep Thor in sight as he loped after the girl.

The roof of the third house appeared above a thick hedge just as the path leveled off and switched from dirt to a concrete slab driveway. Emily was just in time to see the girl, long blonde hair streaming out behind her, dart around the corner of the house. Thor followed her a few seconds later.

"Goddamn it, Thor," Emily yelled between panting breaths. "Stop, you're scaring her."

Emily sprinted the remaining fifty feet to the same corner, working out how she was going to approach the kid to convince her she wasn't a threat. As she rounded the corner of the house, Emily almost tripped over Thor, his body rigid, his ears down, and his teeth bared in a low growl as he stared at the doorway.

Emily looked up from her dog. Standing in the open entrance was the little girl; next to her was a man with a pistol aimed directly at Thor's head.

"Stop!" Emily screamed.

Thor raised himself from his crouch and let out a low growl. The man pulled the girl closer to him and his finger began to tighten on the trigger.

"No," Emily yelled. "He won't hurt you…Thor! Come here. Come on, come here." The dog didn't budge, so Emily took a tentative step closer to him, her hands raised to shoulder height, palms out. "We aren't here to hurt anybody." She spoke as softly as she could, fighting the urge to yell at the man that if he didn't point the pistol away from her dog she was going to take it from him and shove it so far up—

"Who are you?" the man said, nervously waving the gun. The words were directed at Emily, but his eyes never left Thor. "Where the hell did you come from?" Emily noticed the girl glance quickly up at the man, a look of fear in her eyes.

"Dad…" she whimpered.

Okay, okay. So now she knew what she was dealing with: a father frightened for his daughter and his own safety. She could understand that. Just have to keep them—and Thor—calm, she thought.

The girl's father glanced down at his daughter. "It's all okay, kiddo," he said reassuringly, squeezing his daughter's shoulder.

Then his focus snapped back to Emily and Thor. "I won't ask again. Who are you?"

"My name is Emily Baxter. This is my dog, Thor. We aren't here to hurt you. I didn't know anybody was alive here," she explained, then added, "I didn't know anybody was alive anywhere."

When he next spoke, Emily thought the man's demeanor might have softened a little. "Are you with an agency?" he asked, the edge of panic almost gone from his voice, replaced now with a tone of inquisitiveness.

"I'm sorry? Agency?" Emily was confused, but she took advantage of the moment to edge a little closer toward Thor. The malamute was still crouched low, but at least he had stopped growling.

"You're with the government, right? Part of a rescue team. So, which agency are you with?"

Before Emily could say anything further, something exploded from the shadows of the doorway behind the father and daughter and headed straight for the dog.

Emily wasn't sure who was more surprised: the man, herself, or Thor, who now sat bolt upright as the little shape covered the ground in small stumbling steps.

It was a little boy, no more than four or five, and he was running as fast as his legs could carry him straight at Thor, a smile of absolute delight plastered across his face.

"Doggy!" the little boy yelled as he barely avoided colliding with the dog. He threw his arms around Thor's neck and declared again in a singsong voice, "Doggy!"

"Ben!" the man yelled, the pistol dropping to his side as panic gripped his throat. He was either too stunned to react or he was still concerned about protecting his daughter because he gave a single tentative step forward, glanced down at the girl who still clung to his waist, and froze in place, half-in, half-out of the doorway to the house.

Emily took advantage of the man's hesitancy and covered the remaining distance between herself and Thor in two quick steps. She saw the man's eyes go wide as she stood next to his boy and placed a reassuring hand gently on the top of the kid's head. They went wider still when he saw the shotgun slung over her shoulder.

The child—Ben, she reminded herself—didn't seem the least bit interested in her; he had his arms locked around Thor's neck, his face buried deep into his ruff, whispering "doggy" over and over into the malamute's ear.

Emily raised her hands again, trying to look as unthreatening as possible. "Look, I didn't know anyone was here. You're the first people I've seen since leaving Manhattan, and I swear to you we are absolutely no danger to you or your family. I promise."

"Is there anyone else with you?" the man asked.

"No," she answered. "Just me and Thor. And, as you can see, neither of us is a threat to you." The pistol, Emily noticed, stayed at the man's side as he spoke, and she thought she saw a slight relaxing of his posture. Even Thor seemed to have relaxed. He was busy licking the boy's face, which elicited a mass of giggles from the kid.

Emily could see the stranger's mind working through the situation. He looked to each of his children and then to her. Finally his eyes settled back on the little boy, who was still giggling joyfully as Thor continued to wash him.

He slipped the pistol into his waistband and stepped toward Emily, holding out a hand. Thor stopped slobbering over the child, his eyes tracking the stranger as he approached Emily but making no move.

"My name's Simon," he said as Emily took the proffered hand and shook it. "That's my daughter, Rhiannon, and your dog's new-found best friend is Benjamin."

"I'm Emily. This is Thor," she replied with a sigh of relief.

"Pleased to meet you both, and I'm sorry for the reception. It's just that we haven't seen anyone for more than a week now. I saw your dog chasing Rhia and just panicked. We're just glad this nightmare is finally over. We were wondering how long it would be before emergency services got to the area."

"Emergency services? I'm sorry—you think I'm with the government?"

Simon nodded. "Of course. I mean, I know things must be bad out there, what with the terrorist attack and all, but we knew it was only going to be a matter of time before someone found us. That's why we've stayed put." He turned sideways and gestured down the corridor to the interior of the house. "Come on in and make yourself at home. Can I get you something to drink? Coffee? Tea? Something stronger?"

"I...I'm..." Emily was a hairbreadth away from telling him that she wasn't part of any rescue party and that there was zero chance of one ever showing up, but she held the words back when she looked at Rhiannon's face. The kid was obviously as relieved as her father. Now was not the time to break the news that they were the only survivors she had encountered since leaving Manhattan. That could wait until she and Simon were alone. He would be better equipped to break the news to his kids, rather than having them hear it blurted out from a stranger.

"I'll take a cup of coffee," she said instead, stepping past the man and into his home.

■ ■ ■

Emily waited in the entryway for Simon and the children to join her.

He looked to be somewhere in his late thirties, dark-brown hair, athletic build, dressed casually in jeans and a polo shirt. All sense of threat had gone from him now, and Emily wondered whether he would really have been able to use the pistol on either Thor or her.

The children stayed close to their dad. She couldn't blame them, of course. She was a complete stranger who had just chased the girl through the woods with what must have appeared, at least to anyone who didn't know him, to be a bloodthirsty hound.

"Come on in." Simon gestured for her to follow him as he closed the front door behind him and made his way down the entrance corridor.

In the confines of the narrow corridor, Emily became acutely aware of just how bad she smelled. Sweat, dirt, and an underlying aroma of lemon baby wipes. Social anxiety was not something she'd thought she'd ever have to worry about again.

She was amazed at just how incredibly clean and tidy the house was. How very normal it all seemed. From somewhere deeper in the house, Emily could hear the sound of music playing, and it took her a few seconds to realize what that potentially meant.

"You have power here?" she asked.

"Yup," said Simon as he led her into the kitchen area. "Totally self-sufficient. We have a backup generator that we use to power the house, and we're on our own well and septic system."

"You have running water?" she asked, amazed.

Simon looked at her, his face betraying his puzzlement. "Suuuurre. Running water. Hot water, too. We've got a propane tank outside, but I've tried not to use it too much because we only have enough propane for six weeks, a bit longer if we really ration it. I hoped help would arrive before it ran out."

She tried not to allow her astonishment to show.

"We were about to grab some lunch. Would you like to join us?"

"I'd love to," Emily answered with a smile. "But do you think I could freshen up first? I've been on the road for a few days."

"Of course. Of course. Rhia. Why don't you show Emily where the guest bedroom is?"

Thor was still happily engaged with Benjamin. The dog seemed to have settled in quite happily to being the center of the little boy's attention; he was lying on his side in front of a large potted fern while the boy playfully rubbed his tummy and head. The kid hadn't even made eye contact with Emily since they'd arrived; he was totally besotted with the dog. Kids! How very simple life was for them.

"You're very smelly," said the little girl, wrinkling her nose as she took Emily's hand and started to lead her from the living room toward a staircase at the back of the house.

"Jeez, Rhiannon," sighed her father. "At least try to be polite, would you, darling?"

"But she is," insisted the little girl.

"I'm sorry, Emily," Simon apologized. "My daughter is a little forthright."

Emily smiled and gave a polite laugh. "It's okay. She's right, I'm sure. I've been on the road for days." She knew she smelled worse than month-old milk.

"Come on," said Rhiannon, apparently unmoved by her father's embarrassment. "The guest room's this way."

■ ■ ■

Emily was pretty much convinced that she had died and gone to heaven. Either that or she was going to wake up on some strange couch again, extremely disappointed.

That was the only explanation for just how good she felt as the hot water of the shower beat against her skin, washing away the accumulated grunge and dirt of her exodus.

Emily pushed the many questions fighting for her attention about how this little oasis had survived the red rain from her mind, luxuriating instead in the delightful feeling of warmth that enveloped her. Within a few minutes, she felt the pain and fear slough away from her as she soaked in the wonder of simply still existing.

When she was done, she toweled herself dry and dressed in the fresh blouse and jeans she had set on the bed. The blouse was wrinkled from her hurried packing, but she didn't think her hosts would mind too much.

Emily realized her mouth was watering even before the smell of roasting meat wafting in under the door registered in her mind. Fastening the last few buttons on her blouse, she slipped her feet into her shoes and headed in the direction of the glorious scent.

■ ■ ■

"Better?" asked Simon as Emily walked into the kitchen.

"Much. Thank you," Emily replied. And she really did mean it. But it wasn't just the shower and the smell of hot food that had lifted her spirits. It was being around people again. She hadn't realized how lonely she had become these past few days.

Thor padded over to Emily, his tail wagging enthusiastically but dipped a little as if he realized he had abandoned his mistress to the first person willing to show him any attention.

The two kids, Ben and Rhia, were sitting around a table set for four in the breakfast nook just off the kitchen. Rhiannon looked up and smiled at her, but the little boy kept his eyes fixed on the plate in front of him, his hands clasped around a knife and fork in readiness.

"You're not a vegetarian, I hope?" Simon glanced over his shoulder at her as he reached into the top compartment of a double oven and slid out a tray with a steaming roast. The smell was just overwhelmingly delicious, and Emily knew that even if she had been a vegetarian, the aroma of that cut of meat would have convinced her of the delights of being a carnivore, without a doubt.

Simon sliced the roast with practiced aplomb, then pulled a second dish from the bottom oven.

"Fresh from the garden," he said, nodding to the roasted potatoes, carrots, and onions.

"You seem very self-sufficient?"

"The nearest supermarket is about ten miles away, so I like to keep a decent stock of food. You know…just in case," Simon explained as he spooned the food onto each plate. "The vegetable garden's a pet project of ours. It was something we started after my wife died. The kids and I like to work out there. Don't we, kids?"

Both Ben and Rhiannon nodded, their mouths already full.

If the shower had been heaven, the taste of roasted beef and potatoes was nirvana.

Emily said nothing about the death of his wife; the statement had been made so offhandedly that she assumed it must have happened well before the red rain appeared. Emily wasn't sure how much Simon would want to discuss about the red plague that had swept across the world in front of the kids, so she kept the conversation light.

"So, how long have you lived here?" she asked.

"All my life," said Ben, which brought a burst of laughter from both adults.

"Almost fifteen years now," Simon said, playfully mussing his son's hair. "Elise, my wife, and I moved in right before we were married. I'm an architect, so this was the perfect location for me. Close enough to the city that I could get in when I needed to." He paused to chew and swallow a piece of meat before continuing. "We lost Elise just over two years ago, and I decided I'd spend as much time with the kids as possible, so I left the firm I worked for and went freelance. It gave me the time I needed with the children."

"I'm sorry about your wife."

"It was cancer," said Rhiannon, her head bowed. "Pancreatic cancer."

"Cancer sucks the big one," whispered Ben to a lone carrot skewered on his fork.

"Yes. Yes, it does," replied his father.

■ ■ ■

After lunch, Simon insisted Emily sit at the table until he and the kids had finished washing the dirty dishes and stacking them on a plastic draining board next to the sink.

"It's a family ritual," he explained. "Besides, you're our guest."

With the chores out of the way, Simon joined Emily back at the breakfast nook table.

"Rhia. Why don't you take Ben outside and play for a little while?" The little girl looked as if she was going to object, but she resigned herself with a deep sigh and shrug of her shoulders. As the kids pushed away from the table, Thor jumped to his feet and padded alongside them before stopping and looking back toward Emily.

"Go ahead," said Emily with a nod toward the children. "If that's okay?" she added, looking at Simon.

"Well he doesn't seem like the killer I first thought he was, so why not? Just don't get him too excited, kids. Okay?"

Both children promised they wouldn't, then rushed out the door, Thor leaping alongside them. Within a couple of minutes, the two adults could hear the joyful screams of the kids accompanying the playful barks of the malamute.

"I know it's a little early, but can I get you a drink?" Simon's voice had lost the playful tone it had assumed around the kids.

Emily shook her head. As much as she would like to, alcohol would go straight to her head, and she wanted to keep her wits about her. Simon poured himself a shot of whiskey and sat back down at the table, sipping at it occasionally as they began to talk.

"The day the red rain fell, we were all here at the house. The kids were off school for the day. I don't even want to think what I would have done if…well, best not to think about how blind luck could save your life, the life of your kids. I like to think keeping them alive was chance's way of making up for taking their mom. Stupid really, don't you think?"

Emily smiled gently and allowed him to continue.

"Have you ever heard of a microclimate?"

She shook her head.

Simon leaned forward in the chair, illustrating his words with his hands. "It's a localized weather effect. The weather in a microclimate area can be absolutely opposite from that surrounding it. So, it could be raining where you are and, just a few feet away, completely dry. Amazing, really, when you think about it." He took another sip of his drink. "This whole valley is in a microclimate zone, something to do with the trees and the lake at the base. Last winter it snowed, we got nothing here. Dry as a bone."

"Actually, I think I saw it in action yesterday," Emily said. "I only stopped at the house across the valley because it had begun to rain, but it seemed to stop almost right at the driveway of the house."

"It rained yesterday? Well, that's a perfect example. I never even noticed. The day the red rain came, it was much the same. We saw it on the news after it had happened, and by the time I went outside to check, there wasn't any sign of it except for a few puddles down the hill toward town. Then of course I saw what happened on TV..." His voice trailed off. "I think I saw a couple of bodies on the street the first day. It was hard to be sure, though, and I didn't want to risk going down to look. Then of course there were dead birds almost everywhere. The next day, they were gone. I made sure we all stayed inside for a couple of days, just in case, but there seemed little reason to keep them in after that. I called everyone I knew, everyone in town. I even called the Pentagon. There was no answer from anyone."

He leaned forward in his chair and looked her straight in the eyes. "I was beginning to think we were the only ones left. Again, I'm sorry for the reception I gave you. It was just such a shock to see the dog...then you."

"How about Ben and Rhiannon? How did they take it?"

"I've done my best to keep the truth from my kids," Simon said. "Ben is too young to really notice, but Rhiannon, she's old enough to know that something very serious has happened. But I've managed to keep them both distracted." He took another sip from his whiskey, and Emily realized that he was steeling himself for the answer to the question he was about to ask. "So, why don't you tell me what's going on out there?"

Emily recounted her story: how the rain had come from nowhere; the dead birds falling from the sky; the mass panic; and, finally, how everyone in New York, and probably around the world, had died.

Simon sat in shocked silence for a while. Then: "Everyone? They're all dead?"

"As far as I know, yes. But there's a group of survivors, scientists, in the Stockton Islands in Alaska. That's where I'm heading. They think the cold has some kind of effect on the rain, which is why they survived." Emily went on to explain how she had been contacted by Jacob and why she was traveling north.

It was only when she began to explain how she had witnessed the dead transformed into the spider-aliens and how they had in turn created the strange forests of alien trees that she felt Simon pull back. He was still nodding attentively, but his energy had turned from sympathetic to politely cautious.

"Look," she said. "I know it sounds insane, and I know that you probably think that I am crazy, but I'm not. You must have noticed the way the weather is changing? I mean, it's almost permanently red out there now. I think the dust I saw being released from the trees is spreading and changing everything that it touches. You didn't see the rainstorm yesterday, but if you had, you would have seen how red it was. That's how it's spreading. And it's not just humans that it's changing—there are new animals out there, too...look."

She stood and unbuttoned the first three buttons of her blouse. Simon's eyes went wide, and he glanced away.

"You can look now," she said as she slipped the blouse off her shoulder and turned to show Simon the still-healing wounds on her back.

"Jesus! How did that happen?"

She explained how she had been attacked by the creatures in the forest, how she had nearly died and would have if it had not been for Thor showing up and saving her butt. "I know it's hard to comprehend," she said as she buttoned her blouse back up, "that this is some kind of alien attack, but I've seen them and they're real. And it's spreading…fast."

"But I thought…I thought it was a terrorist attack. You're telling me there's nobody left out there?"

She shook her head. "Apart from the group in the Stocktons, no, none that have made contact with us. But look at it this way—they survived, I survived, and you and your children survived. The probability is that there are others out there, too."

Simon slumped back in the chair and gave her a long appraising stare, then he finished what was left of his whiskey in one swig, refilled his glass, and downed that in one go, too.

"Are you insane?" he whispered eventually. It was a question asked by a man who Emily thought was doing his best to understand what was surely the most ridiculously crazy story he had ever heard. She stood up and walked to where he was standing, staring blankly into the kitchen.

"No," she said. "I'm not crazy."

"You have to understand," he said in the same soft whisper. "It's all a little too much to take in…in one go. But what am I going to do about the kids?"

CHAPTER FIVE

Later, after Simon had settled the children into their beds for the night, he joined Emily in the living room.

"I hope you don't mind, I helped myself," she said, raising a quarter-full glass of brandy. Simon nodded, picked up a glass, and poured himself a double before sitting down in the chair across from Emily.

"So," he said after taking a sip, "what do you think our options are?"

Emily considered the question, sipping from her brandy. "I don't think we have any options other than to get out as fast as we possibly can."

Simon seemed unconvinced. "You have to see this from my perspective, Emily. My kids and I are safe here. We have enough provisions to last us for a couple of months. That should be more than enough time for any federal rescue to reach us and"—he paused choosing his next words carefully—"I don't know you. Until today, I'd never even met you. You show up out of nowhere with some crazy story about people turning into alien monsters and constructing giant trees that are churning out this red dust." He paused as he let the words sink in, more for himself than her benefit, Emily thought. "And now you're asking me to leave the one place that has kept us safe and follow you to Alaska. I mean, come on, if you were in my position, taking care of two kids, I'm sure you'd be just a little skeptical. Right?"

Emily could, of course, empathize with his position. In just the few short hours she had known this family she had become fond of the kids. They were just adorable, even Rhiannon with her blasé response to almost every situation and her almost continual state of ennui.

"I'm not asking you to follow me," she said eventually. "I'm asking you to protect yourself and your kids. Of course I understand how crazy it all sounds. I'd be less than convinced if I were in your position, but look at it like this. If you're right and everything I've told you is nothing more than some elaborate, crazy joke, then you have nothing to lose by coming with me." She let the words sink in for a few seconds. "You have to take the risk, Simon. Please."

She saw a flicker of anger, possibly fear, cross Simon's face. "I really don't appreciate you using my kids as bargaining chips."

Emily placed her drink down on the table, reached out, and took both of Simon's hands in her own. "I'm not trying to bargain with you, Simon. Whatever you decide, I'm still leaving tomorrow and heading north again. If I'm right and you stay here...you, Rhiannon, and Ben are all going to die. And you better hope to God that you die first because I would not want you to witness the agony your kids will go through in their final minutes."

Simon met her gaze, pulled free of her hands, and swallowed the remaining brandy in a single gulp. He walked back to the wet bar and poured himself another double. When he turned to look at her, Emily could see that the dilemma was tearing at him: Did he stay where he thought he could keep his kids safe? Or did he listen to this stranger who had suddenly materialized in his life and head north into the unknown?

"Can you guarantee that if we leave here, the instant we set foot outside of the valley we won't die? Will you look me in the eyes and guarantee the safety of my kids?" His words were delivered without emotion or anger, but as a simple question that he already knew the answer to.

"I can't guarantee anything other than everyone else is dead. There will never be a rescue party. But whatever is happening out there"—her hand fluttered toward the darkened window—"will reach in here at some point and snatch away the lives of you and your kids. Just like it did to everyone else on this planet."

Simon placed the glass onto the wet bar, its contents untouched, and looked into the darkness beyond the window. "If Elise was here, she would know what to do. It would be simple for her. She would have liked you."

Emily allowed a smile to part her lips, put her own glass down, and walked over to stand behind Simon. She placed a hand gently on his shoulder. "You know what you need to do, Simon. You have to leave here because it's your only hope. You have to take the chance because soon you won't have any choice left."

Simon turned to face her, his eyes glistening with tears. "This is all just so damn hard to take in," he whispered. "Jesus. How am I going to explain this to the kids?"

"Don't worry about it tonight," she answered. "Just get a good night's sleep and we'll deal with it all in the morning, okay?"

CHAPTER SIX

Emily woke with a start.

In her sleep-fogged mind, she thought she had heard some-thing. Had she? Or was it just an already forgotten nightmare?

Seconds ticked by, and the only sound was Thor's deep rhyth-mic breathing as he continued to sleep, undisturbed.

Only nerves, she told herself eventually, allowing her chest to sink as she inhaled. She was no stranger to bad dreams, she reminded herself. Not since she'd left Manhattan, at least.

She had just begun to allow sleep to claim her once more when she heard a scream, shrill and sharp. It sounded like Ben.

Her eyes flickered open again. Disoriented, heart racing, she fumbled for where she thought the lamp was, cringing as she knocked over the glass of water she had placed there. It didn't smash, but she heard the water slosh over the carpet.

"Damn it," she cursed just as her probing fingers found the switch and flooded the room with light. Smarting at the sudden assault on her eyes, she glanced around the unfamiliar room just to make sure there was nothing in there with her. The place was empty except for Thor, who, in the space of a couple of seconds, had somehow managed to go from sleeping to standing with his nose pressed against the crack of the bedroom door, his hackles raised and his back ramrod straight. The malamute glanced at Emily as she swung her feet out of the bed and stumbled toward the door. The instant she opened it, the dog slipped through the gap and padded quickly toward the sound of the commotion as Emily stumbled behind him.

The screaming continued, but now she could hear Simon's voice echoing down the corridor as he called out to his boy, "Ben! Ben! It's all right. Daddy's here. It's just a dream. Ben, it's just a dream."

By the time Emily reached the child's bedroom, Ben was clinging to his father, tears streaming down his face as Simon rocked the child back and forth, cooing gently to his son, "Hush! Hush! It's all okay."

Ben looked up as Emily entered his room, his hazel eyes moist with tears. "Monsters," he cried, choking back more tears. "The monsters are coming."

■ ■ ■

Thor lay on the bed next to Ben, his head resting gently against the child's arm. It had taken a quarter of an hour for Simon to quiet his hysterical son, but with a mixture of soothing words and gentle rocking, Ben's sobs had gradually grown fainter. Finally they faded to nothing but a trembling upper lip. His eyes had begun to droop as Simon laid him softly back down on the bed.

Thor nuzzled in beside the child. Ben opened his drooping eyes momentarily and looked at the big dog. "Love you, For," the child whispered, throwing an arm around the malamute's neck. Moments later the child fell back to sleep. Emily didn't have to tell the dog to stay; she knew there was no way Thor was going to move from his spot unless she commanded him to. Emily, Rhiannon, and Simon retreated into the corridor and quietly closed the door behind them.

The house was quiet again except for the distant muffled thrum of the generator. Simon sent Rhiannon back to bed with a kiss on the cheek and the reassurance that her little brother had just had a nightmare and was going to be fine.

"I think this is all finally beginning to take its toll on them," Simon whispered once they were alone, as he walked with Emily down the hall, their bare feet falling silently on the carpet.

Hoping she wasn't pushing her luck too far, Emily spoke her mind. "All the more reason for you all to come with me." She caught a glimpse of a smile cross Simon's face through the dimness and saw his eyes flit momentarily to her legs before looking back to her eyes. She couldn't be sure, but she thought she caught his cheeks flush; then she realized why. In the rush to get to Ben's room, she hadn't even thought to throw on her pants; she was only wearing a tee and panties.

Embarrassed, she crossed her arms across her chest and tried not to blush. As the light from her bedroom caught them both in its glow, Emily could see Simon's cheeks had turned a deep crimson, and she couldn't help but notice his overt attempt to keep his eyes fixed firmly above her shoulders. She felt her own cheeks burn even more fiercely.

Christ, here they were, facing an uncertain future and possible death from an unknown invader, and yet they still found themselves reacting like teenagers at the first glimpse of skin. At least it proved they were both still human, and that was a trait that had become the most precious of commodities in this world.

"Okay," said Simon, "I think we all need to get some rest. Good night." He took two steps toward his own room, stopped and turned: "Emily…"

"Yes?" she said, in the process of closing the bedroom door behind her.

"Thank you." He gave her a firm nod of his head and disappeared down the corridor.

"You're welcome," Emily whispered into the emptiness and closed the door, Ben's cry of monsters still echoing in the back of her mind.

CHAPTER SEVEN

"Good morning," Emily said through a hand-covered yawn. Her stomach grumbled its own greeting as the smell of bacon sizzling on the skillet filled her senses.

"I'd ask you how you like your eggs, but all we have is this…" Simon shook a carton of liquid egg whites above his head with one hand while he poked at the contents of a frying pan on the stove. "So, it's scrambled or scrambled, I'm afraid."

"Sounds perfect," Emily replied as she moved to join the two children at the breakfast nook table. Thor jumped up from his spot next to Ben and met her halfway across the kitchen, fanning the air with his tail while pushing his head between her knees until she patted his head and scratched behind his ears.

Ben and Rhiannon were bantering back and forth about some comic book hero figure the little boy had insisted on bringing to the table. The boy didn't seem any the worse for wear after his nightmare.

"How are you guys this morning?" she asked.

"Fine," said Rhiannon.

"I'm fine, too," echoed Ben, almost in sync with his sister.

"Here you go," said Simon as he brought the frying pan to the table, sliding portions of the fluffy eggs onto each plate, closely followed by a couple of slices of bacon.

"Oh. My. Goodness," said Emily as she swallowed the first bite of bacon. "I never thought I'd taste fried meat again."

"Why not?" asked Ben, a quizzical tone taking his voice up an octave.

That was a loaded question, Emily realized. Simon had kept both of the kids shielded from the reality of the situation they faced, and until their father had spoken with them, she was going to have to watch what she said. She certainly didn't want to frighten them.

Emily glanced across the table at Rhiannon; she was busy shoveling the remainder of her breakfast into her mouth, head bopping to some internal melody only she could hear. But Ben, his big hazel eyes regarding her with almost adult raptness, waited patiently for her to answer his question.

Simon must have sensed her reticence. His eyes moved first to Ben and then Rhiannon, lingering momentarily on each of them. "Kids, we're going on a road trip for a couple of days," he announced without any kind of preamble.

That got their attention, Emily's included. At some point during the night, he must have finally decided she was telling the truth. She smiled at Simon as she felt a swell of relief wash over her.

"Where are we going?" asked Rhiannon, her fork paused halfway to her mouth.

"There are some people, a little way north of here, that we're going to see. We're going to stay with them for a little while."

Rhiannon just rolled her eyes and continued eating.

"Is For and Emily coming, too?" Ben asked, spitting bits of bacon onto the tabletop.

"What have I told you about talking with your mouth full? Hmmm? And yes, they are most definitely both coming with us."

Ben's eyes drifted to Emily, who smiled and nodded. "Yup, we'll be joining you guys."

"Cool," replied Ben as his face broke into a huge grin.

"Now, why don't you and your sister finish your breakfast and then, if it's okay with Emily, you can take Thor outside for a walk. He looks like he could use some exercise to burn off all that junk you've been feeding him, Mr. Benjamin Keller. That okay by you, Emily?"

Emily thought about it for a second. She didn't want to scare the kids, especially now that Simon was convinced of the need to leave, and tell them to stay inside. "Of course it is. Just, don't stray too far," she said. Using the kids' affection for Thor, and his equal exuberance for their company, was about as obvious a manipulation of their emotions as you could get, but it was a means to an end. What the adults had to talk about was not for kids' ears. Even Rhiannon brightened, quickly finishing the remains of her breakfast in a couple of bites.

Emily noticed Ben sneak the final piece of bacon from his plate and slip it to Thor as the three headed out the back door, the echo of their laughter and excited chatter floating back down the corridor.

■ ■ ■

Simon disappeared into the garage, reappearing a couple of minutes later with a large red plastic gas can in one hand and what looked like a bicycle pump in the other. The pump had two long lengths of thick orange hose attached to it, one at each end of the body; on its side was a crank handle.

Emily and Simon had quickly figured out that the Honda Accord parked out front was not going to be of much use to them. They needed something larger that could carry more supplies, Thor, and the four of them. Emily had remembered the Dodge Durango SUV parked in the garage of the house across the valley, and Simon had decided he would go and try and find the keys and bring it back. While Emily wasn't particularly happy about them splitting up, it would save time and time was their most valuable commodity right now.

"It's a hand pump," said Simon, placing both items on the table. "That should solve our gasoline problem, but I'll have to siphon gas from other vehicles. SUV's are gas hogs, but as long as we're careful and take every opportunity to keep the tank full, I think we'll be okay." He placed a large spiral-bound book he'd been carrying under one arm onto the table. "This might also come in handy," he said. Emily canted her head sideways to read the book's title: *Michelin Road Atlas—North America: USA, Canada, Mexico*, it read in large black letters.

Simon flipped open the atlas, found the page for New York State, and tapped his finger against Stuyvesant. "This is where we are," he said. "We could head north up I-87 into Canada. Or we can head north for about twenty miles and can cross over the Hudson into Albany. Route 90's right there, and that'll take us west all the way into Michigan."

Emily followed Simon's finger on the map. The Mackinac Bridge was a suspension bridge that ran for close to five miles across the Straits of Mackinac, bisecting Lake Huron to the east and Lake Michigan to the west, and connecting Mackinaw City on the southern Michigan peninsula with Saint Ignace on the northern peninsula. From there it looked like it was about fifty miles to the Canadian border at Sault Saint Marie in Ontario.

"It's a toll bridge," said Emily, lifting her face to smile at Simon. "Better make sure we bring exact change."

He gave her a toothy grin back. "Ah! A sense of humor…I'll have to watch out for that." Simon's eyes dropped back to the map and he was all business again, flipping across pages of the atlas as he talked. "Once we're in Canada, we can just head northwest toward Edmonton. From there it's basically a straight line to Fairbanks in Alaska. I'd estimate it's going to take us about a week or so if we drive a maximum of eight hours a day, maybe less if we don't hit any bad weather." He glanced up from the road map at Emily, his eyebrows raised questioningly. "What do you think?"

Emily wasn't happy about the detour. It was going to take them into areas that were more populated than she was really comfortable with, but there was no arguing with Simon's logic. It would shave so much time off the trip doing it his way. Still, she couldn't help but feel uneasy about the decision. She had already seen how fast the world had changed; who knew what had happened since her last encounter?

Emily was still studying the route when Rhiannon and Benjamin, closely followed by a barking Thor, came tearing into the house. They were yelling at the top of their voices, "Dad! Dad! You have to come see what we found."

Emily spun around in time to see the kids almost collide with their father. He threw his hands up as they skidded to a stop next to him. "Whoa! Whoa! What's going on?" Thor padded along behind them, ignoring the two kids and heading straight to Emily's side. Instead of sitting next to her, he circled her, stopping momentarily to sit, only to be up and pacing again a second later.

"Dad, you have to come see," pleaded Rhiannon, tugging at Simon's sleeve. "Come on."

"Kids, I can't. We're going to have to leave very soon, and we need to plan. Okay?"

"But, but…you have to come see this." Rhiannon's voice had turned shrill. Her little brother stood quietly off to one side now, silently staring up at his dad with those big hazel eyes.

"No!" Simon almost snapped, probably a little more forcefully than the children were used to, because she saw them both flinch.

Thor was still restlessly pacing back and forth around her. Something had obviously spooked both the kids and Thor.

"Simon," she said, trying to be heard over the children's excited chatter as they pleaded with their father to follow them.

Simon apparently didn't hear her because he kept on talking. "Ben. Rhia. Please. Emily and I are trying to talk here. Could you give us just a little time, please?"

"Simon!" Emily snapped, loud enough that everyone, including Thor, turned to face her. She managed to force a smile through the growing miasma of anxiety she could feel settling over the room. "I think it would be best if we let the kids show us what they've found."

Simon met her gaze for a few long seconds. She thought she could see anger behind his eyes, but then it was gone, replaced by a look of bemusement as he stared down at his two children, as if seeing them for the first time since they had rushed into the house. He sank down to one knee and pulled first Rhiannon and then Ben to him, kissing them both on the tops of their heads. "I'm sorry, guys," he whispered. "Dad's just a little stressed out right now."

The children hugged him back, then each grabbed a hand and pulled him in the direction of the back door.

On the way out, Emily stopped by the bedroom and pulled her shotgun from the shelf in the cupboard, where she had stored it out of the kids' reach. She checked the chamber to make sure it held a round, then slung the weapon over her shoulder and went to join her newfound family.

■ ■ ■

The kids were pulling Simon along a path that led away from the back of the house up toward the summit of the hill, still babbling excitedly. Emily jogged to catch up with them. All signs of the tension she had seen in the man just minutes ago had disappeared and he was now laughing, playfully leaning back to make their job of towing him that little bit harder.

Ben and Rhiannon were both giggling and laughing between complaints of "Daaaaad! Stop it. Come onnnnnn" as they tried to drag him faster.

"All right, I'm coming. Hold your horses." He laughed, winking at Emily as she caught up with them. Then he noticed the shotgun slung across her shoulder and raised a questioning eyebrow. She smiled back at him and gave what she hoped was a reassuring nod. She didn't want this family to find out the hard way just how dangerous their world had become.

The sky above the valley was free of the previous day's storm clouds. Emily could still see rolling clouds of red to the east, beyond the border of their sanctuary, as the sun struggled to push through the veneer of red dust that had turned the day into a permanent twilight.

The path wound upward toward the summit of the hill. Closer to the ridge the trees began to thin out, replaced by grass all the way to the top. Emily watched as the kids began getting more excited and finally pulled their stumbling father to the ridge. As he reached the top, Simon straightened and pushed his kids behind him.

By the time Emily walked the final few feet to join the silent trio on the hilltop and looked out at the sight that lay beyond them, she knew that she had been right to insist on following the children.

CHAPTER EIGHT

"See?" said Rhiannon, her young voice emphatic with an adult sense of vindication that she had done the right thing.

They looked out across the sprawling landscape that had, until only a day ago, been lush with grass and trees. Now it was nothing but a swirling mass of red. Gone was the grass; gone were the trees. Replaced by a jungle of alien red plants and vegetation that stretched from about a mile or so from the base of the hill below them toward the southern horizon.

A very obvious line of delineation separated the old world from the new—the planet's original life from the invaders that had taken hold like some vicious weed, consuming everything they touched. On one side there was green; on the other nothing but red. It undulated off into the distance like some incoming tide of blood. To the east, the old world still remained, but once you stepped past that line of demarcation, you might just as well have stepped onto another planet.

"Jesus Christ," she heard Simon whisper.

All this had happened in the space of just a day? While she had slept and eaten and talked with the family, this transmutation had been taking place at an incredible pace, far faster than she would ever have imagined possible.

As she looked out over the distant swell of red, she could see a shimmering distortion in the air right above the point where the red vegetation met with the grass and trees of her world. It looked like the kind of heat shimmer she had seen hovering over the road during a hot summer day, and it followed the line of contact almost perfectly, creating a wall of distorted air that rose a few feet above the ground. Was it something to do with the rapid transformation of earth vegetation into the new alien variety? Some kind of indication of the energy that was being used up as it relentlessly marched across the landscape?

Emily surveyed the area below her, trying to pick out some kind of familiar landmark in the red zone that she could define as still belonging to her planet. Her eyes flicked back and forth over the landscape until she finally found the distant glint of a lake. If she hadn't been looking so intently, she would probably have missed it; the surface reflection was almost as red as the sky above. But it wasn't the lake or the coppice of half-built alien trees bunched together in one corner, their thick roots clearly visible as they snaked down below the water's surface, that made her reach out and grasp Simon's arm just above his elbow.

No, it was the area just beyond that—a clearing, almost perfectly circular and completely devoid of both invading vegetation and earth life. Unmistakable even from the mile or so distance she guessed she was from it. It wasn't even the huge tree she saw sprouting up from the center of the clearing, its limbs heavy with the unmistakable bulbous white-skinned fruit that had caused such unfocused terror in her when she'd found them in the forest as she fled Manhattan.

No, what caused her heart to race and her breath to freeze in her lungs was that she could see one of the fruit lying broken and discarded on the ground beneath the tree.

And whatever had been inside it was nowhere to be seen.

■ ■ ■

"We need to get out of here now," hissed Emily into Simon's ear. Whatever had come out of the sack could be out there right now, watching them. Or…stalking them.

Simon didn't react; he just kept staring out across what had once been lush green fields and forests. "My God," he finally said, his voice filled with awe or fear, Emily wasn't sure which. "I honestly wasn't sure whether I believed you, Emily. Maybe it was just wishful thinking, but this…" He swept a hand across the horizon, then returned it to his son's shoulder, pulling him closer. "This is just surreal."

"Isn't it beautiful, Daddy?" said Rhiannon, blissfully unaware that she was witnessing the inexorable destruction of her world. If this kid survived long enough, Emily realized, she would be one of the last generation who would ever remember what the earth had looked like before this great transformation.

"Fantastic," replied Simon as he released both kids from his grasp. "Now we have to go home, okay?"

As the kids raced ahead, Emily placed a restraining hand on Simon's arm, holding him back until they were just out of earshot, but not so far that she lost sight of them—she would be keeping them all close from this point on.

"We have a problem," she said.

"You aren't kidding. Did you see that? It's just so…so…alien."

"Okay, let me rephrase that. We have a bigger problem. Did you see the weird-looking trees down by the lake?"

"Of course," said Simon. "How could you miss them? Those things must be eighty feet if they're an inch."

She quickly reminded him of her disconcerting encounter with the lone tree and its white pods when she was traveling through the forest outside Valhalla. "Oh, shit," said Simon. "That's what those things were down there? I thought it was just some kind of trick of the light."

Emily shook her head. "Don't ask me to explain, or how I know, because I won't ever be able to give you an adequate explanation, but whatever was growing inside those sacks it's…it's evil."

She realized how ridiculous that must sound, but it was the truth. She didn't mean "evil" in the religious sense, though. Her encounter in the clearing was simply the most incredible sense of concentrated malevolence Emily had ever experienced. It had been like the frozen blade of a knife had been laid against her soul, and it had left an indelible scar. Even now, as she thought back to her first brush with the globes, she shuddered. More than anything in the world, she did not want to know what was inside those milky-white sacks.

CHAPTER NINE

"Lock the doors and keep the children inside," Emily warned as Simon ushered Rhia and Ben back inside the house.

"Where are you going?" he asked as she and Thor turned and began to head back toward the path that led down into the woods.

"I won't be long," she called back over her shoulder. She heard the door slam shut.

She had left her backpack, bike, and, most importantly, her satellite phone at the house on the opposite side of the ridge when she had left yesterday morning.

Emily followed the path back down the hill toward the Jefferson house, Thor trotting beside her. She had learned the home owners' name from Simon. Mr. and Mrs. Jefferson had, apparently, left the day of the red rain, heading off to be with their parents in DC. They were probably dead now.

The trail dropped down, then leveled out as she headed back past the pond. The ducks she had seen earlier were back, but

Thor seemed uninterested in harassing them this time, preferring instead to stay close to her.

At least one of those sacks they had seen growing on the tree had disgorged its contents. She thought back to the similar tree she had seen in the forest outside Valhalla and the slowly rotating shadow she had seen hidden within the orb's pink-liquid-filled interior. Whatever had been inside, it was now out and roaming the area. The knowledge that she might not be alone had turned the surrounding woods and deep shadows from a pleasant distraction to a potential ambush, and she found herself jogging along the path, the shotgun off her shoulder and held tightly in both hands.

If she had brought the phone with her, she would not have risked coming back to the house and would have abandoned her supplies, but it was her only means of contact with Jacob and his team, and she would be damned if she was going to leave it behind.

The muffled electronic call of the sat-phone greeted Emily like a long-lost friend as she pushed open the door to the Jeffersons' home and stepped inside.

She raced upstairs and jogged into the living room. Pulling the case holding the phone from the backpack, she quickly opened it, pulled out the phone, and flipped up the antenna, simultaneously hitting the Talk button.

"Hello," she said, breathless. "Jacob?"

"Emily. Thank God. I've been trying for hours to get in touch with you. Are you okay?" Jacob's concern was obvious, but Emily had no idea why he would be worried in the first place.

"Yes. Of course. Why?" she finally answered.

"Listen, I have some news that I need—"

Emily cut him off. "I have better news, so I get to go first. I found more survivors."

Emily heard Jacob's sharp intake of breath. "What? Where? How many?"

"They're a family, a father, son, so damn cute, and a daughter. I found them yesterday."

"That's astonishing. Amazing," Jacob stuttered. "Wait? Are they immune to the effects of the red rain, too?"

Emily realized that she hadn't actually given any thought to the possibility that Simon and his little family might not be immune to the red rain. She had simply made the assumption that they were, for whatever reason, resistant like her. They'd had zero exposure to the event thanks to the quirky weather system of their little valley. But what if they were not immune? What if once they stepped outside of the hill's border the virus—or whatever the rain actually was—was still active, and what if it killed them?

No! She was convinced that once the original red rain had turned to dust, its ability to infect human life had become negated, but there was no way to find out if her theory was correct without risking the lives of Simon and the kids.

"I don't know," she answered Jacob eventually. "Maybe they are immune, but I think they were probably just lucky." She took a couple of minutes to explain what Simon had told her about the valley's microclimate and how it had shielded them from the red rain. "There are even ducks here, too," she blurted out excitedly, resisting the urge to add a comic quack to emphasize the point.

"Fascinating. Just fascinating. This makes my news even more important." She heard Jacob's voice grow fainter as if he was holding the phone at arm's length. "I'm going to send you some images that you need to look at," he continued, raising his voice to ensure he was heard while he apparently fiddled with some controls on his sat-phone. "You'll need to share them with your new friends as quickly as possible. You'll need to convince them to get out of there."

The sat-phone gave a beep, and Emily glanced at the little LCD screen; it read, "Downloading Files...1 of 4."

Emily waited for all of the files to download. The resolution on the screen was not optimal for viewing the kind of detail she was looking at, but as she scanned through each of the images while Jacob explained what she was looking at, she felt a growing discomfort in the pit of her stomach.

"You can see what you're facing, Emily. It's imperative that you get yourself and the family out of there as soon as possible. If you don't there's no way—"

Emily stopped him midsentence. "I need to get back to the other house. You'll need to explain this to Simon, or I don't think there's any way he's going to believe me. He's already skeptical of what I've told him. Without proof from you, he'll think I'm out of my mind. Can you give me half an hour to get to them and then I'll call you back?"

"Make it fast, Em.," Jacob said. "I'll be waiting by the phone." Emily heard the click of Jacob hanging up and immediately began to collect the remainder of her belongings. She shoved them into the backpack and swung it over her shoulder and called for Thor to come with her.

Making her way through the house to the garage, she found her bike on the side of the house and walked it around to the back path. Once she was down the steps and back on the dirt trail, she began pedaling toward the house on the opposite side of the valley.

She barely felt any of the bumps of the rough trail as she and Thor raced back to Simon and the kids. The implications of what Jacob had shown her flooded her mind with questions, and it was all she could do to keep her pounding heart from exploding out of her chest.

■ ■ ■

"What exactly is going on?" Simon asked as he followed Emily into her room.

"Do you have a computer? One that's charged," she asked.

"What? Why do you need a computer?"

Emily dropped the backpack onto the bed and turned to face Simon. "Please, Simon," she said. "Do you have a computer?"

Simon stared at her for a moment, then disappeared. When he came back, he was carrying a laptop computer under one arm. Emily pulled the sat-phone from the backpack, pulled the computer from under Simon's arm, and walked into the living room.

"Jesus, Emily. Are you going to tell me what the hell is going on?"

"I don't know what's going on," she replied as she set the equipment down on the coffee table and attached a USB cable from the laptop to the phone. She pressed the On button of both machines and, once a connection had been established, hit Redial on the phone. "But I think I know someone who might be able to explain it to both of us."

She pressed the Speakerphone button and listened to the ringing phone. It chirruped a couple of times before Jacob answered. "Emily. Are your new friends there?"

"It's just me and Simon," she answered, keeping her voice as low as possible in case the kids overheard her. "I didn't think this was something we should discuss with the children around." Emily glanced up from the phone at Simon, and she realized by the surprised look on his face that he hadn't believed a word she had told him when she had tried to explain about Jacob and his crew of scientists. "Simon, meet Jacob. Jacob…Simon." The two men exchanged greetings before Jacob took control of the conversation again.

"I don't know how much Emily has explained to you about what we think is actually going on here, Simon, but I have someone else that I want to introduce to the both of you who I think will be able to clear up any doubts you might have about the threat you are all facing. Hold on a second while I bring them in…" There was a sharp beep followed by a short burst of electronic tones. A few seconds later, a woman's voice filled the room.

"Hello all, can you hear me okay?" There was a slight static buzz behind the transmission, as though the stranger was speaking from a great distance. The woman's voice was accented, certainly not American. British maybe?

"We hear you," said Emily and Jacob almost simultaneously.

Jacob's voice broke in to the conversation. "Everyone, this is Fiona Mulligan. She's the commander of the International Space Station."

CHAPTER TEN

"My God," said Simon, his voice a stunned whisper.

Huddled around the computer screen, Emily could see exactly what Simon saw: a panoramic view of what looked like Venezuela, Colombia, and Mexico. Of course, she could only assume it was the uppermost part of South America because the majority of the image she was looking at was obscured by a red haze. The only way she could be sure of what she was seeing was because she could still make out the rough outline of the Gulf of Mexico on the right side of the image. The east coast town of Veracruz was just vaguely visible, but everything else was covered by the same cloud.

"Are you looking at the first image?" Commander Mulligan's voice crackled over the speaker.

"Yes," replied Emily.

"Jump to the second image, if you would." Again Commander Mulligan caught a gasp of astonishment from the two civilians;

this time it was followed by an expletive from Simon and a quick apology.

"That image was taken twenty-four hours later. It's the same location as the first image. I'm sure you can see now why I thought it was so important for Jacob to let you see these pictures as quickly as possible."

The image on the screen could have been anywhere for all Emily and Simon knew. It was impossible to tell because there was nothing but a swirling mass of red that looked like some kind of crazy kid's finger painting or Rorschach image. No land or sea was visible at all.

"This cannot be happening…" Simon whispered.

"I assure you it is, Mr. Keller," came Fiona's voice from the phone. "And I am sorry to tell you that the news does not get any better. Please skip ahead to image three, if you would." The third image was of a clearly distinguishable US East Coast. Small spots of red were splattered over the image like drops of blood. Emily could see the largest spot was hanging over New York. "That was taken two days ago," continued Fiona. "You can see the phenomenon is less pronounced than you just saw over South America, possibly because, as Jacob has already postulated, whatever we are seeing here is retarded by colder climates. But if you would be so kind as to move to the fourth image."

Fiona waited a second before continuing.

"You will see that although the progression is slower on the US mainland, there appears to be a much larger storm, if that is the right word, rapidly approaching from the east. The picture you are looking at now was taken six hours ago."

Emily sucked in her breath as she looked at the aerial photograph on the screen. It was mind-blowing. While the outline of the coast was still clearly visible, what had been spots of red in the previous image had now grown to three or four times their size. She could just make out tendrils of red extending out from each spot; each one seemed to be reaching in the direction of the nearest red splotch of its neighbor. Here and there she could see some of the tendrils had already made connections, and the originating red stains seemed to be uniformly larger than the ones that had not yet connected.

But that paled into insignificance next to the huge red storm that occupied most of the right side of the screen, a swirling mass of red hues with thick branches extending out in front of it, as though searching blindly for the land mass that lay just a few hundred miles ahead of it.

"What we believe you are seeing is a huge body of this substance you called 'red dust' that we first saw amassing in Europe. It broke off from the main body of the red storm over that continent and began heading in your direction several days ago. You may already have experienced some preliminary effects from its approach. If this was a normal meteorological event, I would be recommending you simply hunker down and try to ride it out, but given the information I have received courtesy of Jacob and Emily, my only advice to you is to reiterate what Jacob has already advised you: run as fast and as far north as you possibly can."

"Daddy, what's that?"

The sound of Rhiannon's voice shattered the shocked stillness that had settled over both Simon and Emily. Simon's hand flashed out and slammed the screen of the laptop shut. "It's nothing, sweetheart," he said as he turned to face his two children, who had somehow managed to sneak into the house unheard. "Just some photos that Emily took that she wanted me to see."

"It's pretty," said Benjamin, standing next to his big sister, a coloring book in one hand and a green pencil in the other.

While the implication of what the kids had just seen had passed by Benjamin, Rhiannon didn't look convinced by Simon's explanation.

"Who were you talking to?" she asked, nodding at the sat-phone next to the computer, as Benjamin, apparently already bored by the conversation, took a chair next to Simon and began coloring the remainder of his picture.

Before Emily or Simon could reply, Fiona's voice filled the kitchen. "Hello, children. My name is Fiona, and I am a friend of Emily's and your father." The ISS commander's strong British accent instantly grabbed the children's attention. "I was just telling your daddy how nice it would be if you and your brother might like to come see me and my friends. Would you like that?"

Rhiannon's response was to simply raise her eyes to the ceiling, spin on her heels, and head out of the kitchen toward her bedroom. "Whatever!" she called back over her shoulder. Ben continued to concentrate on filling in his coloring book, biting his bottom lip as he carefully worked the color between the lines.

Simon watched his daughter disappear, then took his son's hands in his own. "Why don't you go and take Thor to the kitchen and give him some cookies?" he asked. The little boy's face instantly brightened as he turned toward Emily, his eyes fixed on the carpet.

"Can I?" he asked.

Emily tried not to let the surprise she felt creep into her voice. Benjamin had barely acknowledged her existence since she had stumbled across his family. She nodded, not trusting herself to speak.

The little boy turned to the dog: "For. Want a cookie?" Emily smiled at the sheer sweetness of it. The malamute didn't seem to have any problem understanding the boy, though. He rolled to his feet and trotted after Benjamin, and they both disappeared into the kitchen.

"We have some other problems to contend with," said Emily when the boy was out of earshot. She explained what they had seen happening over the hill, quickly filling in the commander on her experience in the Valhalla forest and what the empty sack might mean for their safety.

"This is a very interesting development," said the commander after a pause. "And you have no idea what this egg sack contained?"

"No, all I know is that when I encountered the first one, I was almost overwhelmed with fear. Just take my word for it, whatever is on the loose out here isn't thinking happy thoughts."

There was a burst of static, then Jacob's voice cut through it. "... all that you have told us, I'd advise you leave as quickly as possible. While I can't speak with any certainty about the storm, given your previous experiences and observations, and the unprecedented size of the storms, I can only assume that this is the next phase in the geoengineering of the planet. In short: you don't want to still be there when that thing makes landfall."

Emily stared at Simon. She could almost hear the cogs in his brain whirring as he tried to process this avalanche of information.

"Okay," he replied, finally. "We leave now." The tenseness Emily had seen in him seemed to drain from his muscles in resignation, all resistance finally leaving him.

"If there's nothing more? I think Simon and I need to get cracking. There's not much of the day left and the sooner we're out of here the better."

"Good," replied Fiona. "Don't waste time. You have no more than twelve hours in our estimation before that storm makes landfall and starts heading inland in your direction. You'll want to be out of there well before then to stay ahead of it."

Jacob added, reinforcing the commander, "Whatever you two are going to do, you need to do it quickly, guys."

"We will," Emily said, then added, "And, commander, thank you."

Emily glanced across at Simon as she hung up the sat-phone. His face was ashen, and she wondered how she would be handling the same news if she had been in his position.

Simon looked up and met her stare. After a few moments he gave a single solemn nod of understanding.

"Let's get started."

■ ■ ■

As soon as they were off the sat-phone, Emily followed Simon into the living room. Simon called Rhiannon and Ben in and told them they would be leaving within the next hour or so.

"Is For still coming?" said Ben.

"Yes, he's still going to be coming with us," said Simon, smiling at his little boy.

"We're leaving *now*?" Rhiannon asked. She had a look of incredulity on her face that telegraphed she was going to have a hard time believing anything she was told unless it was the absolute truth.

Simon looked at Emily for support, but she just smiled back at him. The ball was completely in his court, and he had to tell the children what he chose to tell them.

"There's a very big storm coming," Simon said. "So, we have to leave sooner than I thought."

"Why?"

"Because, if we stay, we might be hurt…or worse. Do you understand what I'm saying, Rhiannon?" said Simon, glancing at her brother.

Rhiannon took a moment to analyze what had been said. "I suppose," she said finally.

"Okay, well I need you and your brother to stay out of Emily's way for a while. She's going to pack some clothes for you both for the trip."

"Where are you going to be?" Rhiannon asked, suspicion back in her voice.

"I'm going to go and see if we can borrow the Jeffersons' SUV. I won't be long."

As much as Emily hated to split the family up, they had decided it was for the best if Simon took the Honda Accord over to the Jeffersons' place, located the keys to the SUV, and brought it back to the house while she packed some supplies and got the children ready to go.

"It's not perfect, but under the circumstances..." she said.

Simon nodded. "It's our only option." He picked up his car keys from the table in the hall and headed out the front door. "I'll be back soon," he said and closed the door behind him.

■ ■ ■

Emily moved from bedroom to bedroom, carefully pulling a selection of clothing from hangers and packing it into a couple of small travel cases Simon had set aside. When each case was full, she placed them in the hallway near the front door so they could be quickly loaded once Simon returned with the SUV.

She did the same for Simon, quickly selecting and packing enough clothes to last him at least three days. One side of the master bedroom's walk-in closet was filled with slacks, designer jeans, and summer dresses—they were all his wife's clothes. How long had she been gone? Two years, or so, and he had never gotten around to emptying her side of the closet. It was a painfully sweet observation of a man who was still deeply in love with the memory of his wife. By the time Emily had filled and added several cardboard boxes of food supplies to the luggage waiting at the front door, she was beginning to worry.

Where the hell was Simon? It had been at least ninety minutes since he had left on what should have been no more than a thirty-minute round trip, an hour tops if he had to track down the keys for the Jeffersons' SUV. Either way, he should have been back long ago.

Maybe there was some kind of problem with the SUV? Something he thought he could fix but had taken longer?

Something was wrong here. He could have had an accident or run into something else that delayed him. Emily didn't even want to think what that "something" might be.

She gave him another thirty minutes, just in case.

But when there was still no sign of his little silver Honda, Emily realized she was faced with two choices. She could stay put and hope that Simon showed up, but if he hadn't come back by dark then they would be stuck there at the house until morning. Then they would have to go searching for Simon and, if he was injured, they might be too late, and with the storm less than eleven hours away now...

On the other hand, if she left now, she could make it to the house in twenty minutes, locate Simon, and, hopefully, figure out what to do next. But that would mean she would have to take the kids along with her, because there was no way she was going to leave them alone in the house, not even with Thor to guard them.

Every second she wasted brought the red storm closer and would make it even harder for them to get out. It was too late for her to leave by bike now; she would never outrun the storm, and it would mean having to leave the kids behind to whatever fate was heading their way. No, she would have to risk heading to the other house. She'd take the kids with her but leave the supplies here. Hopefully, they would be able to swing back once they had found Simon.

She found pen and paper and left a note on the kitchen table, where it couldn't be missed.

Simon,

You've been gone for over two hours. I am heading to the house, through the valley. The kids are with me. If you read this, that's where we will be.

Meet us there.

The kids had both fallen asleep on the sofa, Ben's feet resting in the lap of his sister, her arm draped over her little brother. Beyond them, through the window, Emily could see they had about an hour of daylight left. That would be enough for what she had planned.

"Rhiannon. Ben. Wake up," Emily said, gently shaking the girl's shoulder. Rhiannon opened her eyes and sat up, looking a little confused. She pushed her brother's feet off her lap and scowled at him as his eyes fluttered open and he yawned. Rhiannon's scowl grew deeper when she saw it was Emily who had woken them.

"Where's Dad?" the girl demanded.

"Grab your jackets," Emily said. "We're going to go find him."

CHAPTER ELEVEN

By the time Emily and the children were halfway to the Jeffersons' house, the sun had dropped closer to the crest of the valley's ridge. In the rapidly dimming light, long shadows stretched through the woods, crisscrossing over the path ahead, and Emily was beginning to reconsider her decision to go look for Simon.

"I want my daddy," said Ben for the umpteenth time since stepping outside. She couldn't blame him, of course, but dear God, it was annoying.

"Shut it, dweeb," his sister shot back.

Emily suppressed a smile. The banter between the kids was rather cute, she had to admit. The constant poking and prodding of egos that were as fragile and underdeveloped as the children themselves. That same malleability would ensure no damage was done...probably.

"Okay, you two. That's enough. Let's concentrate on where we're going. This ground is pretty rough." Emily clicked on her flashlight and shone it into the growing darkness ahead of them, highlighting the uneven ground and occasional rock that poked through the earth. "The last thing I need is for one of you guys to trip and break something. 'Kay?"

Both kids nodded back at her.

"All right. Stay close to me and Thor."

Emily was surprised when she felt a small hand reach for her own free hand, clasping it tightly in its soft warmth. She looked down at Ben; his full-moon face looked up at her with such utter trust. Her heart missed a beat, and for a second, the pain and loss of an entire race that was carried within her softened. In the eyes of this little boy and his sister resided the hope of humanity. If there was to be a future, it would be through these kids. And, who could tell, but if this family had survived the red rain and carnage that followed, there must surely be more survivors. More kids. Hope.

A fighting chance. Maybe. If she managed to keep them all alive.

"Dweeb," she heard his sister mutter under her breath. Emily sniffed back a tear and replaced it with a smile. The moment was about as emotionally poignant as she had ever experienced. Leave it to the kid to go and ruin it.

The moment gone, Emily concentrated on maneuvering the group along the path she'd walked earlier in the day.

With the dying sun now lost behind the far horizon, a three-quarter moon had peeked through a break in the clouds, saturating the forest in a dim silver light. At the duck pond, a white mist wafted off the water, coating the ground in an eerie fog that almost came up to Ben's knees. The kid was fascinated by the shroud of water vapor as he moved his free hand through it.

"Pretty," he whispered.

More like spooky, Emily thought. But then, at his age did he have any idea of just how much trouble they were all in? Of course not. Emily sensed Rhiannon step closer to her. The girl looked nervous. Good. She should be, and an extra pair of nervous eyes to add to her own and Thor's could only be a good thing.

The ducks were nowhere to be seen. Probably huddled together deep in the reeds, if they had any sense. Even Thor was more subdued, pacing alongside Rhiannon's right side, panting gently.

The path leading up to the Jefferson place was a lot easier to negotiate thanks to the moonlight lighting the way. As the house came into view, Emily felt her pulse begin thrumming in her wrists. What if Simon wasn't there? Worse, what if something had found him before she did?

As they topped the steps, Emily saw Simon's car parked off to the left of the house, just beyond the corner of the garage. So he had made it this far, at least.

A shape materialized just beyond the car, and Emily let out a sigh of relief as Simon stepped out of the shadows and onto the gravel path.

He was alive.

CHAPTER TWELVE

Emily's feeling of relief disappeared as quickly as it had arrived.

There was something wrong with Simon. The way he stood, his hands draped at his sides, his eyes wide open, staring directly at them, his mouth a thin slit, the way his chest barely seemed to move. It looked like Simon, but it just didn't feel like Simon. His energy just felt unnatural.

She felt Ben start to move from her side toward his father. Heard his ecstatic cry of "Daddy" as he took a step closer.

"Stop!" Emily yelled, her voice like a crack of thunder in the stillness of the virgin night, her hand automatically reaching out and grabbing the little boy's shoulder, slowing him before he could get out of her reach. "Stop," she said again, more gently this time, as she swung the boy around and dropped down to face him. "That's not your daddy, Ben. That's...someone else."

"No!" he yelled at Emily while at the same time tearing loose of her grip. He turned and sped across the grass toward Simon, his little legs eating up the ground at a frighteningly rapid pace.

The spell that had grasped Emily so firmly broke; she was back in reality watching as the boy raced across the fifty or so feet separating them from Simon.

"Oh, Jesus," she whispered, casting a quick glance over her shoulder. Rhiannon must have sensed something was not right with the scene because she seemed glued to the spot of grass she was standing on, a look of horror and confusion painted across her pale face.

"Stay here," she ordered the girl. Then Emily was off, chasing after the kid, her feet sliding on the damp grass, searching for traction.

Simon did not move to intercept them; he stood as still as the trees behind him, his face expressionless and his hands resting flat against his thighs, like a soldier at attention.

There was maybe twenty feet left between the kid and his father when a blur of motion exploded past Emily on her right and made like a missile directly for the running boy. It caught up with him in a second, skidding to a stop between the child and Simon, blocking the kid's path. Ben collided with the flank of Thor, bounced off him, and flew three feet backward through the air, a surprised "Oomph!" whistling from his throat as he landed on his butt on the grass.

"Bad For! Bad doggy!" the little boy cried, his voice a high-pitched wail as he struggled to get to his feet. Thor was back at the kid's side in a second, dancing around the child and keeping him from standing.

It was all the time Emily needed to scramble after the boy and close the final gap separating her and Ben. She grabbed the spluttering kid with one arm under both of his shoulders, scooping Ben up in one fluid movement, even as he struggled and kicked against her, pulling him tight to her side.

Despite his son's obvious distress, Simon did not move to help him.

"Daddy!" Ben cried, both hands reaching out to Simon. "Iwannnnntmyyydaddddddy."

Perhaps the sound of his son's voice struck a chord deep within Simon's mind or perhaps it was simply coincidence, but as Ben's sorrowful howl faded into the dark, Simon took a single jerking, almost robotic, step toward them.

"Oh, shit!" The first step was followed by another hesitant, wobbling step toward Emily and the boy.

Thor was back at her feet now, his attention focused on the boy under Emily's arm, until he caught sight of Simon's tottering steps in their direction. Snarling, the malamute turned and faced the advancing man.

"No!" Emily yelled. "Come here, Thor. Back up." The dog threw a look at Emily, then back at Simon, who had moved another step closer. For a second, Emily thought Thor was going to disobey her and attack, but an instant later he was at her side.

She began to back away from Simon, unwilling to turn her back on him for a second. Ben cried his father's name, both hands reaching out toward the shuffling figure.

Simon's face remained expressionless, seemingly unmoved by his son's dilemma, but with each step he took his head swayed slightly—first right, then to the left, as though the muscles in his neck were unable to hold the weight of his head. If it hadn't been for the almost ramrod-straight posture of the rest of his body, she might think he was drunk.

With each faltering step forward Simon took, Emily managed two backward. If she didn't have Ben tucked under her arm, she would have simply turned and run for her life, but she had to think about Ben and Rhiannon. She had no idea what was wrong with their father, but there was no way she was going to let him get close to either of them until she figured it out. She didn't want to hurt him, but if he had suffered some kind of breakdown or the red dust had managed to affect him in some way, then she was going to have—

Simon teetered out of the long shadows of the trees and into a bright pool of moonlight.

He was fully illuminated now, and Emily could see there was something very wrong with him.

Slick black tendrils, each edged with small wicked-looking barbs, glistened in the light of the moon. Emily could see two of them jutting out from either side of Simon's spine just above his shoulder blades. They arced up above his head and back into the shadows, as though they sprouted from the very darkness itself. A third snakelike tentacle spiraled from the darkness and attached to the back of Simon's head, terminating at the point where Simon's spine met his skull. An instant before Simon took each step, Emily could see the barbed tubes pulse as though they were moving liquid under pressure from whatever was hidden in the darkness to Simon. Or maybe they were issuing instruction, she thought, as the tentacles throbbed again and Simon took another faltering step, as if on the command of some strange puppet master.

Emily swung a struggling Ben around so his head was pressed deep into her shoulder; there was no telling how he would react if he saw his father like this. The boy squirmed and complained, but she kept him pressed as tightly to her as she could without risking suffocating him. She took another step backward, then braced and forced herself to turn away from Simon and whatever was controlling him.

Standing in front of her, rooted to the spot, was Rhiannon, her jaw hanging loosely open, a look of abject terror spread across her face. Emily could see the girl's eyes were wide and fixed on her father; there was little doubt the girl had seen what Emily had seen. Well, there was nothing she could do about that now. She had no idea what had captured Simon, but, if her previous experience with the new life-forms wandering the planet were anything to go by, they weren't there to say hi and invite themselves to a Mets game. The most important thing right now was to get them all as far away from here as possible. She could figure out what to do next when they were all safe.

"Rhiannon," Emily said as loudly as she could without frightening the girl or the still-wriggling boy clasped in her arms. The girl didn't even register Emily's presence; she just kept staring back at her slowly advancing father. Emily chanced a look back over her shoulder. Simon had moved a few steps closer; he was near enough now that she could make out the bloodless pallor of his skin and the black pits of his eyes.

"Rhiannon!" Emily spat, her voice sharp enough to cut through the terror enveloping the girl. Her eyes flicked to Emily, then darted back to her father, then back again to Emily. This time they stayed fixed on her. "I need your help, baby. I can't explain what's happening to your dad, but we have to get out of here, right now, okay?"

Rhiannon's eyes stayed locked with Emily's for a second, then drifted back toward Simon. He was close enough now that she could hear his feet dragging through the damp grass, snapping twigs underfoot like a character from some bad zombie movie. It was all Emily could do not to scream and run. Instead she spoke as calmly as she could, "Honey, we have to get out of here. We have to get you and your brother to the Jeffersons' house, now." The words tumbled from her mouth in one breath, but still the kid refused to move.

Shit! Think. Think.

"We have to get the dweeb out of here, Rhiannon. Do you understand me? We have to save the dweeb."

Recognition flickered across Rhiannon's face for a moment; it wasn't much, but it was enough. Emily shifted the boy from her right arm to her left, grabbed Rhiannon by the sleeve with her free hand, and pulled her in the direction of the house. The girl stumbled backward for a few paces, still looking back at her dad, but then she shook free of Emily's grasp, swung around, and started to stride toward the house. Emily could see a glint of tears trickling down her cheek, but there was a resoluteness to her face now that Emily thought she had seen in her own face during the first few days after the rain. The fear was there, too, in her eyes, but the kid was doing her best to keep her foot firmly on its throat.

Thor ran right alongside Rhiannon. Occasionally he would stop, look back, and glare at Simon. Then he'd wait for Emily and the boy to catch up and then run on to catch up with Rhiannon, who was quickly increasing the gap between Emily and her brother.

"Rhiannon," Emily yelled between panting breaths. "Head for your dad's car." She wasn't sure the girl had heard her, but Emily saw her change course away from the house and head toward her father's parked car. Rhiannon reached the car and pulled open the unlocked passenger side door. Instead of jumping in and slamming the door she stood in the V of the open door and waited.

"Give me my brother," she demanded, holding her arms out for the boy as Emily caught up with her a few seconds later.

"Here," said Emily, lowering the boy down to the ground. Ben immediately grabbed his sister around the waist, burying his head into her stomach. "Don't let him out of your reach," she warned the girl.

Emily looked back to where Simon was. He was still advancing toward them, inexorably placing one foot after the other, but he was terribly slow, plodding almost. It was as if the dynamics of walking were alien to whatever had taken hold of Simon, which, she surmised was probably closer to the truth than she cared to admit. Emily had a sense of something dark looming in the shadows just out of sight, but it kept to the darkness as though trying to convince them that it really wasn't there. That was fine by Emily. It gave her time.

She ran around to the driver's side of the car and pulled open the door, feeling for where the ignition should be and, hopefully, the keys. The ignition was empty. She slipped her hand between the center console and driver's seat, checked the cup holders and glove compartment, just in case. Finally, she flipped down both sun visors, hoping Simon might have stashed the keys there. He hadn't of course. And why would he have? They were probably in his pants pocket.

There was no way she was going to head back through the woods in the dark with whatever this thing was on the loose. Under its control, Simon was barely able to move at the pace of an eighty-year-old, but who knew how fast it really was? And who was to say what would happen if it suddenly decided to drop Simon and come after them directly? She had to get the kids to safety, and the only thing resembling that was the Jeffersons' home.

"Come on, Rhiannon. Bring your brother. We're heading to the house," Emily said as she jogged back around the vehicle to the passenger side. Ben was back on his feet and standing next to his sister; her hand was clamped firmly around his. He seemed to have calmed down a little but refused to look at Emily, shrugging off her hand when she ushered him gently in the direction of the house, allowing his sister to lead him instead.

Emily walked behind the kids, occasionally glancing back in Simon's direction, as she and Thor herded the two children in the direction of the front door of the house.

Ben clung to his sister, his legs unable to keep up with her faster pace. He had to give a little skip every other step to keep up with her. Emily was surprised at how quickly Rhiannon had seemingly accepted the situation and adapted; gone was the prissy "Valley girl" demeanor, and in its place was a cold determination, almost a fatalistic acceptance. Emily wondered whether the whole attitude thing had simply been a coping mechanism for her, a cloak to cover her fear and a wall against the reality that existed just beyond the safety of her family's valley.

Their feet crunched over the gravel path leading up to the front door of the house. Emily sprinted ahead and tried the door; it was unlatched. She pushed the door open and turned on her flashlight, illuminating the hallway.

"Thor," she called. The dog sprinted from the kids' side and into the house, disappearing into the darkness beyond the reach of her flashlight. Emily looked back at the kids stumbling toward her. She stopped them at the threshold. "Let Thor check the house for us first, okay?" She did not want to risk trapping them all inside the house, only to find there was another of whatever that thing behind Simon was waiting for them.

Thor reappeared at the end of the corridor; tail wagging, he rushed to the kids' sides and wheeled around them.

"Okay, move, kids. Get inside now."

Rhiannon pulled Ben inside, and their two shapes disappeared into the blackness of the corridor, quickly followed by Thor. "Turn on your flashlight," Emily called out, her voice echoing through the empty house. A second later she saw the faint orange glow of Rhiannon's flashlight flowing back to her as the children moved through the house.

Simon had stopped moving and was standing about a hundred feet or so away, his hands back at his sides in that strange stance of attention, his body swaying slowly back and forth, his eyes staring directly at her, framed by an expressionless, emotionless face. Behind Simon, backlit by the moonlight, the silhouette of something huge blotted out the tree line. Emily caught a glimpse of long angular arms articulated at odd angles like the legs of a praying mantis. The shadow towered over Simon; it looked as though it was stooped at an angle, leaning down toward the man. The tentacles were still attached to him. She could see them move slightly in the darkness, but could not make out any more detail, as the thing hid itself in shadow.

As she continued to stare, Simon's head turned slightly to one side, his eyes fixed on hers, and he smiled, a wide, shit-eating grin.

Emily closed the door, flipped on her flashlight, and sprinted into the house. In an anteroom off the living room, she found a large wooden desk. It weighed a ton, creaking and complaining as she dragged it down the corridor. She pushed it flush up against the front door. It should at least slow Simon down and give her advance warning if he tried to force his way inside the house.

She had to think clearly. If she had been alone, she would have tried sneaking out the back door and avoiding Simon and whatever the thing in the shadows behind him was, relying on her own ability and Thor to avoid contact. She could have headed back to Simon's house and hid out until dawn. But with the kids there, she couldn't risk it, and there was no way she was going to leave them behind. They would just slow her down if she tried to escape and sneak away.

There was only darkness and the woods beyond the four walls of the home, and Emily would bet her last can of peaches that the alien was better equipped to find them than she and the children were at avoiding it. Besides, Ben was too upset. The kid just would not shut up. They wouldn't get ten feet before Simon heard them making a run for it.

She took a deep breath and exhaled slowly. For now, the children were safe in the guest room—it was the only place in the house that was not directly adjacent to an external wall—with Thor standing guard over them. Neither of the kids had spoken a word to her since they had entered the house. By the light of the flashlights, she had seen Rhiannon's frightened, accusing eyes staring at her as she cradled her baby brother in her arms.

The front door had a five-by-ten-inch glass window with fake leading set into it at about head height. Switching the flashlight off so she wouldn't be seen, Emily clambered up onto the desk and shuffled forward on her knees until she could see out through the tiny window into the front yard.

Simon had not moved from where she had last seen him. He was still swaying back and forth. The disconcerting grin had been replaced with that emotionless nonexpression. She could see the moon glinting off his eyes as he, unblinking, continued to stare at the front door. She felt a chill run down her spine, chased by a frigid drop of sweat. Even though she was sure it was impossible for him to see her hiding there in the darkness, she had the distinct impression that he was aware of her presence. It was almost as though the door and the walls and the distance did not matter; she could feel his awareness of her. She supposed it should scare her. Instead she found herself angry, pissed off at the thought of yet another one of these intruders on her world trying to frighten her, trying to kill her and the kids.

If it wasn't for the fact that the man standing out there was the children's father, she would risk storming outside with the Mossberg and facing off with the thing that hid in the shadows behind Simon. That was, of course, assuming the thing even had a face.

She had to curb her instincts to blow the thing away and think about the safety of the children. She had no idea if Simon was still alive or dead, but after her past experience, she would not place bets on the first option. There was no way she was going to jeopardize the children, and she surely didn't want to be seen as the person responsible for Simon's death in the kids' eyes. At this point, she had to consider Simon a lost cause and concentrate on figuring some way of getting the children to safety.

Emily looked up to check on Simon one final time and screamed. Simon had moved, and he had moved fast. Now he was standing just a few feet from the house, directly in front of the door, staring through the window at her.

"Oh, shit!" she squeaked as she stared back at the man outside the door. This close she could see the three tentacles, each as thick as her wrist, snaking up over Simon's head. Jesus! The thing must be on the roof of the house, she thought as her eyes followed the barbed tubes up until they disappeared above the rain gutter running along the edge of the roof.

Simon continued to focus on the little window. Emily stared at Simon, unable to look away, fascinated by what she was watching. As she continued to watch him, she saw the muscles in his face convulse once...then again. His dry, chapped lips began to move, only slightly at first, but then his mouth opened and closed repeatedly. Emily could see his tongue, white and flaccid, begin to twitch behind the wall of his teeth.

Simon spoke.

At least, he tried to speak. What came out of his mouth was a weird half yell, half-slurred cry, like a deaf person trying to enunciate clearly or a child trying to grapple with a particularly difficult word for the first time, sounding out the vowels and consonants individually.

"Chaaaaadaaaaannn."

Whatever it was he was trying to say was utterly indistinguishable, the word too slow and slurred for her to understand. Simon's mouth contorted asymmetrically, the right side of his upper lip moving upward while the rest of his mouth stayed rigidly still. She watched in horrified fascination as Simon tried again; this time he seemed to have more control of his lips.

"Chaalldraannnn."

There was no look of frustration or annoyance on the man's pale face. His eyes remained facing forward, his body unmoving. Another pause, and then he spoke again. This time, although still distorted, Emily understood exactly what he was saying.

"Chhilldrennn." The single word came out as a whisper, as though he was checking the feel of it against his tongue and lips. Her mind raced to grasp the implications of the situation: was he trying to lure them out there? The shadow of the thing she had seen standing behind Simon in the darkness, the owner, she presumed, of the tendrils attached to him, had seemed massive, far too large to get into the house. But why would it need to use Simon to lure them to it? Maybe it was too slow, or wanted to take them alive? Simon had taken forever to stumble jerkily across the lawn when they'd first arrived, but he (and whatever was controlling him) had made it from his stationary position on the gravel to the front door as fast as a normal person while she had been distracted. So maybe the thing was getting used to operating its host, like a human becoming familiar with a new car. Whatever the reason, this thing was able to control a human and assume complete authority of his mind and functions, controlling him as if he were a puppet. It spoke of a whole new level of weird…worse, it spoke of a dark intelligence, an intelligence that was motivated.

"Children," Simon yelled suddenly, the word enunciated perfectly this time, shouted rather than whispered. Simon's voice had returned, and that single word held all the warmth and emotion that she had heard whenever he'd spoken to Ben and Rhia over the past couple of days. But his face remained as impassive and unemotional as a statue, the black tubes attached to his back a hideous reminder that the words were not his own. It was like he was simply repeating a recording; he was a mechanical entity regurgitating the words perfectly.

"Children," he called again, his voice rising to the point where there was no doubt the two kids could hear him. "It's Daddy. Come on out here."

Emily stumbled back from the door. She could still see Simon's silhouette through the small glass window.

"Ben? Rhee. Ann. On? Come out. It is okay. Daddy is here." Simon's voice echoed down the hallway and into the house, pushing the silence aside. While it reached the same emotional amplitude she had heard Simon use with his children, it sounded false, almost robotic, to Emily.

A gruff bark from Thor and the padding of paws and feet alerted Emily to the children heading her way.

"Daddy?" Rhiannon's voice called from behind Emily. She turned and illuminated the little girl with her flashlight at the opposite end of the corridor. Ben was next to her. His sister's arms wrapped around his fragile frame as they both blinked in the beam of the torch.

"Jesus," she muttered, realization flooding her mind. This thing wanted the kids, and it was using their father to lure them out. It must know that she was here with them, and there was no way she was going to surrender either herself or the kids, and there was no way it could get to them while they were holed up in the house. So it would pull the kids to it, knowing that she would not be far behind. And if it couldn't lure them outside? Then it would be only a matter of time until it figured out how to get inside.

An even more frightening thought crossed her mind: What if he was still aware of what was happening to him? What if behind those eyes he was aware of the pain of each cracking bone as his body was reorganized to his captor's will? What if he was aware of the motivation of this thing that wanted to use him to lure out his children and...what? Kill them? Consume them? Make them like him? And what if there was nothing he could do about it as he was bent and molded to the will of the thing controlling him?

Emily had read about a bird called a shrike. It would impale its prey on thorns and wait for it to die, slowly consuming it over time. She glanced back at the tentacles extending from Simon and the row of barbs running along its length. She searched Simon's pale face for any sign of the man she had met, but all she saw were his lifeless eyes and marionette-like stance.

She made an instant and unemotional decision.

Emily stalked down the corridor and crouched down in front of Rhiannon and the boy. Ben still refused to look at her, hiding his head in his sister's shoulder, but Rhiannon stared right back at Emily from the dimness of the shadowy corridor. Emily could see that the child understood what was coming next—maybe only on some subconscious level, but she understood.

Emily took a deep breath and spoke, not even sure what words to use. "Your daddy is very sick," she began. "I know you can hear him outside and I know you want to go to him, but he's not feeling very well and I'm afraid that he might"—she paused as she searched again for the right words—"I'm afraid he might make you sick, too. So, we're going to get out of here and, when your dad's better, we'll come back for him, okay?"

Ben's sobs grew louder. Rhiannon pulled her brother closer. "It's all okay, Benny," she whispered. "It's okay. Daddy's going to be fine. We have to go with Emily right now, though."

Ben's sobs stuttered and finally stalled. Emily's heart wanted to break for these two kids whose life she was sure had been changed forever this night. She resisted the urge to reach out and stroke the little boy's hair; that would probably set him off again. His cries had faded to the occasional sniffle, and she was not exactly the flavor of the month with him right now. Instead, Emily smiled at Rhiannon. "All right, kids. We have to be really quiet from now on. Let's go."

■ ■ ■

Emily held her breath and shone the flashlight into the corridor, searching for the hook with the car keys she thought she had seen when she'd first arrived.

There it was. She could see the glint of the keys hanging from a hook plugged into the wall. She plucked the keys from the hook, noting the embossed Dodge logo on the black plastic fob. These had to be the right ones.

Emily turned to the children and moved her forefinger to her lips. Both kids nodded they understood, and Emily was relieved to see that Ben's tears had dried up, his big hazel eyes, bloodshot and pitted in the beam of the flashlight, gazed back at her with just a hint of trust behind the fear and pain. She pushed the door to the garage open. The former owner must have been handy with the WD-40 because the creak of dry hinges she had expected never materialized. She ushered the children and Thor past her as she held the door open. When they were all safely inside, she closed the door again as quietly as possible.

The big Dodge SUV was exactly where she had seen it when she'd first arrived at the house.

The handle was locked. Her thumb was hovering over the alarm disable button on the key fob when she stopped herself. If she used the key fob to turn off the alarm, wouldn't it make that *whoop-whoop* sound she'd heard so many times on the streets of New York? She couldn't risk any noise alerting the Simon-thing to the fact that they were at the other end of the house.

If she used the key to unlock the door manually, would that have the same effect? She had no idea, but the door had to be opened. She slipped the key into the lock and turned it. The locks unlocking sounded like gunshots in the silence of the garage, and the sudden illumination from the automatic interior lights sent flashing motes zooming across her eyes, but there was no alarm.

She reached back and pulled open the rear passenger door. "Come on, kids. Quickly, jump inside," she hissed.

Thor didn't need to be asked twice. Tail wagging frenetically, he leaped into the back row of seats and positioned himself behind the front passenger seat. Rhiannon helped to get Ben up onto the kick plate with a push on his butt. He clambered the rest of the way inside and was met with a barrage of licks from Thor that teased out a giggle from the little boy.

Well, that was a good sign. At least he was not irreparably damaged. Rhiannon pulled herself up into the backseat next to her brother and immediately pulled the seat belt across him, fastening it into the receiver, then clicking her own belt into place.

Sure that the two children were safely locked down, Emily pushed the door closed as quietly as she could.

Climbing into the driver's seat, she pulled her own door quietly shut behind her. Now came the hard part.

She had no idea what any of these dials, switches, and levers did. She mentally kicked herself in the ass again for not having taken any driving lessons. At least she knew what the steering wheel and gas and brake pedals were supposed to do. She looked down between the driver's and passenger's seats—thank God it was an automatic and not a stick shift.

"Okay," she whispered. "Now what?"

Emily found the ignition on the steering column and slotted the key into the receiver. She turned the key and felt it slip into the first position with a reassuring click. Instantly the interior lights turned off, replaced by a neon-blue glow from the dashboard instruments. Emily breathed a sigh of relief. Part of her had been sure that the battery would be dead.

She took a few seconds to familiarize herself with the layout of the cockpit. The gearshift handle was on her right, a lever jutting from the left of the steering column. It had some kind of a twistable selector at the end of it, covered in white icons. They obviously represented headlight settings, so she turned the selector to the first position. The interior of the garage lit up, pushing back some of the shadows. She twisted the switch to the next setting and was pleased to see the headlights become even brighter, illuminating the entirety of the garage and the flat metal of the retractable garage door in front of her.

The garage doors…Shit!

How was she supposed to open them without any power?

If this were a movie, she would probably just start the car, rev it up, and burst through them before speeding off into the darkness. This wasn't a movie, though, and the shuttered metal looked pretty strong to her. There must be some way to manually open them, she reasoned. After all, what would happen if there was a power outage? Were people expected to be locked out of their garages?

"Stay in the car, kids," she said, turning to face the children. "I'll be right back."

Emily took a deep breath to steady her breathing and exited the vehicle, her heart thumping in her chest. She made sure the SUV's door was ajar, then checked that the door leading from the interior of the house was still closed securely; she didn't want the Simon-thing creeping up behind them.

A large plastic box was fixed to the ceiling right above the Durango's roof. A thick chain, much like the chain of her bike, ran from the box along a metal beam to the door. Fixed to the garage door was a curved arm that extended upward, connecting to the pulley system that raised and lowered the door. That was how the door would open normally, but how the hell was she supposed to raise it now? She spotted two aluminum handles at the base of the door, near the floor. She grasped one and gave it a gentle tug. The door rattled, moving up about an inch but then hit resistance and refused to budge any farther. Looking up at the arm attached to the door and the pulley illuminated in the beam of the SUV, she could see there was some kind of hook attachment that meshed into the chain like the spokes of a gear. A nylon cord with a red plastic handle at the end hung from the arm, swinging back and forth gently.

The handle screamed, "Pull me!"

Again, she found herself holding her breath as she grasped the plastic handle in her hand and tugged. There was a very distinct click as something disengaged from the chain, but there was no other indication of anything else happening. Was that it? Only one way to find out, she told herself. Emily moved back to the door and, ever so gently, pulled the same handle.

This time the door continued to move past the stop, rumbling and rattling along its tracks. When the door was a foot off the ground, she stopped. What if Simon was outside right now? Waiting for her. He could grab her legs and pull her under the door, and that would be it. She let the door drop to the floor with a clang of rattling metal.

There was no doubt in her mind that whatever controlled Simon was going to hear them trying to escape. When it did it would do whatever it could to get to them. What would happen if she opened the garage door and it was waiting outside? She would have a matter of seconds at most to get to the vehicle, figure out how to drive it, and get out of there. And then what? Where would they go? They had no supplies. Everything, including her bike, backpack, and sat-phone was at the other house.

That was the least of her problems.

She needed to figure out whether she should lift the garage door first and then hope the car started before Simon found them. Or did she start the car first and hope the garage door would open?

"Jesus," Emily hissed. Despite the cool night air, she felt sweat trickle down the insides of her arms.

It made no sense to raise the barrier between them, she reasoned, only to find that the Dodge would not start. That would leave them completely exposed. Car first. Then worry about the garage doors. She climbed back into the driver's seat and looked at the kids. "Okay, you two, here we go." Reaching for the ignition keys, she twisted them all the way forward.

Nothing happened.

"Shit," she cried and thumped the steering wheel. The engine was dead. They had been through all this only for the fucking SUV to not start? You had to be kidding.

"You have to step on the brake," said a voice from the back-seat. Emily flashed around to face Rhiannon, trying to keep the anger and disappointment from her voice.

"What?"

"You have to step on the brake to start the car," Rhiannon repeated. "It's a safety feature," she added proudly, probably repeating some tidbit of information she had learned from her dad.

Emily looked down at her feet. Which pedal was the brake? It had to be the larger of the two, she reasoned and pressed her left foot down and twisted the ignition key again.

The big V-8 engine of the Dodge Durango exploded into life. It was incredibly loud in the enclosed space of the garage. Emily flipped around and shot a huge smile at Rhiannon, all anger dissipating with the deep roar of the engine. She could already smell the acrid stench of the vehicle's exhaust seeping through the open driver's door and gave a little cough. It wouldn't do to breathe this crap in for very long, but she needed to leave the door open, every second would count. Sorry, kids, she thought as she leaped from the driver's seat and ran over to the garage door.

She grasped the metal handle again and began pulling with all the strength she had. If there had been any doubt that Simon would not be alerted to their escape attempt, it was quickly dispelled as the door rattled along the tracks, even louder, it seemed to Emily, than the rumble of the SUV's engine. With the door halfway up, Emily dipped her head under the gap and scanned the area beyond the garage. The light from the SUV illuminated the ground directly in front of the garage, pushing the darkness away. There was no sign of anything waiting outside to grab her. Thank God.

Flipping her grip on the handle she began pushing the door up rather than pulling it. The door was almost at its zenith when

Emily heard the clattering of dislodged roof tiles as something huge scrambled over the roof toward her.

"Oh, shit! Oh, shit!"

What was she supposed to do now? The door was still only three-quarters of the way up. She let go of it for a second and watched as it began to slowly slide back toward the ground. She grabbed the handle again and began pushing. There was no way she was going to get back into the car in time to figure out the controls and get out of the garage before the door closed on them again or the thing scrambling across the roof reached her.

Run, her frightened mind screamed. Just leave the kids and run.

No way! There was not a chance in hell that she was going to do that. She would rather just—

She felt the metal garage door click into place. Looking up, she could see the hook had engaged itself again onto the stud on the pulley. She let go of the handle and the door settled back slightly but stayed exactly where it should be, suspended above her head.

"Thank you," she sighed and sprinted back to the SUV. She was about to clamber into the driver's seat when a cascade of adobe-colored roof tiles fell to the concrete just outside the entrance of the garage, shattering like broken plates across the drive. Before the last broken piece had skittered across the concrete, a shape dropped from the roof, landing low to the ground just on the other side of the door, red eyes staring unblinking into the lights of the SUV.

"Simon," she whimpered as she leaped into the driver's seat, slamming the door behind her.

CHAPTER THIRTEEN

"Rhiannon," Emily yelled. "Cover your brother's eyes...*now!*"

Emily pushed the accelerator to the floor and slipped the gear stick into the drive position. There was a squealing noise, and, in the rearview mirror, Emily saw smoke begin to fill the garage. What was she doing wrong? Why weren't they moving?

Through the windshield, Emily could see Simon, and for a second her heart seemed to stop. He had undergone a stunning metamorphosis. His arms had rotated 180 degrees in their sockets and now jutted forward from each elbow. His legs were impossibly twisted at the knees, so he now walked on all fours rather than upright. The tentacle trailing from the back of Simon's head pulsed once as it pushed something dark and viscous down its elongated length. Whatever that stuff was had an instant effect on Simon; his neck began to stretch inch by inch until, finally, it had grown in length by six inches or more.

"Oh no," she squeaked as she fumbled with the gear stick, pushing it back into Park. What the hell am I doing wrong? What? She chanced another look outside.

Simon's head arced back on his newly elongated neck, like a snake rising to strike. A trickle of black liquid that could have been blood, or spillover from whatever shit the thing controlling Simon had pumped into him, dribbled from the corners of his mouth. And then he leaped into the air, pushing himself into the air like some weird, alien grasshopper.

He landed with a resounding thud on the hood of the SUV.

Emily screamed and pulled the gear stick back into drive. The screeching of tires and the roar of the engine filled her ears again, but still they did not move, and with only a quarter inch of glass separating them, she stared into the black dead eyes of a monster that had once been Simon Keller.

"You have to take your foot off the brake," Rhiannon yelled from the backseat just as Emily realized her mistake and yanked her foot from the pedal. The SUV shot forward, and Emily was pretty sure everyone inside the vehicle screamed at the same moment. It was hard for her to tell because her attention was completely focused on Simon; his twisted body blocked her view ahead of her.

He flew forward, hitting the windshield face-first, leaving a smear of black fluid behind as his body rolled up and onto the roof of the SUV. A second later and his misshapen face appeared at the passenger door window, his eyes searching for some way into the vehicle.

"Don't look," Emily yelled as she fought for control of the rapidly accelerating vehicle, but the warning came too late as she heard Rhiannon's sorrowful scream of "Daddy?"

Anger flowed through Emily. She was going to end this…
right here…right now.

She took her foot off the accelerator and hit the brake. The
Dodge came to a sudden, jarring halt, and Emily saw Simon's
body fly through the air, the three tentacles trailing behind him
like marionette strings. He landed on the concrete driveway in
front of the car, rolled three times, then flipped to his feet and
began to scuttle toward them again.

Emily floored the accelerator, and the SUV lurched forward.

Simon froze midstep, caught like the proverbial rabbit in
the lights of the rapidly accelerating SUV. A fraction of a second
before the vehicle would have flattened him, he leaped into the
air and landed on the hood of the Durango, one misshapen hand
clinging to the seam of the hood below the windshield wipers.

And then he was gone, as his fingers lost their grip and he
tumbled sideways off the hood.

In the rearview mirror, Emily saw Simon's body disappear
into the white bank of smoke from her tires and then even that
vanished as the SUV was swallowed by the darkness.

■ ■ ■

"Oh my God! Oh my God!" Emily yelled as the SUV continued
to accelerate, careening along the gravel driveway, sending stones
and rocks flying into the dark as the back end fishtailed wildly
from side to side, its tires scrabbling for grip on the loose rock.
The children's screams from the back row of seats rang in her ears,
but they were nothing compared to the screaming in her own
head as she careened into the darkness.

Technically she had never learned to drive, never even been
behind the wheel of a car or a truck before. But as her mind raced

to find some kind of previous experience that might help her out, she remembered a visit to Coney Island and the bumper cars attraction. The principle had to be the same, right? Press the pedal to go and release it to slow down while using the steering wheel to point the SUV in the direction you wanted to go.

In the fear-induced clarity of the moment, her mind seized that little bit of knowledge and held on to it like a shipwreck survivor holding on to a life preserver in the middle of an angry ocean. Who had she been trying to fool all this time? How freaking hard could it be to drive one of these things? After all, it was just an oversize bumper car at heart. Right? She glanced down at the speedometer; the arm was just below the forty-five miles per hour mark. In the second or so that she stared at it, the speedometer climbed up to just under fifty miles per hour.

Outside the rapidly accelerating vehicle, it was as though someone had dropped a curtain of black all around them as it plummeted through the darkness. She could see nothing on either side of her but vague shadows; the only light was the swath cut ahead of her by the powerful headlights. Emily had no idea where she was going, but for now the gravel path led only one way: forward. Away from the house and the Simon-thing that she had left there.

She glanced in the rearview mirror to check on the kids. She could hear both of them whimpering in the backseat, but she couldn't tell if they were hurt or just frightened. Looking back over her right shoulder, she saw the two kids huddled together, still strapped in by their safety belts. Thor had disappeared from the seat, and she could not see him. A whimper from somewhere behind the passenger seat told her he had decided the floor of the Durango was probably a safer place to be for now.

When she turned back, the gravel road before them had disappeared, replaced by blacktop that curved away at a ninety-degree angle to the right. In that split second of recognition, she already knew she was going too fast to make the turn, and before she could even decide whether to hit the brakes, the SUV had left the road and was in flight.

The Dodge smashed through a corrugated aluminum barrier that had been placed there to stop just such a thing from happening, although she was sure whoever had erected the barrier had never anticipated a nondriver with a vehicle full of kids being chased by their late father under the control of some shadowy alien. The SUV exploded off a grassy berm, and for a few long moments Emily knew what Commander Mulligan must have felt when she first experienced the weightlessness of space.

A second later the Durango hit the ground with a bone-snapping thump, teetering on its two left wheels before collapsing back down to the ground with another rattling crunch. The force of the impact lifted Emily from the seat, and, as the screams of Ben and Rhiannon filled the cabin again, her head whipped hard to the left, colliding with the glass of the window.

Her last thought before everything went black was that she was sorry she had not been able to save the children.

CHAPTER FOURTEEN

One second the world was normal, and the next Rhiannon was weightless, at least until the strap of the seat belt tugged her back down into the leather seats with a jarring slap. She was aware of her little brother next to her, his arms flailing as the SUV bumped and rattled over the ground. Her own limbs were useless to her as she was thrown around like the raggedy doll she had played with when she was little.

The first hint she had that the car had stopped was when she realized that the interior dome lights were on and there was a really annoying pinging coming from the front of the car. That was weird because just a second ago the entire cabin had been dark except for the instrument panel's glow. She tried to lean forward, but the seat belt still held her firmly in its grasp, pinning her to the seat. The leather squeaked like one of her little brother's farts as she wriggled her butt to try to free herself of the belt.

Rhiannon pushed against the restraints again, but they still held fast. When she dipped her head to look for the belt's release button, her neck spasmed painfully. "Owwww!" she cried, but she strained a little more anyway, until her thumb found the button and pressed. The clip popped from the receiver, and Rhiannon felt the belt's grip loosen as it slid away.

Using the two front seats as leverage, she pulled herself forward until she could see Emily slumped in the driver's seat, her head lolling forward, her hands loosely draped at her side.

Even in the dim glow of the car's interior light, Rhiannon could see a bright splash of blood on the window of the driver's door; strands of Emily's hair were caught in the congealing blood. Rhiannon wasn't sure whether the six-inch stain on the window was a lot of blood or not. It looked like it was a lot, but other than a few cuts and grazes, Rhiannon had rarely seen blood before. She reached out and tentatively touched Emily's shoulder, shaking her gently. "Emily," she whispered. "Are you okay?"

There was no response from the still form in the driver's seat. Rhiannon leaned farther between the seats, ignoring the dull ache in her shoulders and across her chest. Emily's eyes were closed, and Rhiannon could see a line of blood, already beginning to dry, trickling from the woman's bottom lip and down her chin, dripping into a small pool that had soaked into her pants.

"Emily?" She gave her shoulder a final shake. Emily's body slipped slowly sideways until her head once again connected with the bloody window.

■ ■ ■

A low whine from the backseat dragged Rhiannon's attention away from Emily. Thor was standing on the ground outside the car, just visible in the umbra of the open rear passenger door. Rhiannon's shocked mind began to assess exactly what was wrong with the picture: the door was wide open—that was why the interior lights were on and the annoying pinging was still pulsing through the cabin. The seat next to hers, the one where her little brother had sat, was empty, the seat belt snapped neatly back against the back of the leather seat.

Something was missing.

Ben! He was nowhere to be seen.

How had she not noticed that? How had she forgotten about her little brother? Her head, still buzzing with that really annoying pinging from the front of the car, felt like it was going to explode any second. How had she forgotten Ben? The little dweeb was so annoying, he was going to be in soooo much trouble when Dad got ahold of his butt. He was going to be grounded for—

Thor's bark cut through the static filling Rhiannon's head. What had she been thinking? She had to find her little brother right now! She scooted over the seats to the open door. Thor was doing the canine equivalent of shuffling his feet nervously; his tail wagged enthusiastically when he saw Rhiannon moving his way.

The second Rhiannon's feet hit the soft grass, Thor jumped into the space she had just exited. He sniffed curiously at Emily's body; first the dried blood that had congealed on her chin, then down her neck and torso, and finally her arm that hung at her side. He gave a sad whine and pawed gently at her unmoving body.

Rhiannon turned slowly in a circle, scanning the wall of darkness for any sign of her missing brother. The SUV was front-down in a shallow ditch, but Rhiannon could hear the engine still running and the lights were still on, which she guessed was a good thing.

"Ben!" she yelled, surprised at how weak and croaky her voice sounded against the weight of the cool night air. She listened, waiting for a reply. Instead, all she heard was the desperate whine of Thor, still perched on the center console behind the two front seats, pawing at Emily.

What was wrong with this dumb dog? Rhiannon wondered. Didn't he know a dead person when he smelled her? She glanced around the outside of the car. Maybe the dog could be useful. She had seen how her little brother had taken to the big mound of fur.

"Thor!" she snapped. "Where's Ben?" The dog glanced her way, then went back to sniffing Emily. "Thor," she called again, this time a little less sharply. "We need to find Ben. Where's Ben?"

Thor turned again at the sound of Ben's name. He glanced back at Emily one last time, then jumped down from the backseat and started sniffing around the grass. "That's it. Good boy. Find Ben."

The malamute sniffed left and right a few more times, gave a single bark, and started up the embankment the car had fallen down.

"Wait up, you dumb dog," Rhiannon shouted as Thor was swallowed up by the wall of blackness. Then she took off running as fast as she could after him.

■ ■ ■

Rhiannon scrambled up the embankment after Thor, her sneakers slipping on the loose earth. The dog stopped at the top for her, waiting patiently in the last of the light from the SUV's headlights as she pulled herself up the twenty feet or so of incline, his tongue lolling from his mouth.

"Just slow down, dog," Rhiannon panted as she finally pulled herself over the top of the embankment and onto the graveled curve of the road, but the dog was already off again. She could hear his paws scattering the gravel as he loped down the road, back in the direction of the Jeffersons' place.

"Benjamin!" she yelled the next time she stopped. Sweat, sticky and salty, trickled down her forehead and into her mouth. "Yuck."

The stupid dog had already taken off again, but Rhiannon wasn't going to just blindly follow him. She waited patiently for a reply from her brother, then, when there was none, she called out into the darkness again, this time a little louder.

As she waited for her brother to reply, she thought about her dad. She had hoped that maybe she had imagined it all, but she knew that something was very wrong with him. She had seen the shape in the shadows that had those…hooked things stuck in him. Although she would not admit it, she knew her dad was badly hurt, maybe even worse. But her little brother wasn't going to know that. He wasn't going to sense the danger he might be in, that his daddy was no longer who he thought he was.

Although the fear was almost overwhelming for her, she was not going to let the thing that had taken her father take her little brother, too. If there was some way that she could rescue them both, she was going to figure it out. Dad always said she was much brighter than all her friends she hung out with.

The sweat from her climb had begun to cool as the chilly night air slowly claimed her body heat. Her breath formed a white cloud in front of her face. It was so incredibly quiet out here. Except for the occasional rustle of leaves from a light breeze blowing through the branches of the forest, there was no sound. Even the air felt absent, somehow—so still it might as well not be there.

The silence was broken by the sound of scattering gravel as Thor padded back to her location. He looked unhappy that she was not following him, but he could just stuff it. It was her brother that they were trying to find, and she was not going to put all her trust in some dumb dog. She was going to do things her way.

To prove the point, Rhiannon let out a long, loud "*Beeeennnnnnnnnn!*" into the night. Her voice echoed through the woods. She winced at how loud her call actually was. Who knew how many more of those things were out there in the darkness? And now they knew where she was for certain. God! She was *so* dumb sometimes.

In the distance, carried on the breeze, Rhiannon heard a faint but unmistakable answer to her call: "Rhiaaaa!" It was barely audible to her, but Thor's ears pricked up and he was gone in a second, heading off down the path in the call's direction. It was her brother. She knew the little dweeb's voice as though it were her own.

He was alive.

A second after Thor had been swallowed up by the darkness, Rhiannon began sprinting after him.

CHAPTER FIFTEEN

"What happened?"

Emily heard the voice ask the question again before she realized that it was she who was speaking. For a moment she was confused. Hadn't she been in the SUV? Wasn't she supposed to be going somewhere? There was something important she was supposed to be doing, she was sure of it.

Then, like a mistuned radio that finally found the right station, her mind cleared and the confusion was replaced by a heavy aching pain in her head and a nauseating dizziness that forced her to her knees. For a few moments, she thought she was going to throw up, but after a couple of deep steadying breaths, her vision cleared. A loud continuous whirring sound filled the inside of her skull where her brain had once been. The noise finally resolved into the dull drone of the Durango's engine. Somehow she had managed to get out of the driving seat and walk a few feet away from the vehicle.

How the hell had that happened?

The children! She pushed herself to her feet, almost collaps-ing again as the world swam in front of her eyes. She staggered toward the lights of the SUV, her hand in front of her eyes to stop the screaming bolts of pain bouncing around her head.

The driver's side door was wide open. She saw the congealed bloodstain on the glass of the window, and her hand moved invol-untarily to her head. She felt a sting of pain as her hand found a raised egg-size lump on the left side of her head, a couple of inches back from her hairline. She pulled her fingers away and looked at the clean tips. Well at least she wasn't bleeding anymore, but good grief, did it hurt like a mother.

The inside of the SUV was empty. Emily made her way around to the passenger side, leaning hard against the body of the Durango in case her vision betrayed her again.

There was no sign of the children outside the SUV, and she let out a small sigh of relief when she saw that there was no blood on the seats the kids had occupied. That could only mean that they had survived the crash and had left her for whatever reason. There was also no sign of Thor. She knew there was no way her dog would have abandoned her unless he had had to, so he must be with Ben and Rhiannon.

Standing in the dim glow of the SUV's light, Emily realized with a growing unease that she knew exactly where the children were: they were on their way back to the last place they had seen Simon.

■ ■ ■

The pain in Emily's head pulsed harder and lightning lanced through her brain as she tried to jog back to the driver's seat of the big SUV, forcing her to stop and lean against its rear door while her swimming vision and whirling stomach returned to normal. Was she concussed? Maybe, but she had to get to the kids before they reached the Jefferson house. She had no idea how much of a head start the two children had, so she was going to have to get the Dodge out of the ditch and drive it if she was to have any chance of finding the children before they got to Simon...or he found them.

She edged around the SUV, leaning hard against its body for support. The front-left wheel of the Dodge was lodged in a ditch, canting the vehicle to the left, and the front-right wheel was half-way up the embankment; just a few more feet and the SUV would have rolled over, she realized.

Emily pulled herself through the open door into the driver's seat, slamming it shut behind her, and instantly regretting it as the thud reverberated through her head. She gave a startled cry when the cabin lights went out, plunging her into darkness.

The engine was still rumbling, reverberating through the leather seats and steering wheel as she gripped it. She was going to have to reverse this thing out of the ditch if she wanted to go anywhere.

The headlights illuminated the opposite side of the ditch the SUV had landed in. It was a couple of feet higher than the hood, and she had no doubt the SUV could make it over it if it wasn't for the fact that it was lined with trees.

She slipped the gear stick to the reverse position and lifted her foot off the brake. The engine revs increased slightly, but the SUV barely moved an inch. She glanced in the rearview mirror; everything beyond the back of the Dodge was bathed in the red glow of the vehicle's taillights. The white of the reverse lights stretched barely beyond that but were next to useless for seeing anything.

Sliding her foot onto the accelerator, Emily eased it toward the floor, slowly increasing the revs. The vehicle edged up the side of the embankment, then slid back down when it was almost halfway. Frustrated, Emily pushed harder on the accelerator pedal; the big SUV's rear wheels spun as they fought for traction on the grass, finally found it, and catapulted backward out of the ditch and onto the field.

Emily's head flew forward then back again as her seat belt lock engaged. Blackness began to creep into the edge of her vision, but she willed herself to stay conscious, pushing it back until she realized her foot was still on the accelerator. She slipped it off the pedal and slammed on the brake. This time her head flew backward into the head support of the seat, and she saw motes of blackness float across her eyes, blocking the console gauges.

"Jesus," she hissed when her vision finally cleared again. "I've about had enough of this shit."

Taking a deep breath, she slipped the gear stick back into drive and slowly pushed on the accelerator, pointing the grill of the Dodge in the direction she thought the road should be. If she could find the embankment she had crashed over, she would follow it and hope she could find a way onto the gravel road that led back to the Jeffersons' place.

The SUV's headlights cut through the darkness in front of her, illuminating the ground ahead. Everything else beyond that was pitch-black. Wasn't there something brighter? Emily glanced down at the stick with the light controls; the twisty-knob thing had one more selection to it. She turned it, and instantly the field of light in front of her widened and heightened.

"That's more like it."

With the high beams on, she quickly spotted the curve of the embankment rising up in front of her. There were no tire tracks coming down the slope, but she could see a chunk of earth and clots of muddy grass near the base of the embankment, a weaving track of crushed grass and broken earth leading away from where she had landed. What she also saw, as she slowed to a stop at the base of the embankment, was a line of divots, presumably leading up to the road above. She could be wrong, but to her it looked almost like the kind of marks she thought Rhiannon's sneakers would make if the little girl was trying to climb it.

It was hardly conclusive proof, but it would have to do because it was the only clue she had right now to what direction the children had taken.

Emily accelerated slowly until the Dodge was parallel with the base of the embankment and began slowly following the base around as it curved to match the road above. About two hundred yards farther on, she saw the dusty-gray reflection of the gravel road as it dipped down and leveled out.

Turning hard right, she directed the SUV up onto the road. She heard the ping of gravel bouncing off the frame of the SUV as the front tires scrambled for grip. Then, with a final stab of the accelerator, she felt the rear tires dig deep into the soft earth and push her up and back onto the road.

Stealing herself against the coming confrontation, Emily carefully accelerated the SUV and headed back along the road toward the Jeffersons' house.

CHAPTER SIXTEEN

"Rhi-annnnn-on!"

Her brother's frightened voice drifted through the trees like a ghost toward her and Thor. The dog's ears pricked up at the boy's voice; then he dropped his nose to the ground again and bounded forward between two sprawling sycamore trees.

"I'm coming, Ben," Rhiannon yelled back. She tumbled after Thor. The laces of her left sneaker had come undone and would occasionally catch under her opposite foot, almost tripping her. She knew she should stop and tie them again, but her brother's voice had grown more scared sounding with each passing minute. So, she chose to keep on instead, unwilling to stop until she was with her little pain of a brother again.

Not long after she had scrambled up over the edge of the culvert, Thor had suddenly cut diagonally into the forest, leaving the safety of the road for a more direct route to Ben. That might be great for a dog with his superior sense of smell, but for Rhiannon, it was a painful and frustrating diversion. She bumped into trees, almost lost an eye to a low-hanging branch, and tripped over roots seemingly with almost every other step she took. She could feel rivulets of blood trickling down her arm, and her cheek stung from a collision with a branch.

The black shadow of the Jeffersons' house suddenly loomed large in front of her. She had emerged from the woods on the west side of the house, adjacent to the garage they had escaped from earlier.

Thor suddenly stopped, growling menacingly. The dog backed up until he was parallel with Rhiannon, his eyes fixed squarely on two shapes that slowly resolved from the shadow of the house.

Ben was at his dad's side, one of Simon's hands resting heavily across his back, cupping the little boy's left shoulder. Behind them, that same indistinct shadow she had seen earlier loomed, blocking out the shape of the house and moving with the boy and the man.

"Hello, sweetie," said her father. Rhiannon felt a shudder of fear run down her spine at the sound of Simon's voice. Thor gave another growl and backed up even farther until Rhiannon was between him and Simon.

She could see Ben's face, pale against the black night, splotches of dirt on his cheeks bisected by the tracks of tears that still ran from her brother's rheumy eyes.

"Rhia," he sniveled, and he flinched as Simon's grip tightened against his shoulder.

"Come here, Rhiannon. There's a good girl." The voice sounded like her father's, but it wasn't. There was none of the warmth usually present when he spoke to her. And no way would he ever have let Ben cry like that. Besides, the only time Dad ever called her by her full name was when he was pissed at her. And if he was angry, then why was there a permanent smile fixed to his face?

No, whoever this was that had her little brother, it was no longer her dad.

Her father was gone. The pain of the realization was like a dagger thrust into her heart, and she felt her own tears begin to soak her cheeks again.

"Rhiannon," Simon called again, this time a little sharper, utterly oblivious to her pain. "I said…come…here." As he spoke, Rhiannon could see her father's hand slip from Ben's shoulder and move around the back of the boy's neck. "I won't ask again." The threat to her brother was obvious.

Simon's head suddenly dipped sideways until his ear was almost touching his right shoulder. It was as if he expected this position to give him some new perspective on this strange little creature before him. The smile grew wider, and Rhiannon saw his hand tighten around Ben's neck. His fingers enclosed her little brother's throat completely as simultaneously he lifted the boy up until his feet were just inches off the ground.

"Noooo!" Rhia pleaded as her brother began to choke. His feet jittered and kicked, and his eyes, still fixed on hers, bulged as his mouth opened and closed like a fish stranded on the bank of a river. Though she wanted to move, she was glued to the spot by fear. Her feet might just as well have been roots for all the good they did her. She wanted to run, to head back into the darkness of the woods and never look back. "Let…Let Ben go," was all the resistance she could muster.

"Come here, Rhiannon," repeated Simon, still holding the boy. Rhiannon could see Ben's face slowly turning redder and redder as his convulsive kicking began to grow slower and slower.

"Not fair," whimpered Rhiannon as she took another reticent step toward her father and brother. "Please," she sniffled, "let him go."

Her father's head moved from horizontal back to its normal, upright position. As his head moved, he lowered the little boy back to the ground until the kid could at least rest the tips of his toes on the grass. It was low enough that the pressure was removed from Ben's throat, but easy enough for her dad to quickly lift him off the ground again if he wanted to.

Her brother let out a gasp as he sucked in air, and Rhiannon felt a surge of relief as she saw his eyes, which had been tightly shut, flicker open and meet her own gaze. She had no doubt that if he wanted to, he could easily tear her brother in half. The only reason it needed Ben was that whatever was concealed in the shadows was just too slow to catch her. It had to lure her to it. It wanted them both.

This close to what had once been her father, she could make out webs of fine black veins that spread out maplike across his face and his arms. In fact, every exposed piece of skin seemed to have those lines just below the surface. And, although shrouded in shadow, she could see his eyes were no longer the comforting pale blue she remembered; now they swirled with shades of darkness that foretold violence as surely as a thunderstorm promised lightning.

She was almost within arm's reach when she froze and stared past both her father and brother into the deeper darkness that lay just behind them. A smell, powerful enough to make her want to throw up, permeated the air and wafted to her on the cool evening breeze. Transfixed, Rhia saw the shadow shift, saw the three thick tubes running from her father back up into the darkness pulse and flex in synchronicity. Instantly, the arm holding Ben relaxed, dropping her brother the final inch or so to the ground and sending the boy coughing and spluttering to his knees. The other hand shot out toward her, grasping her upper arm in an iron grip that was far stronger than her father would ever have contemplated using.

Rhiannon stared helplessly as Simon's face drew closer to her own; then he sniffed her. He drew in a deep breath through his nose, his head moving first to the left of her and then to the right, like a wolf scenting its supper.

Simon's lips, laced with the same threading of black veins, drew back in a wide smile as he pulled Rhiannon and her brother to him. He wrapped one malformed arm around her waist and the other around Ben's, scooping them both off the ground as he turned and carried them into the darkness.

CHAPTER SEVENTEEN

As Emily rounded the final bend, the high beams of the SUV pushed back the darkness and revealed the house they had fled from directly ahead. The garage door was still up, but there was no sign of the children inside. She guided the SUV around in a slow turn, sweeping the area in front of the garage with the headlights, her eyes searching for any clue to where the children might have gone.

A flurry of motion off to her right caught her attention. A shadow was running across the open space toward her from the darkness of the woods: Thor!

He bounded across the yard in a few powerful lunges and was at the passenger door before she had managed to bring the SUV to a full stop. Emily fumbled for the door switch, found it, and heard the thump of the locks releasing. Unfastening her seat belt—no way was she ever driving without it, after tonight—she leaned as far across the passenger seat as she could and pulled on the door release handle. The door popped open, and she pushed it with the flat of her hand until it was open enough for the mala-mute to clamber, rather ungracefully, she noted, up into the pas-senger seat. She had to fight her way past his furry body and the excited licks and slurps of his tongue to pull the door shut again before slamming a clenched fist down on the Lock button.

No sooner had she clipped her safety belt back on and she was off again, slowly maneuvering the SUV around the perimeter of the house, trying to saturate every inch of the night-blanketed property with the high-intensity headlights.

Thor seemed unusually quiet. As soon as the SUV had begun moving, he had stepped off the seat and curled up in the leg space under the passenger side of the console in the equivalent of a doggy fetal position, his eyes never straying from her face. She didn't think he was hurt; he just seemed…afraid.

She passed the open garage and swung the vehicle around the farthest corner of the house. Slowing to a crawl, she carefully navigated the SUV around the blind corner, almost dislodging a drainpipe with her mirror.

Beyond the corner of the house was a clear stretch of field sev-eral acres deep and at least as wide that spread out toward a copse of trees on the farthest border. Just outside the umbra of the headlights' reach, Emily caught a brief flash of movement. It was too quick for her to be certain she had actually seen what she thought she had seen. She began to accelerate gently in the direction she thought she had seen the movement, then braked hard as the lights revealed Simon, moving away from her, a limp bundle tucked under each arm as he scuttled across the open field toward the trees.

Emily accelerated a little more until her lights fully illumi-nated Simon and his load. She was right; he had the children.

But there was something else with him, too. Something mas-sive that seemed to shrink from the touch of the SUV's light.

Emily had a sense of thin pale limbs that disappeared into the nearest shadows when her headlights played over them.

Simon halted midstride as the light engulfed and surrounded him. As Emily pulled closer, she could see the three black tentacles she had noticed earlier. Now that she could see them more clearly in the headlights, she thought they reminded her more of umbilical cords; rotting, serrated umbilical cords from some monstrous birth. They flexed and arced as the thing they were attached to maneuvered deeper into the shadows.

Simon turned and faced her, his eyes boring through the darkness to her.

Both children hung limply from the arms that cradled them. Emily had no idea whether they were alive or dead. Their arms and legs draped limply toward the ground like they had been caught trying to touch their toes. Then both kids' heads lifted—first Rhiannon, then her brother's—and Emily could see their faces grimace as they looked directly into the light.

Alive! They were both alive.

In that split second of recognition, Emily saw a smile spread across Simon's face. It was like he was tempting her, taunting her to try, just try to get the kids. Come and get them, that smile said. Try to take what's mine. Come and see what they see.

Emily knew the sane thing to do would be to turn the vehicle around and head back to the other house, pack the supplies waiting there, and leave. But she could not leave these kids to a fate decided by the hands of a father controlled by an alien mind.

"Fuck that," she spat and floored the accelerator.

She felt the power of the V-8 engine surge up through the steering column, along her arms, and set her head ringing. She welcomed the pain this time; she embraced it and allowed it to fuel her anger as nearly a ton and a half of made-in-Detroit gas-guzzling metal and leather leaped forward like a bull with a matador fixed firmly in its sights.

The Durango sped from zero to forty-five, racing across the open space and devouring the distance between them in just a few seconds. By the time the speedometer hit fifty, there was less than ten feet separating her from Simon and his captives. She saw Rhiannon look up again, her attention drawn by the roar of the oncoming SUV. Emily saw the glint of the headlights reflect off the girl's eyes and the look of sheer terror when she realized how fast the SUV was bearing down on the three of them.

This close, Emily could see that Simon no longer looked completely human. His skin was tinged red with lighter blotches here and there that made him look like an oddly colored cheetah. His chest rose and fell in rapid succession as though he had just run a marathon. Dark varicose veins, plump and seemingly close to bursting, crisscrossed his face just beneath the skin and the exposed flesh of his arms, pulsing obscenely. Despite the imminent impact, Simon's expression did not change.

"Sorry, Simon," Emily whispered.

When there was less than five feet between them, Emily threw the steering wheel hard left. Instead of Simon, she aimed for the darker shadows where the alien hid, and she yelled in triumph as the lights finally illuminated the monstrosity.

It was balanced on six impossibly thin legs that hung like wilted, wet stems from an elongated corpse-pale body. An extended compound eye stretched around its bulbous head.

There was no mouth that Emily could see in the brief flash of time the thing was visible in her headlights, but she could see the three tentacles attached to Simon as they writhed and flexed their way back to three nodules extruding from just above the insect-like eye.

The Durango tore through two of the creature's fragile legs with a satisfying crack like snapping branches that she could hear even over the roar of the engine. Black liquid splattered across the windshield as chunks of the creature's legs, the color of dried wheat stalks, bounced off the hood and spun off into the darkness on either side of her.

From the corner of her eye Emily saw the thing stagger sideways, illuminated by the bloodred paint of her taillights. She pulled hard on the steering wheel while stomping on the brake, swinging the SUV around to face the direction she had just come.

Emily cautiously edged the SUV toward the group. Emily could see the creature, Simon, and the kids he still held firmly under his arms. She had managed to smash through the creature's two front-left legs, tearing them from the body about two-thirds of the way up. More of the black liquid spewed from the open wounds, cascading to the ground as the creature silently writhed and bucked, sending a spray of its blood over the three figures beneath it.

The tentacles suddenly detached from Simon with three wet pops and a spray of liquid, rewinding back to the creature like a power cord on a vacuum before disappearing into the nodules on its head. Instantly Simon collapsed into an unmoving heap on the ground, the children spilling from his grasp next to him. Emily saw Rhiannon pick herself up and glance at her father's still form with a look of horrified despair, then at the towering wounded creature blocking the route to Emily, the SUV, and safety.

Emily could see the cogs working in the girl's brain. Could she risk it? Could she make it past the thing to Emily? No, Emily thought, run, just run.

Maybe the kid was psychic or maybe she was just smarter than Emily gave her credit for, but she grabbed her little brother's hand, pulled him to his feet, and began to run back toward the house, pulling her stumbling brother behind her, his free arm windmilling through the air as he struggled to keep up with his sister.

The thing could barely stand; its legs splayed out wide to counter the loss of the two front limbs as it teetered for a moment, regaining its balance. Emily was sure it was going to fall, but somehow it managed to stabilize itself. Its head swung from side to side in a weird caricature of Simon's earlier head movement; the single eye focused on Emily, then swung back to the fleeing kids. It was deciding which it had a better chance with, Emily thought.

It made its decision, and, with ridiculous agility for something that had just lost two of its six legs, spun around and began to limp after the children, its remaining oh-so-thin legs undulating across the ground in a wave of motion. Emily had no doubt that if the thing had its full set of legs still, it would have caught up with the fleeing kids in a matter of seconds. While it was certainly slower, it still moved with a swift rolling flow that reminded her of the graceful movements of the tai chi practitioners she sometimes saw in Central Park. There was no way the kids were going to make it to the house before the thing caught up with them, no way.

Emily gunned the engine and drove straight at the thing. Its head swiveled momentarily in her direction as she accelerated toward it, that single extended eye boring into her with a dark malevolence that far outstripped the expressionless features of the creature, sending her stomach into free fall.

It was closing on the kids fast. Ben's legs just couldn't move quickly enough, and Rhiannon was half dragging her brother as they raced toward the house. Rhiannon must have heard the monster's click-clacking footfalls closing on her because Emily saw her throw a glance back at the creature. Then her head whipped left and right as she searched desperately for somewhere else that would give her cover. She suddenly dashed to the left, almost pulling her brother's arm from the socket as she tugged him along after her. She was heading back toward the driveway. Did she think she could make it to the forest beyond it? Rhiannon might have made it on her own, but Ben was slowing her down; they would never make it to the trees before the creature caught up to them.

The SUV was rattling and bouncing over the rough ground as Emily fought to keep the vehicle under control. Within seconds she was alongside the thing; the broken stumps of its reed-thin legs still spurted black liquid as it chased indefatigably after the kids. It was too close to the children now for her to try to get between it and them, and if she hit it, it could career right on top of them. The best she could do was feint at it. She pulled the wheel to the left and swerved the Durango at the creature, pulling back just before she hit it, all the time hoping she would not inadvertently run over the kids. If she could just get enough room to get the SUV between them and it, she could buy them some time to get to the woods.

Emily saw something flash from the head of the creature and crack through the air like a whip. It was one of the tentacles the thing had used to control Simon. The tip of the tentacle fell just short of the back of Rhiannon's head, spraying liquid across the shoulders of the two stumbling children. The thing wasn't trying to kill them, Emily realized, it wanted to capture them. Use them like it had Simon. Maybe it thought it could use them as some bargaining chip to control Emily?

Wrong. She hit the accelerator of the Durango and swerved sharply into the path of the creature. It swerved away from her, momentarily slowing its pace, giving Emily the opening she needed. It was now or never. She wrenched the steering wheel hard left and forced the SUV between the advancing monster and the children. Pounding her foot down hard on the brake, the SUV fishtailed over the grass and came to a stop directly in front of the monster.

The creature tried to stop. Apparently realizing it wouldn't make it in time, it tried to use its remaining legs to vault over the SUV. Emily stared through the open window as the thing passed overhead; its smooth underbelly flashed by and its trailing legs almost cleared the Durango. Then one slammed into the top rim of the passenger side door, sending Emily diving for cover and the thing crashing to the ground on the opposite side of the SUV.

Emily raised herself up and stared out the passenger window. The creature had come to rest about eight feet away from the right side of the SUV; the leg that had crashed into it was bent and useless as the thing tried to push itself upright again.

The children had come to a stop and now stood about twenty feet from the crumpled monster. Ben's arms were thrown around his sister's waist as he clung to her; Rhiannon's arms held her brother close.

The creature began to crawl toward the two children, pulling and pushing itself forward with its remaining legs. It looked like a broken grasshopper, she thought as the creature's legs scissored back and forth in the dirt.

But it was still moving and the kids weren't.

"Run!" Emily yelled through the open window.

Pulling her brother behind her once again, Rhiannon began to sprint for the house. Emily pushed the gear stick into reverse and pulled the SUV back until she was sure she was where she wanted to be. Slipping the gear back into drive, she aimed directly at the crawling monstrosity and accelerated toward it.

Emily knew it must have sensed the onrushing vehicle, must have known that she was going to send it back to whatever hellhole of a planet it had come from, but the thing didn't even glimpse at her, it just kept crawling toward the kids.

As the SUV's four twenty-inch wheels rolled over the back of the creature, crushing its miserable life, Emily saw a tentacle flick out from its head into the darkness…and both kids tumble to the ground.

CHAPTER EIGHTEEN

The SUV had barely come to a stop and Emily was out, sprinting to where she had seen the children tumble into the darkness. She was vaguely aware of something black and sticky smeared from the front wheel well all the way along the driver's door. Somewhere in the back of her mind, she took deep satisfaction in knowing she had caused such grievous harm to the creature.

"Rhiannon? Ben? Where are you?" she yelled, her flashlight dancing through the darkness.

An almost silent whimpering came from just up ahead, and Emily flicked the beam of the flashlight to the source. Benjamin and Rhiannon were huddled together in the open mouth of an aluminum drainpipe used to direct flash floods along a culvert and away from the house. Rhiannon had the little boy pulled close to her, his head pressed to her chest as they cowered in the shadows.

They were both alive. Thank God. They were alive.

"Are you both okay?" she asked, her voice breathless. Ben's head swiveled to focus on Emily, his big eyes like two bright moons above dirty, tear-streaked cheeks. "The bad thing hit me," he said. Then, "Where's Daddy?"

How do you tell a little boy his father is most likely dead? She couldn't be sure if Simon was, but she wasn't about to go over there right then and find out. So she chose to ignore the question, instead offering her hand to the children. "Why don't you two get out of there and we'll go back to the car, 'kay?"

Emily pulled them one by one from the mouth of the drainpipe. Ben flinched a little as she pulled him to the grass beside her, but Thor instantly began licking the boy's face, which seemed to brighten him up a little.

"Did the"—she searched for the right word—"the bad thing hurt you, Ben? Let me see." She gently took the quivering boy by the shoulder and turned him around, lifting the back of his shirt. She could see a small bruise just below his right shoulder blade, a small red bump at its center, barely visible in the light of her flashlight. It wasn't anything serious. She pulled the boy's shirt back down and tucked it back into his pants.

"You'll be fine, kiddo. We have to get back to your house now and pick up the stuff we left there."

"I don't—" he began to object.

"It's okay, dweeb," his sister interjected, her voice rattling from her throat as she choked back tears. "We have to go with Emily and help her."

"Don't call me that," the boy snapped back. The insult from his older sister seemed to pull him back to reality. "You're the dweeb."

"Am not."

"Are too."

Emily took a hand of each of the children and walked them back to the waiting SUV, leading them to the passenger side so there was no chance they would see the dead creature, then bundled them inside. Thor jumped in with them and sat between the two kids, who had lapsed back into a stunned silence.

Emily climbed into the driver's seat, glimpsing back at the shadowy outline of the dead alien, its limbs sticking up like huge broken twigs from the ground, a faint steam rising still from its spilled fluids.

Beyond the creature's remains, Emily could see the outline of Simon's body. He was lying in the same crumpled position as when the creature had released him. One arm rested across his stomach, the other was draped across his face, his legs splayed on the wet grass. She stared at his still form. She knew she should get out and check whether he was still alive, but she knew already that Simon had been dead long before she'd found the kids.

Her hands were trembling as she gripped the steering wheel of the Durango, pulled slowly away, and swung the vehicle around toward the gravel road leading away from the house.

Simon had said he was taking another shorter route to get to the Jeffersons'. Emily scanned the trees ahead of her for any hint of a turnoff as she slowly advanced along the same road they had left along earlier; the darkness was repulsed by the SUV's high beams. She had been too focused on keeping the big vehicle on the road when they had first traveled this road, speeding away from the creature. Now she saw the turnoff, a gravel path leading into the woods to her left. She turned on to it and accelerated gently up to twenty, still nervous and unsure of her driving ability but more concerned with the way the hand tremors had turned into a case of the full-on shakes.

The children sat quietly in the backseat; Rhiannon stared directly ahead and Ben cuddled up to Thor. The dog's head rested in the boy's lap.

Shock. Disbelief. Horror. Each time Emily glanced in the mirror above her head, she would see a new emotion on one of the children's faces. If things had been normal and something of this emotional magnitude had occurred, there would be people to turn to, experts to help. Someone would know how to deal with the turmoil these kids were about to experience. Emily had no idea how to handle their feelings. God! She was only now beginning to get a grip on her own. What was she expected to do? She couldn't stop, couldn't hole up with them and try and explain what had happened. A storm was coming. A storm unlike any other ever experienced on this world. What was she supposed to do?

The trees disappeared, and Emily found herself bumping over a graveled road that followed the contour of the ridgeline; in the distance she could see the glow of the lights she had left on in the house to help guide them back.

She focused on those lights as they grew closer and brighter; this must have been how sailors felt. Lost on the sea, with only the stars to guide them until they found the light of some distant port to lead them back to safety.

She had to prioritize. There had been more orbs hanging from that tree, unopened; each one would contain one more of the creature she had just killed. They could be out there now, waiting, watching. Commander Mulligan had said they had twenty-four hours maximum before the storm caught up with them if they stayed here. The choice was obvious, she supposed, she had to get the kids out now and run. Right now. Run to anywhere that was not here.

CHAPTER NINETEEN

Emily drove all night and into the next day, stopping only when the children complained they needed a bathroom break, then ushering them back into the vehicle and speeding away again. That evening, exhausted and barely able to focus on the road ahead, Emily had finally pulled the SUV over to the side of the road.

They spent the night in the vehicle, camped in the breakdown lane of Route 90. Emily had tried to sleep, but the occasional whimper from one of the children and a pounding headache had all but ensured she got little rest.

Emily woke in the morning to the storm Commander Mulligan had warned them about—it had arrived with a vengeance. The sky ahead was masked by normal clouds. But the sky behind them was choked with red and pregnant with foreboding. The storm had already consumed most of the eastern horizon. Thick tendrils stretched across the sky ahead of a main bank of billowing red that filled an entire third of the visible eastern hemisphere from horizon to horizon. An occasional flash of lightning lit up the interior, illuminating the clouds with thick bands of white light.

With the children still sleeping, Emily pulled the Durango away from the shoulder and headed northwest. They had been silent for most of the headlong flight out of Stuyvesant, the mock disdain and sniping between the siblings forgotten as Rhiannon had silently consoled her brother, cradling him in her arms.

Clots of alien trees lay in almost every direction Emily looked as she cruised up the freeway. These weren't the half-finished variety, either; they were fully constructed and already giving off a red fog of dust that hung above the skyline like smog, scintillating in the early morning light. It was almost as if the construction had sped up in anticipation of the approaching storm. Here and there, along the tree-lined grass embankments on either side of the road, Emily would spot stretches of red where the indigenous foliage had been converted to something not of this world.

They had plenty of supplies—despite her fear, Emily had circled back to Simon's house before they'd left. She'd thrown boxes and boxes of food into the back of the Durango, along with the children's bags. But there were other worries. The SUV was down to under half a tank of gas. Emily had no idea how much they had started out with, and she wasn't sure how far what was left would get them. She was keeping her speed down to fifty, but even so, the needle on the fuel gauge quickly slipped sufficiently close to the quarter-tank mark that she decided now would be as good a time as any to start looking for gas. If she could fill the tank up, that should give them enough to get them close to Flint, Michigan, their next major goal.

A few minutes later, she spotted a Hilton Garden Inn ahead. Perfect. She hung a right at the next junction and pulled around back of the roadside inn. There were a couple of cars parked in the back lot, but otherwise the building looked empty. She was sure the kids would appreciate using the facilities despite the fact there was no water; kids appreciated their privacy. She followed the driveway around to the front of the building and pulled up outside the entranceway. There were a couple more vehicles parked in random spaces out front, and she could see the occasional evidence that the inn had not been empty when the red rain struck; she counted seven windows that had near-perfect circles cut through their glass.

She surveyed the terrain through the window of the SUV—it looked clear—then turned off the engine.

Emily undid her seat belt and turned to face the children, feeling the bones in her stiff back pop as she twisted. Rhiannon was already awake, but Ben was still asleep.

"Are we staying here tonight?" the girl asked, looking out at the hotel.

Emily had intended to try to get a couple more hours of driving in before calling it quits, but the storm was now just a distant collar of red around the eastern horizon, and this seemed like the perfect place to spend the night. Besides, Ben did not look right to her. His face looked puffy around the eyes, and he looked paler than when they had first set off that morning.

"Sure," she replied. "Looks nice, doesn't it? How's your brother doing back there?"

Rhiannon gave her brother's shoulder a gentle shake. His eyes fluttered open—they were a little bloodshot, Emily noted—and swept around the interior of the SUV as if unsure of where he was before finally settling on Emily. She gave him a broad smile. "How you doing there, kiddo?"

"I wanna go home," he croaked, his lips dry and cracked.

"I know you do. I know. But we're going to spend the night at this motel, and then, in the morning, we'll talk some more, okay?"

Ben nodded from behind a pout.

■ ■ ■

They found a room on the second floor. With the power out, the electronic locks had all automatically failed to the locked position, but they lucked out. The room they would spend the night in had been occupied. Whoever had been staying there had died and transformed into one of the spider-aliens, but instead of chewing through the window, it had exited through the front door. The hole it left was large enough for Emily to reach through and use the internal handle to open the locked door.

There were two queen-size beds in the room, both empty, thank goodness, but Emily found the desiccated husk of a pupa behind the love seat at the opposite end of the room. When she tried to pick it up to move it, it crumbled to dust between her fingers, leaving nothing but a black shadow of powder on the carpet.

They were all still wearing the same dirt- and alien-gunk-stained clothes from the previous night. Both the kids looked like bedraggled street urchins, their faces spotted with mud, their clothes dirty and stiff with sweat. Emily tried the faucets in the bathroom, but nothing came out, just a deep rattle of empty pipes. They would have to make do with the baby wipes tonight.

Emily caught a glimpse of the old Rhiannon's petulance when she handed her the packet of lemon-scented wipes and suggested she might like to grab her bag of clothes and head into the bathroom to clean herself up. In the meantime she would help her brother, Emily told her. She smiled as Rhiannon snatched the wipes from her hand, grabbed her bag, and stomped into the bathroom, locking the door behind her.

Ben was lying on the second bed, his back to her. She made her way to the opposite side and knelt down beside the boy. His face was bathed in the gray sunlight flowing through the room's only window.

"How are you feeling, Ben?" she asked softly.

"My tummy hurts," the boy said weakly.

Emily smiled reassuringly. "Would you like a little water?" The boy nodded. "Let's sit you up then, and I'll bring you some, okay?" She slipped her hands under Ben's armpits and raised him upright. The kid weighed about as much as a sparrow; she was going to have to make sure he ate regularly if he was going to stay healthy. She pulled a disposable cup from its wrapper on the side table and poured it half-full of water from her bottle. Ben took it and gulped it down in three swift swigs. He held the empty cup out for more, and Emily happily obliged, pouring in the remainder of the water. It disappeared almost as quickly as the first time, and Emily thought she saw a little color returning to the kid's face.

"Hey, Ben," she said as he handed the cup back to her. "How about we get you into a change of clothes?" Ben raised his arms above his head and waited for Emily to pull his shirt over his head. He unbuckled his belt, kicked off his shoes, and wriggled out of his jeans. Emily pulled off his socks, holding her nose in mock-disgust as she deposited them into the trash can at the side of the bed, which elicited a brief giggling fit from Ben.

"Okay, big guy. Let's get you cleaned up." She pulled a fresh towelette from a second packet of baby wipes and began to methodically clean the dirt from his face and his neck, then down his arms to his fingertips. She gave his chest and legs a quick once-over. "Up you get," she said when she was done with his feet. "Let's get your back next."

Ben stood and turned.

The bruise on his back from where the creature's whiplike tentacle had hit the boy was ugly; a mix of angry purple-and-black blotches overlapping each other around a raised bump of skin. Emily carefully probed the area with the baby wipe, cleaning the wound as gently as possible. The wound looked a little inflamed to her. She'd need to disinfect it.

She finished cleaning the boy up, then led him over to where she had set her backpack down. She opened a side flap and pulled out the first aid kit, then opened it and unwrapped an antiseptic wipe.

"That itches," he said as she used the wipe to go back over the welt and bruised area beneath his shoulder.

"All done," replied Emily, balling the antiseptic wipe and tossing it in the trash. She pulled out fresh clothes for him from his backpack and helped him into them. By the time she was finished, the kid looked a lot more like the little ball of energy she had come to adore over the past couple of days.

She stared into his eyes for a moment, pushing an errant lock of hair from his face. There was so much sadness behind those young eyes. She was about to ask him how he was feeling when Rhiannon flounced out of the bathroom dressed in bright-pink sweats.

"Your turn," she said to Emily, tossing the half-empty pack of baby wipes to her.

Emily pulled another antiseptic wipe from the first aid kit and headed into the bathroom. The gash on her forehead was ugly looking and inflamed. She cleaned the area with the antibacterial wipe. By the time Emily was done wiping the grime from the rest of her body and slipping into her fresh, if rather wrinkled, clothes, the kids were sitting together at the small table. They had helped themselves to a can of fruit each and were happily spooning the contents into their mouths. A third can sat on the tabletop, a plastic spoon resting next to it.

Emily pulled the lid off the can and joined them for dinner.

■ ■ ■

That evening, Emily placed a sat-phone call to Jacob from the corridor of the hotel. In the confusion and headlong flight of the past few days, she had completely forgotten her nightly commitment to update him. And in her earlier rush to pack, she realized as she pulled the equipment from the backpack, she had somehow managed to turn the phone off, so there was no way for him to contact her.

Emily knew he would be horribly worried.

"All that matters is that you are all okay," he said after she had explained. "Tell me more about the creature and what happened."

Emily ran through how she had managed to rescue the kids but how Simon had been overcome by the creature. Jacob, as always, found the subject matter fascinating.

"I'm sorry," he said after he realized he was more concerned with the process of Simon's transmutation by the creature than the loss of the man. "Sometimes the scientist gets the better of me."

His embarrassment quickly dissipated when she told him she was now driving. "That's fantastic." Jacob's voice took on a new dimension of cheerfulness at the news. "You'll be here in no time at all now."

But Jacob's tone fell back to one of concern when he heard the conclusion of her battle with the creature and that Ben had been struck by the alien as it died. "Is he all right?"

"Yes, a little bruised and in shock. But the kid has his sister looking after him. He'll pull through."

After the call ended, Emily found both the children already asleep. She replaced the phone in the backpack and climbed into the second bed, lulled quickly to sleep by the children's steady breathing.

CHAPTER TWENTY

Daylight gently woke Emily, dancing across the lids of her eyes.

She stretched, dressed, and let Thor out into the corridor, waiting at the door as he wandered first up, then back down the corridor. When, for reasons known only to the dog, he settled on a particular door to pee against, he looked back at her and she nodded once, giving him her permission to do his thing indoors. When he was done, she ushered him back in and allowed the door to click closed behind her.

Rhiannon must have already been awake when she'd let Thor outside, because when Emily turned around, the girl was pulling on the top to her sweats—even more shockingly pink in the daylight, Emily noted—but Ben was still asleep, bundled up beneath the blankets next to where Rhiannon had been sleeping.

"Ben," Emily called as she searched the supply bag for something other than granola bars for breakfast. She was sure she had seen a couple of Fiber One bars in here somewhere. "Rhiannon, wake your brother," Emily asked when the boy didn't answer or stir.

"Emily!" The concern in Rhia's voice made all thoughts of breakfast disappear, and Emily found herself instantly at the girl's side.

"What is it?"

Rhiannon pulled back the sheet from Ben's face. The boy did not look well. His face was flushed bright red and his normally bright eyes were dull and even more bloodshot than the day before.

Oh! Dear God, no.

Emily tried to keep her fear at what she saw from reaching her face as she leaned in closer to check if the boy was even breathing. She placed an ear close to his mouth. Yes, thank you, God. She breathed a sigh of relief as she felt the gentle wisp of his breath against her ear.

It's probably just a reaction to the shock of losing his father, she thought. Too much upheaval for the poor kid. That's all it is. She didn't like the way those last couple of sentences sounded in her head; they sounded more like a plea than a statement of fact.

Emily knelt down next to the bed and pulled the covers back from the boy's body.

"Are you okay, kiddo?" she asked him.

His T-shirt was soaked in sweat, and beads of perspiration dotted his hairline and forehead. She placed a cool hand against his brow.

Jesus! The kid was burning up.

"My head hurts," he whimpered.

"Rhiannon, go into the big bag for me, and in the pocket on the left side, you'll see a first aid kit. Will you go get it for me, please?" she asked, then added, "And bring some water, too. And a fresh T-shirt."

Ben's sister remained where she was, staring at her brother.

"Rhiannon!" Emily snapped. "Now, please." The kid jumped and then ran to the backpack that Emily had left near the entrance to the room. When she was out of sight, Emily gently turned Ben toward her so she could get a better view of his back.

"Oh, shit. Oh no," she whispered. She threw a hand over her mouth before more emotion could escape from it. Overnight the bruise from the creature's attack had spread across both of Ben's shoulders and all the way down to the small of his back. The bump that had seemed inflamed had thickened and enlarged to a black pustule with thick black streamers of infection running from its center, stretching out across his shoulders and under his left armpit. A second ribbon of engorged veins had spread to his spine, then followed it upward toward the base of his neck.

"Here," said Rhiannon, appearing beside Emily at the door, the plastic first aid kit in one hand and a T-shirt in the other. Emily quickly rolled the boy onto his back before his sister could see the infection tattooed across Ben's back.

"Thanks." She opened up the first aid kit and pulled out a bottle of aspirin. The bottle recommended a single tablet for anyone under the age of twelve. But this wasn't a kid with a headache; this was a child with a major infection. She broke two of the little white tablets into smaller pieces and popped them one at a time into the boy's mouth, followed by a swig of water from the bottle each time.

When Ben had swallowed the last of the aspirin, she took the T-shirt and tore it along its seam into two pieces, then folded one piece into an oblong bandage. She emptied half of a bottle of water over it until it was completely soaked, then laid it across Ben's forehead. The boy moaned, then seemed to relax a little.

"Is he going to be okay?" Rhiannon asked, her voice quieted by concern.

"Yes, of course he is," Emily reassured her, although she knew it was probably a lie. The kid needed a doctor. But that wasn't going to happen…ever. She felt her guts begin to knot in fear at the thought of caring for this child. She had zero medical training other than some basic first aid. And what this kid had was going to need more than a couple of aspirin and some TLC.

She had to find stronger medication: painkillers and antibiotics.

That meant she had to find a pharmacy, and quickly.

Emily turned to Rhiannon. "Ben's pretty sick, and we're going to need to find him some medication. I'm going to need you to help me look after him, until he's better. Can you do that?"

Rhiannon's eyes got wide. Emily could see the kid was close to breaking apart. First her dad, now her little brother. If Emily wasn't careful here, the kid could implode under the pressure and stress.

"It's okay," Emily said, placing a reassuring hand against Rhia's arm. "All I need you to do is wait here with Ben while I drive and find a pharmacy. You just need to keep that rag on his head wet for him. Turn it every couple of minutes for him. It'll help keep him cool."

Rhiannon nodded, and Emily handed her the half-full bottle of water. "Don't worry about getting water on the floor, and there's more bottled water in my backpack if you need it," she said. "I will not be long," she promised.

And with that she was out the door.

■ ■ ■

It took her almost an hour to find a pharmacy and a place to refuel—a messy process of siphoning from another vehicle—every moment acutely aware of Ben's condition. Finally, she was racing up the stairs to the second floor of the hotel, barging through the fire door, and sprinting down to the room. Rhiannon was already waiting, peering through the hole in the door left by the escaping creature that had been born there. When she saw it was Emily, she pulled open the door to let her in.

"Good girl. How is he doing?"

Rhiannon looked scared. "He just keeps moaning," she said. "I put the wet rag on his head, but he won't keep still and it keeps falling off."

Emily was already at Ben's side. He looked even paler than he had before. He had kicked the sheets from his body, and Emily could see he had urinated; the sheet beneath him was stained a deep yellow.

Christ. He was in a bad way.

They couldn't stay here; the storm was closing in too fast. But if she moved him, she might make this worse. But she knew she had no choice. She had to get him out of here for all their sakes.

She plucked two of the antibiotics from the plastic bag. "He needs to take one of these every twelve hours. It's going to be your job to remember what time he takes them," she told Rhiannon.

"What are they?"

"Antibiotics. They'll help him fight the...the bug he has." Emily took the boy's lower jaw between her thumb and forefinger—God, he looked so very pale—and pried his mouth open, slipping a pill onto the back of his tongue followed by a swig of water. Instinctively, the boy swallowed, choking a little as the water went down. She broke one of the Lortabs in half and helped him swallow that, too.

"We have to move him to the car," she told Rhiannon as she placed the thermometer she had picked up at the pharmacy in the boy's mouth. She held Ben's mouth closed until the thing beeped.

"But he's really sick," Rhiannon protested.

Shit! His temperature was 104. That was not good. "I know, honey, but we have to go. The storm is right on our tail, and if we don't get out of here now, we'll be stuck." She explained all of this as she quickly pulled off the boy's sodden underwear—eliciting an embarrassed yelp from his sister, who quickly turned her back—and gently cleaned him up with a couple of baby wipes. "I'm going to need your help to take as much stuff for me down to the car as you can, because I'm going to carry Ben. Will you do that?"

Rhiannon nodded, still facing away from her brother.

Emily pulled a change of underwear from the boy's bag and quickly slipped them over Ben's feet and pulled them up to his waist. "All right, you can look now," she said, then directed Rhiannon to grab both her backpack and Ben's. "Will you look after Thor for me?" she asked, slipping a pillow from the bed under her arm, then pulling off the comforter, wrapping the boy up in it, and lifting him off the bed. She would need to come back for her backpack once the kids were safely in the waiting SUV.

"Come on, Thor," Rhiannon said to the dog, who had been waiting patiently between the two beds, his eyes never leaving Ben. Now he jumped to his feet and accompanied Rhiannon to the door. The kid opened it and dragged Emily's backpack to the corridor, then held the door open for Emily to slip through, Ben's unconscious form cradled in her arms.

The not-so-distant sound of thunder echoed through the hallway, rattling the windows of every room, as they made their way to the stairwell.

They were quickly running out of time.

Outside the building, the sky was a fiery red; the billowing mass of clouds enveloped the space above them as a dry wind began to rustle the trees on the perimeter of the hotel's parking lot.

Rhiannon jogged ahead of Emily to the back of the Durango. "It's open," Emily yelled to the girl, who popped the tailgate up and slipped both backpacks into the SUV. She had to jump to reach the tailgate and pull it back down into place. She ran back to the driver's side and opened the passenger door, pushing away the trash that had collected on the backseat and pushing the armrest back into the space between the seats.

Emily gently lowered the boy onto the backseat. She took the pillow from under her arm, raised his head, and slipped it beneath him.

The branches of the trees had begun to sway and rustle. What leaves were left on their branches began to fly into the air one by one as the storm broke over them.

With the kids and Thor in the SUV, Emily sprinted back into the hotel, raced up the stairs to the second floor two steps at a time, and grabbed her backpack before retracing her steps back outside.

Emily jumped into the driver's seat and slammed the door closed behind her. The first drops of watery red liquid had begun to splatter on the pavement just a few feet from them. As she pulled away from the parking lot and out onto the road again, the sound of rain beating against the pavement was all that she could hear.

■ ■ ■

Almost three and a half hours later they crossed into Toronto, Canada, via the Queenston-Lewiston Bridge, just north of Niagara Falls.

On the Canadian side of the border, the bridge funneled traffic into fifteen separate inspection lanes, each lane leading into a customs and excise booth blocked by a security arm. About a mile before they had reached the bridge, Emily had hit the tail end of traffic. It was backed up across all of the Canada-bound lanes, almost to the US Border Patrol buildings. Hundreds upon hundreds of residents had tried to flee the oncoming rain, only to die in their cars and block any chance of Emily and her charges from advancing using that route. By comparison, the lanes into the United States were relatively free of traffic, so Emily had driven across the median—a low moan coming from Ben as each tire bumped over the concrete—and headed toward Canada on the opposite side of the road.

Apart from having to navigate around the occasional vehicle, they had managed to bypass the confusion of the border crossing and continue on their way, now riding the 405 Highway west toward where it would intersect the 403 in Burlington. Only now did Emily feel comfortable that they had placed enough distance between them and the threat of the storm.

Better still, the medication Emily had given Ben seemed to be doing its job, because Ben had slept for most of the journey. Rhiannon had sat almost silently next to her brother during the whole journey, but there was little the girl could do other than give Emily periodic updates on her brother's temperature and breathing.

"I really have to pee," she said now, almost as if it was a major imposition.

"Me, too," said Emily. Truth be told she had been holding it for the last thirty miles or so, just to be sure they were clear of the border, and she was becoming more uncomfortable by the minute. "I'll find us somewhere to stop."

She pulled over to the side of the road when she spotted a clump of tall bushes that would provide them with a modicum of privacy. In the distance, Emily could see the branches of a forest of alien trees towering over a collection of office buildings, red dust floating in undulating streamers above them. It was funny how the human mind could adapt to the unusual so quickly; the trees barely registered on her radar as she stepped from the driver's seat onto the road. Emily tossed Rhiannon a roll of bathroom tissue. "You first," she told the girl.

She waited until Rhiannon had disappeared into the bushes, a barking Thor leaping happily along beside her, then turned her attention to Ben.

He was sleeping, bundled in the comforter like a baby, his skin a little cooler to Emily's touch. His breathing was a little labored, and his lips were chapped. She placed the thermometer under the boy's tongue and waited for it to beep: 102 degrees. His temperature was down. Emily let out a small sigh. The meds were kicking in, and Ben was doing a little better. Any improvement, even if it was so minor, was good news right now, she decided.

Tilting Ben's head upright, she dropped another half Lortab into his mouth and washed it down with water from her bottle. She poured some of the water onto the cloth they had used to cool his fever and gently dabbed away at his lips until they were moistened, then cleaned some of the sweat from his forehead. She would have to remember to liberate some lip balm for the poor kid when they made their next stop at a town.

By the time she had finished working on Ben, Rhiannon was back. "Thanks," she said, passing the roll of tissue to Emily.

Emily followed Rhiannon's tracks toward the bushes, realizing that this was her first time in another country and reminding herself she needed to watch for poison ivy.

■ ■ ■

The red rain did not recognize borders. As they traveled west across Toronto toward Michigan, Emily saw the same empty houses, the same red clouds puffing from patches of alien trees. If anything, there seemed to be more of the trees here, maybe because of the concentration of water in the form of the Great Lakes. At the sight of one enormous cluster of trees just outside the town of London, Emily wondered again whether Jacob's theory about the aliens' inability to handle lower temperatures was correct. It had better be, because she was betting all of their lives on him being right. She reassured herself with the fact that the temperature outside the speeding vehicle had only dropped by a few degrees, an insignificant amount in comparison to what she knew was coming. If she had been heading north, she would have expected to see more proof of his theory, but that part of her plan had changed to this headlong flight west to escape the red storm.

Emily's whole body ached from being in the same position behind the wheel of the SUV for so damn long, but she had decided to push through as much as possible, putting as much distance between the storm and them as she could. She did not want it catching up with them again, but her body was telling her it was ready to stop for the night now.

"How's he doing back there?" she asked, keeping her voice low.

"He's asleep still," came the whispered reply from Rhiannon. "But he's not sweating anymore."

"It's almost time for more of his meds, so I'm going to find us a place to stop for the night."

Emily glanced down at the road atlas. The last sign they had passed had said they were about ten miles outside of a town called Sarnia, right on the Canadian edge of the country's border with the United States, virtually on the shore of Lake Huron.

Emily had noticed a trend as they traveled. As they closed the distance on each new city or town, the landscape surrounding them began to switch from forest or field to the slow materialization of civilization, and she would start to see the occasional hotel or motel appear. They would inevitably be far enough away from the city center to be cheaper than staying in town, but not so far away as to be a burden to a tourist or businessperson.

As she neared Sarnia, she began looking for signs that would tell her where she needed to turn off. A few minutes later, she spotted one that told her to exit at the next turnoff for lodging, food, and fuel.

■ ■ ■

It was a simple building. Two stories, no more than fifty rooms—nothing fancy. The kind of motel where a salesperson or business-man might spend the night if they were looking for something on a budget. Certainly wasn't the Ritz, but that was okay. All they needed right now was somewhere to lay their heads for the night.

Emily went ahead and scouted the ground floor, leaving the children in the SUV, engine running. She noticed a large Peg-Board behind the reception desk with sets of keys hanging from hooks. She confirmed her suspicions when she took a short walk to the first set of rooms; they took regular old-fashioned keys. She walked back to the reception area. There were only five or six keys missing from the board. The place had hardly been a hive of activity when the red rain had struck.

She took a key labeled twenty-nine and walked to the room through the dull-looking corridor; obviously fake potted plants on even cheaper-looking stands were intermittently placed along its length.

Unlocking the door to the room, she quickly checked out the interior: two queen-size beds, both made and waiting for the next guest. Well, she and the kids would most likely be the last guests to ever stay here.

Emily dropped her backpack to the floor and walked back to the Durango. She shut off the engine and opened the rear passenger door, allowing Rhiannon to hop out and Emily to step in.

Ben had gotten some of his color back, she noted, although his eyes were still tightly closed and he was very deeply asleep. His breathing sounded a little deeper, too. There was still a wetness to each intake of breath, and she thought she could discern a slight rattle in his throat when he exhaled. Other than that, he seemed to be holding his own.

"I'll grab the bags," said Rhiannon, already at the tailgate.

Emily picked up Ben with both arms, cradling him in the comforter, and waited for Rhiannon to grab everything she needed before she let Thor out of the SUV.

Ben was still running a bit of a fever; she could feel the heat permeating through the material into her hands as she carried him toward the entrance, Thor matching her pace step for step.

Inside the motel room, Emily asked Rhiannon to pull back the sheets of the bed nearest the door, and she laid Ben down in his polyester cocoon. He groaned a little but never opened his eyes. That was good, she supposed. The more rest the boy got the better. Rhiannon had been instructed to periodically give the boy water while they were traveling to keep him hydrated, and Emily had caught sight of her in the rearview mirror dutifully tipping liquid into his mouth, so she wasn't concerned about him dehydrating. What she needed to do was get some food into him. It had been almost twenty-four hours since he had eaten anything.

She checked the box of food supplies they had brought in with them for the night and found a couple of squeezable foil pouches of pureed fruit. If she could get some of it down the boy, it would likely help both of them feel better. She squeezed some of the fruit onto a disposable spoon and began feeding Ben, pushing it carefully into his mouth before rounding up the dribble of grape that inevitably slipped from the corner of his mouth.

Rhiannon hovered for a few minutes, watching Emily feed her brother.

"Why don't you find us something to eat?" Emily asked her after a minute, aware that the girl was uncomfortable watching her brother being spoon-fed like a baby, even if that was what he was—just a baby.

Rhiannon seemed relieved to be given something legitimate to do, and she headed over to the box of supplies and began rooting around. She pulled out a couple of cans of something Emily couldn't make out and placed them on the nearby TV stand.

Emily spooned the last of the fruit into Ben's mouth and reached for the two plastic medicine containers. She set the pills on the bedside cabinet while she went about unwrapping the boy from the comforter.

Emily managed to stifle the cry of revulsion in her throat before it made it to her lips. She glanced over at Rhiannon; the girl was busy riffling through her bag looking for some clean clothes to lay out for the morning, oblivious to Emily's shocked expression.

Carefully Emily lifted the two edges of the comforter apart, exposing Ben's body. Except what lay within the folds wasn't Ben, not anymore.

Emily had been wrong about Ben; he hadn't been getting better. He was transforming.

CHAPTER TWENTY-ONE

Ben's chest was now a mass of black veins that spread out from his right shoulder toward his abdomen. Around his throat, like ivy climbing around the trunk of a tree, fronds edged upward toward his ear. At first Emily thought the plectrum-size overlapping flakes covering his right shoulder were just skin discoloration, but, as she moved her head closer, she could see they were actually scales, like a lizard's but larger.

Emily looked up to make sure Rhiannon couldn't see what she was seeing. She had moved into the bathroom with her toothbrush and a bottle of water. When Emily heard the door squeak closed, she gently rolled Ben over onto his stomach. The kid didn't make a sound; what she had mistaken as sleep was more likely a coma state, she realized.

His back was completely covered in the same scales she had seen on the boy's shoulder. They extended all the way down over his buttocks and upper thighs, stopping just short of his knees, and edged over his oblique muscles toward his tummy. Ignoring her revulsion, she ran her hands lightly over the rough scales; they bristled like the fur on a cat's back at her touch. Something beneath the layer of scales pulsed and undulated.

Emily allowed Ben to roll onto his back again. The child's eyes were tightly closed and his breathing had become faster than normal, almost like a dog's pant. Drawing in a deep breath for courage, Emily eased back the lid of one eye with her thumb.

Gone were his iris, sclera, and pupil, replaced by a solid-red orb pitted with tiny dimples; at the center of each dimple was a small cluster of black spots. She let the lid drop back into place, then closed the comforter back over the boy and took a step away from the bed.

As she watched the motionless boy, her mind replayed the moment she'd killed the alien-puppeteer; that final second as the tentacle whipped through the darkness and hit Ben. She had been wrong all along about its motives. It hadn't wanted to kill any of them; it had wanted to make them like it, to turn them, and in its final desperate second of life, it had managed to infect Ben.

Angelic, innocent Ben.

A feeling of utter despair took her firmly between its teeth and bit down hard, sinking its teeth into her very soul.

"How is he?" Emily hadn't registered Rhiannon coming back in the room, but now she stood outside the door to the bathroom, looking far more concerned than a kid her age should have to.

Emily frantically waded through the morass of thoughts that filled her mind, looking for an appropriate answer. How was she supposed to tell Rhiannon her brother was changing into something alien? And if she told her he was fine, when he very obviously wasn't, what then? While the transformation was only partially complete, what were they to do when he was no longer human at all? What was he becoming? If it was anything like the creatures that she had encountered so far, then he would be intent on ensuring both her own and his sister's demise.

"The same," she said finally as she placed the pills she had set aside in the boy's mouth and washed them down with water. Ben swallowed reflexively. His breath stank like a cesspool, and she quickly turned away from him.

Rhiannon began to walk over to where her brother was laying.

"He's asleep still," Emily whispered, shooing her in the opposite direction. "Best if you leave him be for now. He needs all the rest he can get to fight this bug."

The lie came easily from her lips, and Rhiannon seemed to accept it.

"Why don't we get ourselves something to eat?"

"I'm starved," said Rhiannon, brightening.

Emily popped the lids on the cans Rhiannon had pulled from the supplies and emptied their contents into a saucepan. She heated the food over a low flame on the portable gas stove; all the while her mind was attempting to assimilate what she had just seen and what few options she had to deal with the situation. She could just grab Rhiannon and run; leave Ben here and go. How she would ever be able to explain that to his sister was beyond her, the kid was smart but she was still just a kid. Even if she showed her what was happening to her baby brother, she doubted it would make a difference to her. She was so damn loyal to him.

Emily spooned the warmed food into two waiting dishes.

"Thank you," said Rhiannon as she took one of them.

"Umm-hmm!" Emily was working on automatic now. She opened a can of dog food for Thor and added it to some dry kibble in his bowl. Poured out some water for him and then some into two plastic mugs for Rhiannon and herself.

"I think it's probably best that you sleep in a separate bed from Ben tonight."

Rhiannon looked up from her food. "Why?" she asked.

Why indeed. "I'm not sure if what Ben has is catching or not. And if you get it…you know. That would be bad."

Rhiannon gave it a few seconds thought, then, "Okay." And she was back to eating, the thought that she had been in constant close contact with her brother for the past two days never crossing her mind, apparently.

At the bottom of the beds was a reading nook consisting of a table and a couple of high-back chairs. She would spend the night there, she decided, so she could keep a closer eye on Ben through the night.

After dinner, Emily placed the lamp on top of the table and rested the Mossberg against the side of the chair. She searched through the closet and found a spare blanket; the nights were becoming chillier, and she would need it.

Rhiannon decided she wanted to take Thor out for his evening bathroom run, which Emily was quite happy for her to do. Ben was beginning to show signs of movement. She had noticed it while she was still eating dinner; the comforter would give an occasional, almost imperceptible twitch, as though Ben was suffering from some kind of muscle spasm beneath its material. She couldn't be certain, but she thought that she may have even seen those terrible alien eyes moving back and forth beneath his lids, like a dreamer in the midst of REM sleep. There was no way she was going to leave Rhiannon alone with him. Not now.

As darkness began to pull the remaining light from the window, Rhiannon climbed beneath the covers of the bed. "Good night, Emily," she said.

"Sleep well," Emily replied as she took her seat and pulled the blanket around her. A pillow laid on top of the table would allow her to get some rest, at least.

"Good night, Ben." Emily heard Rhiannon whisper. "I love you."

■ ■ ■

Emily fought her exhaustion in a vain effort to stay awake and aware.

The light from the LED lamp was turned down low enough that Rhiannon could sleep but bright enough that Emily could still make out the still form of Ben in the opposite bed. Her tired mind was still turning over the events of the past few days, flashing first the image of the cute little boy she had met just days earlier, then the terrible images of Ben's deformed skin in front of her eyes, like some warped movie.

Her fatigue gnawed at her thoughts, dragging them in different directions.

At some point, she lost the battle; her head drooped once, twice. Just five minutes, that's all I need, she thought as she laid her head against the pillow. Just—

Thor's growl woke Emily.

—five minutes.

She sat up with a start, her heart doing cartwheels in her rib cage. Where was this place? What time was it? Her disorientation vaporized as Thor's growl sounded again in the dimness of the room.

She glanced over to the spot on the floor where Thor had been sleeping. Her dog was sitting bolt upright, teeth bared as he slowly tried to back away from something on top of Rhiannon's bed. Her tiny snores floated across the gap to Emily.

Emily's eyes flashed back to the bed; Rhiannon was curled up, fast asleep, the comforter pulled up to her head. Ben—or what had once been Ben—was perched on the end of her bed, one side of his face now completely black with the same spiderweb of veins she had seen covering his back. His eyes were open now, those strange red wet orbs glistening in the light of the lamp.

He was crouched over Rhiannon, his head dipped toward her sleeping body as his nose sniffed the air around her; his mouth hung loosely open as rivulets of drool dripped from each corner, collecting in a small damp pool on the comforter.

Ben lowered his head toward Rhiannon. Emily stifled a scream as a thick black tentacle of a tongue snapped from the boy's mouth and flicked into the air just above the sleeping form. The tongue recoiled and slapped back against the boy's lips, then disappeared into his mouth, leaving a slather of puffy foam behind.

"Oh, sweet Jesus," Emily hissed.

Thor gave another growl, and the boy's head slowly swiveled until it faced the dog.

Snick! Ben's tongue flashed into the air between him and Thor. The dog gave a deeper growl, taking a single step toward the bed, his fur bristling.

"Quiet, boy," Emily whispered. "Stay very still."

At the sound of Emily's voice, Ben's head swiveled silently in her direction.

With very deliberate movements, Ben climbed from his perch, dropping to the floor between the two beds on all fours. He scuttled sideways across the floor before pulling himself up onto the bed and burrowing into the folds of the comforter.

As she watched, Ben's eyes closed and his rapid panting slowed until it returned to almost normal.

While it might still bear a passing resemblance to the child, what lay on the bed was no longer human. Emily knew that with a deep, painful certainty. She had already seen the results of the alien's biological technology, its ability to consume and repurpose human flesh to create new creatures as its tools. How long before what lay beneath the comforter woke again and tried to take Rhiannon? Or kill them all?

The change had reached a tipping point within Ben; by the time the sun rose, she doubted there would be anything left of the boy. She had to stop it now, before Rhiannon woke and before it became so strong that she could not.

Emily rose quietly from the seat, picking up the pillow from the table. She checked Rhiannon; she was still soundly asleep.

Silently she made her way to Ben's bedside. He was curled up within the comforter, his head just visible between two folds of material. Asleep he looked almost normal, those hideous eyes hidden behind his lids, but the black veins pulsing against his temple betrayed what he was, what he was still becoming.

Emily leaned in, ignoring the odor of the boy's breath.

"I am so very sorry, Ben," she whispered as she placed the pillow over the boy's face.

Emily pressed down hard on the pillow, using the palms of her hands to ensure a tight seal around Ben's nose and mouth. His legs began to kick against the comforter; she could feel his arms pushing the pillow, trying to tear it from his face with a strength that did not belong to a child of his age. She leaned in harder against the pillow, using her full body weight to force it deeper onto the boy's face. Gradually the thrashing began to subside as he weakened. Eventually, it stopped altogether.

Emily did not let go for what seemed like hours but could only have been mere minutes. She had to be absolutely sure.

When she finally lifted the pillow from the still form, Ben was dead.

Dear God, what had she done?

Survived. She had survived.

That was what it had come down to, pure and simple. She had done what she needed to ensure both her own and Rhiannon's survival.

Having answered her own question, Emily repositioned the body on its side so the black tattoo of veins covering his cheek and chest would be hidden from sight. His hands were clenched into claws against the material of the pillow, and she had to prize them loose, straightening the fingers as best she could before she moved his arms to his sides and finally placed the pillow she had used to smother him beneath his head.

By the time she had finished, he was just a boy in the bed. A boy who had died in his sleep. Peacefully. Painlessly. That was what Rhiannon would see at least. The burden of his true death would be Emily's alone to bear.

She pulled the comforter up to Ben's chin and stepped away, taking a deep breath as she fought back first the urge to vomit and then the desire to scream. Instead, she made her way back to her chair and pulled the blanket around her.

The pain would return tomorrow, when she had to explain to Rhiannon that her brother had died peacefully in his sleep sometime during the night.

Emily's pain would not be so simple to explain away and would stay with her for the rest of her life.

■ ■ ■

Morning crept silently into the room through the dirt-speckled windows of the hotel.

Emily had sat for the remaining hours between darkness and light and waited, her head a jumble of thoughts and dark emotion. Second-guessing her actions was not in her nature, but she had wondered over and over whether there was something else that she could have done, some other way for her to have saved Ben, cured him, fixed him. Every thread of thought led back to the same conclusion: no. There was nothing she could have done. The choice had been clear: wait and put both Rhiannon and herself in mortal jeopardy, or do what she had done.

But her actions hung around her heart like a millstone, and at this point, with Ben's body cold and still, not six feet away from her, she did not think that weight could ever be lifted.

Rhiannon had barely moved during Emily's vigil over her, and, other than the occasional moan or murmured dream word, she slept silently through the night.

Emily had never watched someone wake before. It was oddly fascinating, the way the body started to shift and move as their consciousness began to swim toward the surface of reality. Rhiannon had started to move beneath the comforter, her legs pushing the cover off her torso as she shifted position. One hand was wedged between her cheek and the pillow; the other was cocked over her head, toward the bed's headboard.

Rhiannon's eyelids began to flutter and her hand slipped from beneath her cheek and reached to meet the other above her head in an almost feline stretch. As a yawn signaled the young girl was close to waking, Emily laid her head against her arm on the tabletop, closed her eyes, and pretended that she was sleep.

■ ■ ■

"Emily!"

At the sound of Rhiannon's shrill cry, Emily slipped into the role she knew she would have to play from this point on.

Her eyes sprung open. "What is it?" she said, with as much surprise in her voice as she could muster. Rhiannon was standing at the head of Ben's bed, she had pulled back the comforter and exposed his upper torso, pale in the morning light.

"Ben's not moving," she said, her voice filled with panic. "I don't think"—her voice cracked midsentence, and tears flooded her cheeks as she choked out the last few words—"he's breathing."

Emily leaped from her seat and was at Rhiannon's side in two quick steps. She placed the back of her hand against the boy's head, then tried to lift one thin arm in a show of measuring his pulse, but rigor mortis had set in and the boy's arm was rigid and unmoving. Emily could see the deep-purple discoloration of lividity along his arm, where it touched the bed. She had expected that, but what she hadn't expected was that the change she had seen last night had continued to progress even after the boy's death. Although undoubtedly slowed, the network of black veins had grown in the hours since she had ended Ben's life, creeping inexorably across the boy's face and chest.

Emily took both of Rhiannon's hands in hers, forcing herself to look the girl in the eyes. "Sweetheart, I am so very sorry but—"

"No!" Rhiannon yelled, trying to pull her hands away and push past Emily to get to her brother's corpse. Emily blocked her with her own body and gripped her hands even tighter, determined not to let her see the full extent of the destruction the alien invader consuming Ben's body had wrought.

"He's gone, baby. Ben's gone."

"No! No! No!" She repeated the single word over and over, as if it were some kind of magic incantation that by sheer force of will would bring her brother miraculously back to life.

Emily pulled the weeping girl to her, pressing her to her chest, enveloping her with her arms, as she struggled to break free. Finally, Rhiannon collapsed into Emily's embrace, her tears soaking into Emily's shirt, damp and cold against her chest.

"Shhhhh!" Emily cooed, her cheek resting against the top of Rhiannon's head as she gently stroked the girl's hair.

Emily didn't think she had ever experienced such manifest anguish; it was as though the child's very soul had fractured and now spilled from every cell in her young body. It was heartrending and terrifying in its raw despair.

As Rhiannon's tears turned to a choked sobbing, Emily held her tightly to her and allowed the child's pain to pierce her.

■ ■ ■

They buried Ben in a rose bed near the entrance to the hotel.

Emily searched for a shovel but couldn't find one, so she broke the wooden back support from a chair she found in the foyer and dug the shallow grave using that instead. By the time she had finished, her hands were blistered and cut and a light drizzle had begun to fall, dampening her already sweat-soaked body.

Emily carried Ben from the room, still wrapped in the comforter that would become his burial shroud. She placed him in the grave she had dug just as puddles of rainwater began to collect in the bottom of the hole. The exposed earth around the opening was quickly turning to mud underfoot.

Rhiannon stood at the edge of the grave and helped Emily push the dirt over the body of her brother, until, finally, all that remained was a mound of wet earth to mark his final resting place. They picked the few remaining blossoms from the rose-bushes and laid them on the grave beneath a cross that Emily had fashioned from the wooden legs of the same chair she had used to dig the grave.

Emily could not tell if Rhiannon cried. Her face remained emotionless as the drizzle rained down over them, covering any evidence of tears she might have shed. As the shower turned heavier, a crack of distant lightning was followed seconds later by the low rumble of thunder.

Emily placed her arm around Rhiannon's shoulder. "Time to go," she said as gently as she could and led her slowly back to the hotel room to change out of their sodden clothes, a disquieting thought playing over and over in her mind.

Although she could not be sure, as she had laid the boy's stiff body into the cold wet earth, Emily thought she had felt something move within the comforter.

■ ■ ■

She parked them for the night at a highway gas station some-where just north of Flint. Rhiannon had remained curled up on the backseat for most of the drive after they'd left the motel, silent and morose. She refused to eat, and Emily had to gently chide her into at least taking a few occasional sips of water. She was asleep in the back of the Durango now, Thor watching over her while Emily left the SUV and walked out of earshot.

Emily had promised herself that she would not cry when she spoke to Jacob; she had even considered not telling him about what had happened to Ben. She was sure Jacob had more than his fair share of problems to worry about, and she was not convinced she would be able to vocalize exactly what had taken place anyway. It was all such a mess.

That plan lasted right up until Jacob answered her call, his voice rigid with concern. "Emily? Thank God. Are you all right?"

At the sound of his voice, she began to sob, unable to even reply to his greeting for several minutes. The words just couldn't make it past the paralyzing pain she felt. When finally she was able to speak again, she managed to slowly recount the story of Ben's rapid transformation after the attack.

"I...I had to..." Emily was ready to confess what she had done to Ben, but Jacob interrupted her before she could fill in the remaining words.

"Emily, stop. I don't want to know," he said, his voice calm, comforting even. "For no other reason than I understand that you did what you had to do. This is not our old world—that one is dead and gone. The rules have changed for us all and we have to do whatever it takes to survive. All of us, Emily. Whatever it takes."

"I had no choice," she said, more for herself than for Jacob.

"I know," he said. "It's the past. You have to focus on the future now. You have to survive."

When she clicked the Off button half an hour later, she felt somewhat more at ease with what she had done. But as she walked slowly back to the Durango, she wondered whether that acceptance would come with a price that she was willing to pay.

CHAPTER TWENTY-TWO

They passed through Saginaw (population 51,230, and the home of the Saginaw Sting), Saint Ignace (population 2,435, with the best view of the Mackinac Bridge, this side of the US border), and tiny Rudyard (population 1,315, named after the English poet and writer, Rudyard Kipling).

By the time they crossed over the US–Canadian border for the third and final time, the towns and villages along their route had become smaller, sparser, but no less empty than every other place they had driven through. They spent nights in hotels, homes, offices, and the back of the Durango. In Prince George they stopped for the night at what had been a railway museum, sleeping in the relative luxury of a refurbished coach car.

Gradually, with each new day and every mile farther north they traveled, Emily and Rhiannon began to feel the temperature outside the air-conditioned SUV drop, and the alien forests that had become so prevalent begin to grow thinner and sparser, a final indication that Jacob's theory was correct. And yet, despite the slowing of the alien incursion, they saw no one and nothing to indicate that anywhere north of the border between the two countries had suffered any less of a tragedy than the rest of the continent, or the world.

The space between towns and cities began to grow larger the farther north they traveled.

And they saw not one other soul.

For the majority of the journey, Emily and Rhiannon had sat in relative silence, each numbed by their own despair, a sharp splinter of pain buried deep in each of their hearts.

When they reached Calgary, Emily pulled the SUV to a halt in front of what had once been a store of some kind but was now just a burned-out ruin of blackened beams and melted glass; the soot-strewn interior was littered with the unidentifiable skeletons of what could have once been furniture.

Emily climbed from the driver's seat into the back next to Rhiannon, staring at the young girl, who seemed to be patently avoiding her gaze.

Emily paused as she collected herself; she wanted to get the words in the right order before she spoke them, so Rhia understood exactly what it was that she was saying. So there could be no mistake in her intent, because she knew she would only get one shot at this speech, so it had to be right.

"I'm sorry," she said eventually. "I'm sorry that I couldn't save your dad. And I'm so very sorry that I could not save Ben. If I could have traded places with them, I would have. But I promise you, Rhiannon, that I will never let harm come to you. I promise that I will always be there to help you, and that I will never leave you. We're all each other has now. We are each other's family, and we have to protect each other from now on."

Emily wasn't sure what she was expecting as a reply, but what she got was something as uncomplicated and yet as confusing as this girl on the waning edge of childhood.

"I know," Rhiannon said softly, her lips parted in a sad slight smile as she finally lifted her eyes to Emily. "I know it wasn't your fault, but it doesn't stop me from being mad at you. Even though I don't want to be. Is that stupid?"

Emily choked back a sudden flow of emotion that threatened to overwhelm her ability to even talk. "No, sweetie, no. It's very normal," was the best she could manage.

"I just wish...I wish you hadn't found us. I wish you had just kept riding. Sorry, but I do. 'Cause then Daddy and Ben would still be alive and we'd all still be together." Rhiannon's hand crept across the space between them, grasping Emily's. "But I know that won't happen, and I know you're sorry, so I just want to be safe."

Emily squeezed Rhiannon's hand in return, leaned in, and kissed her gently on the forehead. "I do, too," she replied. "I do, too."

They took advantage of the unscheduled stop and allowed Thor out to stretch his legs. Ten minutes later, as Emily climbed into the driver's seat, she heard the front passenger door open, then Rhiannon pulled herself up into the leather seat and fastened her seat belt into place.

Emily turned and smiled at her. Neither said a word; none were needed, so Emily just slipped the Dodge into gear and drove.

ALASKA

CHAPTER TWENTY-THREE

"It's snowing," said Rhiannon.

"What?"

"It's. Snowing."

Emily looked up from the road and saw fat flakes of white drifting slowly down from the sky. She had been driving for so long on this particular stretch of the Alaska Highway, mile after mile after dreary mile, that her mind had switched to autopilot and she hadn't even noticed the blanket of gray clouds as they had moved in from the northeast.

According to the digital thermometer display, the temperature outside was thirty-two degrees. The temperature had dropped more than fifteen degrees over the past three days.

"Where are we?" Emily asked.

Rhiannon picked up the road atlas from the floor and thumbed it open to a dog-eared page. She traced their route with a finger, holding the book open and angled toward Emily so she could glance at it. "I don't think it's very far now. We just passed a sign for Eielson Air Force Base."

Fairbanks was about another twenty miles or so farther northwest from the military base; another twenty minutes or so drive, Emily estimated.

The road they were driving was what passed for a two-lane highway but amounted to little more than two lanes of concrete with a median of brown grass between them. On either side of the road was an expanse of the equally dead grass. The grass terminated at a seemingly never-ending line of what she thought were silver birch trees. Whatever they were, their skinny trunks and naked branches became ridiculously monotonous after the first twenty miles or so.

When she had spoken with Jacob the previous night, he had told her to make sure her first stop was at a cold-weather outfitters.

"You need to find winter clothing. It'll hit below zero before you know it, and I can guarantee you won't want to be caught outside in any of your regular clothes," he had told her. He'd given her directions to the store he used, and Emily had promised him they would head straight there as soon as they made it into Fairbanks.

Temperatures this far north could vary wildly. At this time of year, daytime temperature might reach thirty or even forty degrees, and at night, you would be lucky if the thermometer stayed above minus fifteen. "The right clothing is the difference between life and a very painful death," Jacob had warned them.

They had stopped the previous night in a small town, weirdly named Tok. Setting out the following morning, it had struck Emily how normal the routine had become for her and Rhiannon. After their talk back in Calgary, all signs of the petulant little girl she had first encountered had completely disappeared as Rhia slipped willingly into the role of navigator.

And Emily had surprised herself at just how easily she had come to rely on Rhiannon. She had never given children a second thought in her life; there had never been enough time to even think about them or a man that she was willing to settle down with or who would be willing to put up with her. She loved the little girl, she realized. If she ever had a child of her own, she would hope that she turned out like Rhia.

"Watch out!" yelled Rhiannon, suddenly bracing her arm against the dashboard.

Emily's attention had been lost in thought again, her eyes off the road, so she had failed to see the debris of the downed airplane splashed across the lane ahead of them. She hit the brakes and brought the Dodge to a screeching halt.

The wreckage looked to be of some kind of fighter plane, probably from the air base. It had crashed nose first into the north-bound lane, leaving a crater gouged out of the earth that stretched across all four lanes. Strangely, the nose of the plane was still intact, severed just behind the cockpit, which was missing its canopy and pilot's seat. The pilot had probably ejected when he felt the oncoming effects of the red rain, Emily surmised. Lot of good that had done him.

The rest of the plane was nothing but blackened bits and pieces scattered across the ground.

"Sorry," said Emily, turning to Rhiannon. "I guess I'm just tired." Who knew sitting down for hours on end could be so exhausting?

Emily glanced up at the rearview mirror and put the SUV into reverse, backing up about twenty feet, then drove off the road and onto the field, steering around the wreckage of the downed aircraft.

Up ahead, on the right side of the road, Emily could see what looked like a line of adobe-colored blocks. She accelerated the

Dodge back up to speed. The blocks quickly resolved into buildings and military aircraft hangars. A six-foot-high chain-link fence topped with razor wire surrounded the air base.

Emily slowed the SUV to a crawl as she eased past the main entrance. The guard post was deserted, but the metal security gate was down, blocking the entrance to the military buildings beyond it. She could make out vehicles parked uniformly off in the distance, and what looked like several commercial-size gray aircraft parked on one of the runways.

The crumpled skeleton of a helicopter, its tail snapped from its fuselage pointing skyward, sat alone in an open field. It was missing one of its rotor blades, and those that remained hung limply toward the ground.

There was no sign of life. No movement except for the flakes of snow that had now begun to settle on the grass and concrete of the road in front of them.

"Do you think the soldiers are alive in there?" Rhiannon asked.

Emily stared at the silent base. She had hoped that maybe, just maybe, the military had figured out how to survive the blood rain. If anyone could have, it would have been them. But that hadn't been the case. Everyone here was dead.

"No," she said with a final glance at the base. She drove on.

■ ■ ■

She wasn't sure what she had expected from the town of Fairbanks. Maybe a small town full of single-wide trailers and strip joints. That was the impression she had always had of these ends-of-the-world kind of places; a backward whistle-stop of a place, in the middle of nowhere, populated by fat bearded men in plaid shirts and aging whores. Instead, as she finally pulled into the town, she found herself in a community that would have looked at home in any Midwest state. Pleasant-looking, well-kept homes, their lawns dead and brown now that no one was alive to maintain them, bland apartment buildings, a theater, a smattering of gas stations and car dealerships. The tiny houses were never going to appear on the cover of *Better Homes and Gardens*, but then again, nothing was.

Emily got the impression that even before everybody had died, this town had been, for the most part, quiet.

Slowly maneuvering through the empty streets, she turned right onto Second Avenue and immediately stomped on the brake. Ahead of her, in a plot of land that had once been a children's playground, a cluster of alien trees sprouted from the ground. She had failed to notice them earlier because they were hidden by a phalanx of spruce trees lining the park's border. There was something different about these invaders, something that was unlike the usual uniform, almost cookie-cutter versions that had become a daily sight since leaving Manhattan.

These were stunted and irregular. The usual black sheen that coated the bark was missing, and she could see gray splotches scattered across their trunks. Where their cousins south of Fairbanks stretched skyward for hundreds of feet, these barely reached the height of the crossbar of the playground's swing set. They should have been towering over them by now.

Emily pulled the Durango to the curb and rolled down her window. A cold breeze stung her face, and she exhaled sharply, sending a pale cloud of vapor out into the atmosphere to mix with the vehicle's exhaust fumes and the flakes of snow that still fell from the leaden sky. The air felt crisp and clean, knife-sharp against the back of her throat.

"Stay here," she told Rhiannon to the whine of the window whirring back up. "I'll be right back."

Rhiannon just nodded her head. Thor shifted uneasily in the back, but Emily commanded him to stay.

Standing on the sidewalk, Emily shivered as a gust of wind sliced through her thin shirt, straight to her spine. She was going to have to find that cold-weather clothing store, soon. Already, a half inch of snow had settled on the low hedge at the front of the playground, and the pavement was quickly becoming slippery underfoot.

She was going to have to make this quick.

Following the path into the park, Emily walked past the set of swings, their rusty chains squeaking loudly in the breeze, and headed toward the group of scrawny-looking alien trees.

Emily froze—an appropriate term, she supposed, given how goddamn cold it was. In front of her, scattered around the base of the nearest trees like fallen leaves, were at least twenty of the spider-aliens, their ugly-ass heads staring straight at her.

■ ■ ■

Emily didn't dare move. A day-long minute ticked by in her head as she stared at the creatures. Like the stunted alien trees behind them, there was something not quite right with them. In every encounter she'd had with the spider-things they had always been the alien equivalent of a hyperactive kid; always on the move, never still. In fact, she thought, the only one she had ever seen not moving had been long dead, impaled by the iron bars of a fence back in New York.

Dead! These things were dead…probably.

She took a tentative step forward. No movement from them. Then another step. Still no reaction. Emboldened, she took another step closer and another until she was standing next to the closest motionless alien. She prodded it with the tip of her sneaker. It didn't move, frozen solid to the concrete playground. It was the same for the rest of them, all deader than dead, their carapaces hard and unyielding she found as she stomped down hard on one with her heel.

It was almost as if they had been flash-frozen, she thought. Caught out in the open when the temperature had dropped. More proof that Jacob had been right about the temperature all along.

Sure that they posed no threat to her, Emily turned her attention back to the deformed alien trees. They looked half-finished. Instead of the geometric keenness of the top edges that had defined the trees she had seen being built, these were irregular. Pieces were missing, and here and there were gaps, long seams that stretched up the tree like cracks. She squeezed two fingers into the gap. Her fingers slipped in all the way to the second knuckle. The gray splotches she had seen were in reality half-formed pieces of the tree; when she touched one, it cracked, sending a large section down into the interior of the trunk.

The red rain had accomplished its mission, killing everyone in the town, but the growth of the trees had been stopped in its tracks. It looked as though they had been completely unable to deal with the cold. Judging by the lack of growth of the trees and the dead aliens scattered around the base of the trees, she would not be surprised if she found thousands of the aliens, or maybe even their precursor pupae stages, scattered throughout the houses in the town. She would have to remember that when they looked for a place to spend the night.

She gave one of the dead spider-aliens a swift kick to the face, breaking off the thing's frozen tentacles with a satisfying clink that sounded like shattered icicles.

"That's for everyone in this town," she said and walked back to the warmth of the SUV.

"What took you so long?" asked Rhiannon as Emily closed the door of the Durango and turned the heater up as high as it would go.

"Nothing. I just needed to check out the trees," she replied as she felt the heat chase the frigidness from her fingers. Emily didn't see any point in scaring Rhiannon with the news of the dead aliens.

"So, what are we supposed to do now?"

"How about I take us clothes shopping?" she answered.

■ ■ ■

The strip mall parking lot still held two cars. Their owners, presumably, had not heeded the warnings about the effects of the red rain and had perished while shopping. *I guess there are worse ways to go,* Emily thought as she pulled the Dodge to a stop out front of the store Jacob had directed her to.

Large red letters over the entrance to the building read FRONTIER OUTFITTERS, and below that in smaller letters: HUNTING. FISHING. CAMPING. APPAREL.

Emily grabbed the shotgun and her flashlight and stepped outside. She left the engine running not just for security, but also because it was so damn cold that the idea of waiting for the car to warm up again was not a pleasant thought.

"Stay here for a second while I check around," she told Rhiannon. "Thor, come on." The dog leaped from the backseat to the driver's, then down onto the concrete. He stretched and fol-lowed Emily as she headed to the store's entrance.

The door creaked open, and Emily pushed it open farther with the barrel of the Mossberg. She stepped inside and scanned the interior with the flashlight while Thor ran around checking every nook and cranny. There were no windows in the build-ing, so the interior was lit only by the meager light that made it through the panes of the glass double doors.

Thor trotted back to her side after a minute, giving no indication they were anything but alone in the store. Emily leaned around the door and beckoned to Rhiannon to join her.

"Bring your flashlight," she yelled to the girl as she exited the SUV.

Inside the store, row upon row of shelves were stacked with heavy-duty boots, camping equipment, dry goods, and fish-ing gear. Clothing racks held cold-weather jackets and trousers, thick wool sweaters, even thicker scarves, gloves, and balaclavas. Everything the modern outdoorsman would ever need to survive in this unforgiving climate and more.

Emily couldn't see any carts, so, after a quick look around, she found a large gray plastic storage container. She discarded the lid and carried the container over to the racks of clothes.

Rhiannon had already found a parka with a fur-lined hood that she had zipped up so far her face was completely hidden.

"A big improvement," said Emily, smiling.

They worked their way down each aisle, pulling what they needed from the racks, filling the plastic container to almost overflowing.

Near the camping equipment, Emily found a selection of heavy-duty sleeping bags. The tags attached to them said they were good down to minus thirty degrees. She added two of them to the container, the electric-pink one for Rhiannon.

Emily double-checked their loot one last time, running over the mental list she had made, making sure they had forgotten nothing.

Sure they had liberated everything on the list, Emily and Rhiannon each took one end of the box and readied themselves to carry it out to the idling SUV.

As they navigated carefully between the racks, Emily's flashlight glinted off a glass display case that took up most of the right wall of the store.

"Hold on a second," she said, lowering her end of the box to the ground. She walked over to the display case and played the light over the contents of the case, then along the back wall behind it.

"Excellent," she called back to Rhiannon. "Guns. Lots of guns."

■ ■ ■

The gun cases were all locked. Emily solved that particular problem with the butt of the Mossberg.

"Here, hold this," she said as she handed Rhiannon her flashlight, the sound of the shattered glass still reverberating in their ears. "Keep it angled like this and be careful of the glass." She used the butt of the shotgun to clear away the remaining broken shards of glass that still jutted from the surround of the case.

There was a selection of about twenty handguns to choose from. Each one had a small plaque beneath it that displayed the make and model. When Nathan had taught Emily how to shoot, she had used several handguns, but her favorite had been the

Glock 19. It was light enough for her to handle easily and held fifteen rounds of nine-millimeter ammunition.

She searched the glass-strewn case until she spotted the model she was looking for. Emily carefully picked up the pistol, shook off a couple of pieces of broken glass, and gave it a quick once-over. The magazine was missing, but she'd probably find that in the plastic case that came with the weapon.

She was about to start looking for the Glock's case when another pistol caught her eye. She picked up the little revolver and placed it next to the Glock on the counter behind the gun case.

She found both pistols' protective cases in a drawer beneath the gun display. She added gun oil and a couple of cleaning kits and a shoulder rig for the Glock along with a leather belt holster for the little revolver. Adjacent to the display case were shelves of ammunition. She pulled several boxes of ammo for each of the guns and added them to the clothing and pistols, then went back and grabbed four boxes of shells for the shotgun.

It took two trips to carry their new "purchases" to the waiting vehicle. They hefted the overflowing container up into the cargo space of the Durango, sliding it in between the remainder of their food and Emily's bike.

"Brrrrrrr!" Both girls were shivering as they climbed back into their seats, glad to be out of the biting cold. Emily cranked the heater back up.

In the thirty minutes or so their shopping trip had taken to complete, a layer of white fluffy snow had covered almost everything, completely transforming the image of the town from empty frontier to classic Christmas card. Emily was surprised at how comforting it was. With the layer of white covering everything, it was easy to think of each of these businesses and homes as containing families huddled around the fire, talking and laughing, safe and warm.

Emily glanced at the digital clock on the dashboard; it read 3:18. Still a couple of hours of light left but with the snow reducing visibility, it was probably better if they tried to find the university as quickly as possible.

Jacob had told Emily that it would be a mistake to try to make the final leg of the trip in the Durango. "It just won't be capable of making it," he had explained. "The engine isn't designed to take the kind of gasoline you'll need, and if it gets cold enough, it'll freeze in the lines and you along with it."

He had told her she needed to find his department at the university. "Look for the Geophysical Institute building. We have a couple of Sno-Cats that will be better suited to the terrain."

When she had expressed her concern about how she was supposed to drive this new vehicle, Jacob had told her not to worry. "If you figured out how to drive the Durango, you shouldn't have a problem."

Emily wasn't sure she agreed with him, but he had been right about most things so far.

"Okay, young lady, buckle up," she said and carefully edged the SUV out onto the snow-covered road.

■ ■ ■

They spent the night on the second floor of the Geophysical Institute building, serenaded by a storm that, come morning, had added a fresh layer of snow several inches deep, completely covering the SUV they had left parked on the narrow road outside the building.

Jacob had told Emily that she would find the Sno-Cat in a storage facility on the north side of the Geo-Phys building, so, after breakfast—soup they found in the second-floor lounge—they threw on their cold-weather gear and headed out, descending down to ground level. Rhiannon found a fire escape that led them out to the rear of the building, but when Emily pushed down on the bar to open it, the door would not budge. She tried again, this time leaning her shoulder into it, and she felt the door give a little, then a little more as she bumped her shoulder hard against it.

Sunlight streamed in through the gap along with a large clump of snow that fell with a splat onto the floor.

Well, that explained the problem with opening the door. A drift of snow, at least four feet high, had piled against the outer door. She thumped the flat of her arm against the door, each time she hit it, the door budged a little bit more until there was just enough room for them to kick the snow away and squeeze through.

The early morning sun bounced painfully off the top layer of snow, blinding them both momentarily as they stepped from the darkness of the corridor into the open daylight.

Thor was off in a heartbeat, leaping like a fox through the snow that came up to his belly.

Emily, her hand pressed against her forehead to shade her eyes, scanned the field of white for any indication of the building that Jacob had talked about.

At the top of an embankment about three hundred feet or so away, past several mounds of snow that were probably buried cars, Emily saw a large building, its roof heavy with snow and its white sides blending almost seamlessly into the surrounding scenery.

Parked outside the entrance were several large dump trucks.

"I think that's where we need to go," she said to Rhiannon. The girl looked like an Eskimo bundled up in her thermal trousers and parka, her warm breath condensing in the frigid air like smoke from a baby dragon.

"'Kay." Another puff of white filled the air.

The pair, flanked by Thor, trudged their way toward the building, the fresh powder crackling and crunching beneath their boots.

By the time they crested the embankment leading up to the building, Emily knew this had to be the right place. It was about the size of an aircraft hangar. They stood in front of two huge fold-back doors, both of which were closed and locked tight. A door on the left of the building opened when she twisted the knob, and they stepped into a small office area with a back wall made entirely of shatterproof glass that looked out into the darkness of the hangar's interior space.

A set of filing cabinets and a small desk with a computer occupied most of the room. Fixed to the wall next to a second door leading out into the hangar was a corkboard with paper fliers and notices pinned to it. Beneath the corkboard was a metal frame from which hung several sets of keys.

There didn't appear to be any windows in the main part of the building, and with the main doors closed, the interior beyond the office was dark as night. Emily hadn't thought to bring the flashlight and didn't much care to trudge all the way back through the snow to fetch it. If she had to, she would, but she decided to see if she could figure out a way to open the doors and let some light into the building first. Much like she had with the garage door back at the Jeffersons' house, she surmised there had to be a way to manually open them.

She opened the second door leading into the main hangar and asked Rhiannon to stand in the doorway and keep it ajar for her. A thin pathway of light filtered out from the office. It wasn't much, but it was at least enough for her to be able to make out the shape of the two main outer doors. Stepping into the larger space, she edged over to the double doors, pausing a minute as her eyes adjusted to the darkness.

Through the gloom Emily spotted a large metal handle protruding from a gray oblong box that came up to her waistline. It was secured to the floor by four bolts. A pulley system ran from the box and disappeared into the darkness high above her.

She took the handle firmly in both hands and rotated it once. The mechanism inside the box made a clacking sound as Emily turned the handle farther and the doors rattled like they'd been buffeted by a gust of wind. Two more turns of the handle and a laser-thin beam of light appeared at the center of the doors running from floor to ceiling. With each turn of the handle, the beam widened and grew, flooding the interior of the building with the sharp white light of the winter wonderland beyond its walls.

A few minutes later and both doors were fully opened. Emily dropped the hood on her parka, putting up with the sudden chill as the sweat on her forehead began to freeze.

"You all right?" asked Rhiannon.

"Fine," Emily replied as she drew in deep icy breaths that stung her nose and throat. She beckoned the girl over to her side.

"Let's find this thing and get out of here."

Two rows of vehicles lined the interior of the storage building. A snowplow and a couple of trucks adapted to spread salt over icy roads waited off to her right. On the left was a second snowplow and, just beyond that, she saw a large bright-orange tracked vehicle that looked like it was designed for a science-fiction movie… or to traverse the snowy wastelands of this world, she thought. That could only be the Cat.

She walked over to the nearest side of the vehicle. It had four powerful-looking triangular tracks instead of wheels. Each was attached to a flat chassis on top of which sat a glass-encased four-door cab that contained two rows of seats. It looked like whoever had designed this machine had taken the cab from an eighteen-wheeler and dropped it onto a tank. In front of the cab was the squared-off engine compartment, and to the rear of the cab was a large silver tank that she assumed contained the fuel. Seven large windows in the cabin gave whoever was driving this thing a 360-degree field of vision.

An emblem etched on the engine compartment read TUCKER SNO-CAT.

"Wow," said Rhiannon. "Are we going to be riding in that?"

It really was more like a tank than the SUV, Emily thought as she slowly circled the vehicle.

"Ohhh-kay!" she said aloud as she stood next to the giant machine. "How the hell am I supposed to drive this?"

■ ■ ■

First things first: she needed to find the keys.

While Rhiannon waited with Thor next to the Sno-Cat, Emily walked back to the office and the sets of keys she had seen dangling from beneath the corkboard. Each pair of keys was attached to a plastic tag indicating which vehicle it belonged with, and Emily quickly located one that had "Sno-Cat 1644" written across it in thick red marker.

Keys in hand, she headed back into the hangar.

The Cat's triangular tracks were almost three feet at their highest vertices. To get into the vehicle's cab, Emily needed to use them as a ladder to climb up to a flat aluminum access gantry running the length of the vehicle. Much like the Durango, the cab of the Sno-Cat had two sets of doors, the first accessed the front section, where the driver's area and a single passenger seat were located. The second was for the passenger section of the cab. The cabin doors were locked, but the keys she had found slipped easily into the lock. She pulled the door open.

Inside the cab Emily was happily surprised at how similar the interior layout was to the Dodge. There was a regular steering wheel with a gearshift stick on one side of the column and one to control lights on the other. The dash had a similar cluster of indicators and dials she had become accustomed to driving the SUV. Even the seats looked comfortable and familiar. She'd been expecting something far more complicated, but the only unfamiliar thing she noticed was a bank of switches on the right side of the console. A quick inspection of these showed her they were most likely heating and exterior lighting controls. There was even a CD player, for crying out loud.

In the time it had taken to drive the Dodge Durango from Stuyvesant to Fairbanks, Emily had become quietly confident in her newfound skills as a driver, but she found herself feeling nervous as she settled her butt into the Cat's driver's seat. This thing was a hell of a lot bigger than the SUV, and like the tank it reminded Emily of, it looked more than capable of causing major damage to anything it hit...or ran over.

"Better if you stand out of the way," she called down to Rhiannon. "And keep a tight hold of Thor."

Rhiannon slipped her gloved fingers beneath the dog's collar and guided him into the space between the snowplow and sander on the opposite side of the building.

"Hurry up," she yelled back. "It's freezing out here."

Emily pulled the cabin door closed and looked over the controls. "Nothing to it," she whispered as she slipped the keys into

the ignition and turned them. The engine turned over once...
twice...then caught, and the cabin filled with a deep rumbling as
the engine sprang to life. A large puff of exhaust fumes coughed
from the engine exhaust and a barely audible thrum vibrated
through the cabin as the engine settled into its natural cadence.
She checked the fuel gauge. It indicated the tank was almost full.

Slipping the gear stick into drive, she slowly pressed down
on the accelerator. The engine revved, but the tracks of the Cat
did not move an inch. What the? Glancing over at the console of
lights and indicators, she saw a large button glowing red. Etched
above it were the words PARKING BRAKE. She pressed it once, and
the light went out.

She eased her foot back onto the accelerator. The Sno-Cat
gave a slight shudder, and then it was moving, inching forward as
its tracks rumbled across the concrete floor.

Emily whooped with joy as she guided the Cat toward
the exit. She beckoned to Rhiannon to meet her outside the
doors.

When she was clear of the hangar doors, Emily brought the
Cat to a halt and pushed the gear stick back into the park position.
With the engine still running, she climbed from the driver's seat
into the passenger seat. Opening the passenger door, she beckoned for Rhiannon to come around to her side of the vehicle as
she stepped out onto the access gantry.

"You're going to have to climb up the tracks. It's easy. Don't be
afraid," she said, yelling to be heard over the rumble of the engine.

The girl hesitated for a moment, then used the deep ridges
of the track's tread as finger- and toeholds and pulled herself up
until Emily could reach down and take her hand. She pulled her
the rest of the way. "Inside," she yelled, pointing toward the passenger seat. Closing the door, Emily moved to the rear door and

pulled it open. The door's hinges were positioned so the door could be laid flush against the cab and not block the gantry access to the back part of the cabin.

Thor waited patiently at the foot of the Cat, his tail sweeping the dusty concrete floor. Kneeling down, at the far end of the gantry where he could see her, Emily called the dog to her.

He didn't hesitate, leaping onto the rubber tracks and using his powerful hind legs to launch himself over the metal lip and onto the gantry next to Emily.

"Good boy," she cooed and ushered the dog into the back compartment of the Cat. He climbed inside and sat facing the front windshield, panting quietly.

Emily climbed down the tracks and walked around to the driver's side, then climbed back up again and retook her place in the driver's seat, closing the door behind her.

"Wagons roll," she called out as she slipped the Cat into gear and pulled out of the storage facility and onto the snow.

■ ■ ■

The Cat was incredibly easy to maneuver, nimbly moving over the snowy surface with no loss of grip; the four huge caterpillar tracks provided a surprising amount of stability and traction. It was a little bumpy in the cabin, but that was something they could put up with. The important thing was that they now had a vehicle that could travel safely over the roads and snowfields that Jacob had warned her were to come.

Before they could head out, they would need to head back to the Geo-Phys building and pack their supplies from the previous night. Then they would have to transfer as much of the supplies they still had in the back of the Dodge over to the Cat. It was going to be a tight squeeze in the backseat for Thor as there wasn't a stowage compartment.

Rhiannon had slipped her parka's hood from her head and sat with her arms braced against the console as she stared out the side window of the cab. She had seemed fascinated by the Sno-Cat's tracks as they'd pulled the vehicle across the snow, leaving a trail of powder behind them like a jet's vapor trail and a smile of joy on her face as the machine raced along the street.

Emily allowed her foot to become heavier against the gas pedal, pushing the Cat first up to twenty-five miles an hour, then, when she was confident of her ability to maintain control, up to thirty-five. Her nerves and the narrow streets of the campus quickly got the better of her, though, and she brought the machine back down to a more sensible twenty-ish as they cruised the street leading back to the Geo-Phys building. She spotted the snowy outline of the Dodge Durango halfway up the street and slid her new set of "wheels" to a stop alongside it.

Switching off the engine, Emily climbed out of the cab and leaped down onto the tracks, then the ground, closely followed by Rhia and Thor.

The Dodge was barely visible beneath the snowdrift that had all but covered it overnight. That was okay, though; they wouldn't be needing it anymore.

"Race you upstairs," Emily shouted. She was already running toward the door before her little companion could yell "Not fair" and chase after her to the accompaniment of Thor's gleeful barks.

■ ■ ■

Twenty minutes later they were back at the SUV. Emily's backpack was already in the backseat of the Cat, and Rhiannon was pushing the snow from the rear door of the Durango, trying to find the handle so she could open it. When it finally popped open, Emily made a quick assessment of everything they had. The food was not as important now that they were so near to their goal. Jacob had told them that he had months' worth of provisions still, so they could leave some of it behind, as much as she hated to let good food go to waste. He had told her that the trip should take about two days to complete, so if she made sure they had enough food and water for five days, they should be golden. Besides, according to the atlas and Jacob's instructions, there were a couple of small settlements they would need to stop at for fuel along the way. They could restock there if they needed to.

Their cold-weather clothing was the most important. They would be traveling several hundred miles farther north, and the weather would become even more unpredictable the closer they got to the Arctic coast. They transferred the remaining supplies across to the new vehicle's backseat, making sure they left enough room so Thor could sit comfortably.

God, she hated to leave the bike behind, but where they were heading, there wasn't going to be a need for it, and short of strapping it to the side of the Cat, nowhere to store it. She checked the panniers for anything that might be useful, but found only a gallon of water and a few cans of food.

It was going to have to stay with the SUV.

Emily helped Rhiannon climb back up onto the gantry, then returned to the SUV and clambered into the back, over the rear seats, grabbing the road atlas and a couple of energy bars stashed in the pocket of the passenger door.

After a final glance around, she dropped the keys onto the driver's seat and climbed out, slamming the door closed behind her.

CHAPTER TWENTY-FOUR

The James Dalton Highway was a four-hundred-mile stretch of road connecting Fairbanks to the town of Deadhorse, just a few miles shy of the Arctic Ocean. The twisting road covered some of the most extreme terrain and weather conditions in the world. Temperatures could drop to minus thirty degrees centigrade and storms could blow in seemingly out of nowhere, reducing visibility to nothing and freezing anything caught unprotected in the open.

"Thanks so much for that," said Emily as she recalled the information Jacob had relayed to her.

"What?" asked Rhiannon, yawning and stretching as she woke from a two-hour nap.

"I said it looks like snow," lied Emily.

Rhiannon gave her one of those withering looks that only an adolescent girl could deliver: a cross between utter disdain and pity. Emily smiled. Maybe it was better that the world's supply of teenage boys was probably extinct. This one would do more than break hearts; she could turn them into mincemeat with a single glance.

"Go back to sleep," Emily suggested.

Rhiannon shook her head and stretched. "Not tired," she said. "How long have we been driving for?"

Emily glanced down at the display panel on the dash. A timer in the top corner of the screen showed they had been on the road for almost four hours now. She had kept the speed down to a manageable thirty miles per hour, occasionally even as low as fifteen when she had to navigate a particularly tricky corner. The tachometer said they had traveled a total of 107 miles. Just over a quarter of their trip was already behind them.

Rhiannon might not be tired, but Emily felt her own eyes beginning to ache. Even though the outside temperature was a frigid fifteen degrees, inside the cab, thanks to the superb heating system, the temperature was a balmy seventy-two degrees. Combine that with the sweeping sheets of white on every side and the occasional rhythmic beat of the industrial-size wiper-blades as they swished away the ice and snow that built up on the windshield, and you had as good a recipe for falling asleep at the wheel as was ever invented. If it wasn't for her unease at driving this thing, she would have probably landed them in a snowbank or off the side of a mountain by now.

They had about another 150 miles of driving ahead of them before they reached the tiny encampment of Coldfoot. Jacob had assured her that they would find fuel and somewhere to spend the night there.

"It's the only stop between Fairbanks at the southern end of the highway and Deadhorse, where you're heading at the opposite end, that you'll find fuel," he had told her.

Ahead, the road curved up a steep slope that ran over and between a pair of hills before disappearing into a bank of fog or low clouds that obscured the top; it was hard to tell exactly which.

Emily slowed the Sno-Cat as they rumbled up the slope.

She had spent some time checking out the bank of switches and had identified what most of them did. As the white mist enveloped them, she switched on the powerful halogen lamps mounted on either side of the cab. The light helped a little, but it also gave the fog/cloud a weird orange glow that strained her eyes even more as the light bounced back at her.

Emily eased off the gas a little as the road rose higher into the hills, curving and dipping unexpectedly. Her heart was in her mouth for most of the next fifteen minutes as they climbed higher and higher; then suddenly they were out of it. Emily could see the road disappear again between two icy peaks about a mile farther up the road, so she picked up her speed a little, quickly chewing up the distance to the ridge.

She glanced over at Rhiannon, but the kid was curled up on the seat, her head resting against the passenger window, eyes closed as her chest rose and descended rhythmically. Asleep again.

The weather had been clear for most of the drive so far, except for the occasional squall that blew in seemingly from nowhere and disappeared just as quickly. Now as they crowned the valley between the peaks, looking down onto the plain below them, she could see for miles ahead of her. It was breathtakingly beautiful. An unspoiled white canvas. In the distance, mountains rose into the air, crowned by thick waves of cloud, their dark outline providing an elegant border to the sheer simplicity of nature's perfection.

Emily guided the Cat down the opposite side of the hill's winding road, the same band of fog/clouds blanketed the descent for several miles ahead, completely obscuring the road from view.

Emily switched the lamps back on as they penetrated the mist and slowed the Cat to a more manageable speed, edging it around a hairpin bend that dropped rapidly and then curved again in the opposite direction.

If Emily had taken her eyes off the road for even a second she would not have seen the eighteen-wheeler splayed across the road. When it materialized from out of the bank of fog there was less than ten feet left between the Cat and it. Emily slammed her foot against the brake pedal. The tracks instantly locked, bringing the machine to an almost immediate stop as its treads dug into the snow. Rhiannon tumbled off the seat with a cry of fear, hitting the console and falling in a pile of waving arms and legs to the floor.

"What was that? What was that?" she demanded as she pulled herself back into the seat. She screamed again when she saw the huge glinting curve of the tanker just feet from the front of the Cat's engine.

"Where did that come from?" she demanded.

"I have no idea," answered Emily. "Are you okay?"

Rhiannon, pouting just a little at the embarrassment of the spill, nodded that she thought she was. The only thing bruised was her dignity.

The lamps cut through the space between the Cat and the tanker, and Emily grabbed the handle of the one on her side of the cab, panning the light through the mist along the length of the other vehicle. The driver's cabin of the truck hung over the right edge of the road, its back wheels the only thing keeping it from falling into the space beyond, snapping the cab from the trailer like a broken neck. The rest of the truck, a huge cylinder trailer of brushed silver, cut diagonally across the road, blocking most of the path.

Emily panned the light left, then back to the right again, but even the powerful beam of the spotlight could not penetrate very deeply into the bank of mist. There was nothing else for it; she was going to have to get out and see what kind of room there was for her to maneuver.

Shit! If this tanker blocked the entire road, they were screwed. They would have to head back to Fairbanks and figure out some other way to get to Jacob's location.

"Stay here," she said to Rhiannon. "And lock the door behind me." Emily saw the look of fear spread over the young girl's face at the thought of being left alone. "Don't worry," she told her. "I just need to look around. Besides, Thor will keep you company. Won't you, boy?" Thor laid his muzzle on the center console between the two front seats and whined quietly, his tail beating a subdued rhythm against the upholstery.

"I'll be right back," she continued as she manipulated the floodlight until it illuminated the majority of the length of the trailer. It would give her some light at least.

She pulled on her parka and zipped it up tight before slipping the hood over her head. The shotgun was hard to handle with the thick gloves, but she took it anyway. Emily opened the door quickly and stepped outside before the heat of the cabin could escape. Slamming it shut, she saw white condensation begin to collect on the window. She tapped the glass and mouthed "Lock. The. Door" to the wide-eyed Rhiannon. She waited until she saw her reach across and click the lock into place, then turned and maneuvered carefully along the ice-covered access gantry, stepped down onto the front track, and hopped the last few feet down onto the snow-covered road. The snow was less than a foot deep here, she noted, as her boots sank down into it with a crunch like dry autumn leaves.

Through the narrow vision of the hood of her parka, Emily could make out the cold steel of the tanker ahead of her. She crunched over to it and leaned a gloved hand against it as she oriented herself with the light from the Cat. Even through the thick pads of her glove, she could feel the cold of the frigid metal permeating to the tips of her fingers.

The mist reduced visibility down to about fifteen feet; her own breath added to it as it swirled around her. She moved as close as she dared to the cab. The rock-strewn curb leading over the edge had no guardrail to protect drivers from the plunge to the valley below. It was probably best to stay back from the edge—the lip of the road looked loose and crumbly. No point putting herself in danger; besides, the driver's cabin was too far over for her to reach, anyway.

Doubling back, Emily followed the trailer toward its rear, walking carefully alongside it. Ten steps beyond that and the truck had completely disappeared from view. The panic that flooded her system was almost paralyzing. Getting lost out there, with no visual cues to orient herself by, could be deadly. Panicking, on the other hand, would be disastrous.

Breathe, she told herself. Just breathe.

She looked down at the snow; the outline of her tracks, crisp and fresh, were easily visible. Unless it started snowing again, they would act as bread crumbs. All she would need to do was follow them back to the Cat.

She started walking again, measuring each step as she watched for some indication of the end of the road. Five more steps and she could just begin to make out a dim form through the mist; another step and the edge of the road materialized, flanked by an embankment that rose up above her before disappearing into the mist. The embankment, an almost sheer face of rock, was too steep for even the multitracked Cat to climb, but she was pretty sure that if she was careful, she could slip the Cat through the space between it and the back end of the tanker. The Cat was about nine feet wide, and she had marked off about sixteen feet from the end of the tanker to the embankment. If she took it slow, they would be okay.

Emily turned to retrace her steps back to the vehicle as a gust of wind swept down from farther up the hill, buffeting and jostling her as she followed her footprints back the way she had come. A sudden, powerful crosswind pummeled her back, sending a flurry of blinding snow into the air. Off balance and disoriented by the sudden pounding wind, Emily fell forward, arms windmilling and then disappearing into the snow up to her elbows. The wind continued to buffet her even as she tried to struggle back to her feet. Every time she managed to raise herself to her knees, another gust of wind would knock her down again. It was futile to try and fight against it, she realized after her third attempt. Instead, she sank back to the ground and pulled her legs up to her chest, dipping her head down to her knees to limit the amount of cold air that could be blown into the hood of the parka. She'd just have to wait until the wind died down rather than risk being blown over the edge of the road.

Seconds dragged into minutes as she was rocked back and forth; clumps of snow lifted from the embankment face, bouncing off the protective coating of the jacket. In the darkness of her hood, the wind sounded like a wolf, baying for her blood.

Slowly, the wind began to die away. When she was quite sure it had stopped, she slowly lifted her head from her knees and looked around. The mist had disappeared, too, dragged away by the wind and revealing the rest of the road as it wound down the hill.

"Oh, shit!" The expletive tumbled from her mouth as she struggled to her feet and pulled the hood from her sweat-soaked head, oblivious to the chill.

Stretching out below her, lining almost every foot of the road, was a procession of frozen vehicles winding the remaining two miles to the bottom of the hill.

■ ■ ■

To Emily, as she gazed out over the line of trucks, flatbeds, snow-plows, tankers, Sno-Cats, and even a snowmobile or two, it seemed as though she had stumbled across some long-lost convoy.

It looked like they had been moving in formation together. Maybe they had been evacuating from the oil fields of Prudhoe Bay when the red rain caught them out in the open? The majority of the dead vehicles consisted of either heavy-goods or commercial-size transportation, suggesting they must have come from one of the support sites that supplied materials and assistance to the oil rigs that plundered the Arctic. Maybe these were even from Deadhorse?

Her own Cat was just fifty feet away, its engine billowing plumes of exhaust into the air. She could see Rhiannon, her nose pressed against the glass of the cab, staring at her and then at the snaking trail of frozen metal glinting in the sunlight.

Emily motioned to her that she was okay—not so easy to do when your hands are hidden in gloves. But she was a smart kid; she could figure out that she was all right.

The jackknifed big rig that had caused them to stop was the lead vehicle of the convoy. Behind that was another rig, which had come to a stop about ten feet or so from its rear end. The second vehicle's flatbed was empty, but when Emily climbed up onto the cab's footplate and wiped away the snow from the passenger window, she could see the cabin was not.

"Jesus!" Emily exclaimed.

Where she had expected to find the frozen body of the rig's driver, she instead found an alien pupa. It was stretched across both the driver's and passenger's seats, and a light sheen of frost covered the outside of the dark-red shell. It was at least twice as big as the pupae she had seen in her newspaper's offices back in Manhattan, and Emily wondered just how many people had been crammed into this cabin when the red rain had claimed them.

She dropped to the snow and moved to the next truck. There were two more pupae inside. Each resting on the seat where the human host had died.

It was the same for the next ten vehicles she checked. Every seat filled. Everyone inside dead.

But some of the convoy's refugees, either trying to escape or maybe stepping outside to see why the convoy had stopped, had not been changed. They lay frozen on the ground, their still-human outlines barely visible beneath the layer of snow that had settled over them, a shroud of pure white. Some had not managed to make it any farther than their open doors and now lay face-down in the snow, their torsos covered by a white veil while their bottom halves remained inside their vehicles.

That was strange. It was as though the extra insulation provided by the closed-off vehicles had allowed the transmutation to progress to its later stages, while for those who made it outside, the lower temperature had arrested the development into the alien pupa form.

It was only after Emily wiped a sheen of sweat from her forehead that she realized how warm it had become. She exhaled heavily. There was no white fog of breath. In fact, she could feel the air warming around her, tingling against her ears and her cheeks.

How could that be?

A minute or so later, as she checked for a clear route between a tanker and what looked to be a decommissioned school bus, she had to unzip her parka. The temperature must have risen at least three degrees in that time. She could feel a warm breeze blowing against her face and hands, like a car heater turned to low. It was sweeping down from the mountainside above her, and, as she looked up the mountain toward the peak, she could see rivulets of water beginning to run down the mountain as the snow began to melt.

She glanced around her at the maze of metal. It was thawing down here, too. The windshield of the school bus that had just a minute ago been covered in a crispy frost was now completely clear, exposing the dim outline of another pupa in the driver's seat. A continual drip, drip, drip of melting ice water ran off the hood.

Emily headed back to the waiting Cat.

There was a sudden loud crack like split wood off to her left.

She started at the noise. It had come from the inside of a Toyota SUV, stopped near the edge of the mountain pass. She paused, listening, then when the noise did not come again, crunched over to the Toyota. A large chunk of snow and ice that had collected on the roof slid off and fell to the ground as she approached.

Leaning in, Emily used the arm of her parka to wipe away the sheen of condensation that had collected on the passenger side window.

There was another pupa inside, but this one was open. A long fissure ran down the center of the shell; there was an inch of space between each side. As she watched, a set of spindly black legs, each with a sharp claw at its tip, rose slowly from the darkness of the pupa's interior, grasped each side of the shell, and pushed them wider apart.

Emily took an involuntary step back. "You have got to be kidding me!" The pupae were still alive? They should be frozen solid.

She glanced back at the row of stalled vehicles. There could be hundreds of aliens gestating inside them, for all she knew, heated by the warm thermals sweeping down off the mountaintop.

"Great. Just freaking great," she spat as she began to make her way back to the Cat as quickly as she could. The top layer of snow was rapidly turning to slush beneath her feet. An occasional spindrift of white still leaped into the air, lifted by the warming breeze.

From all around her now, the cracks of splitting pupae began to resonate, bouncing off the sheer walls of the winding mountain road.

There was still sixty feet left between her and the Cat when Emily heard what sounded like a squadron of mosquitoes buzz into life. She glanced back in the direction of the metal graveyard. A blur of movement behind the windshield of the nearest big rig drew her eyes to it. There was a whirring motion, like a propeller of an airplane, then a screeching sound that was quickly followed by an almost perfect circle appearing against the windshield of the truck. Glass powder began to fly away from the windshield as the alien caught inside began to use its specialized mandibles to cut a way out.

Then the glass circle fell off, and Emily began to run.

She passed the first jackknifed truck just as the alien inside was squeezing through the hole it had made in the passenger side window. Emily could see its black claws pushing through the opening as it pulled itself out onto the hood of the truck.

Rhiannon's shocked face, her eyes wide, mouth agape, pressed against the window of the Cat, staring at the alien as it emerged from the frozen tomb. At her side, Thor barked silently through the reinforced windshield.

The snow had become slippery, almost like mud now, and it sucked at her feet, slowing her pace. She was almost at the Cat's front set of tracks when the newborn alien launched itself into the air toward her from the side of the cab that still hung precariously over the precipice.

Emily let out a gasp as it landed on the lip of the road just a few feet from her, its two front claws furiously trying to find purchase on the slippery surface, while its back legs scrambled against empty air. It managed to hang there for a few seconds then, just as Emily clambered up onto the gantry of the Cat, she saw the creature lose its fight and disappear silently over the edge.

Emily pulled at the door, but it was still locked. She hammered furiously on the window until Rhiannon, still shocked at what she had just seen, reached across and flipped the lock. Emily pulled the door open and jumped inside, locking the door again behind her.

"What is that?" Rhiannon demanded.

Emily ignored the girl. As she repositioned herself into the driver's seat, she looked up at the convoy just in time to see the first wave of twenty or more spider-aliens begin to collect on the flat top of the lead big rig.

"Emily? What are they?" Rhiannon yelled again, almost in tears now.

"They're aliens, Rhiannon. And we have to get out of here, right now."

But where was she supposed to go? She couldn't go back, there was no other way across these mountains than the road they were on. They were still far too high up to try a direct descent over the side of the mountain; it was virtually a sheer drop all the way to the bottom at this point. There was only one way: forward, through the maze of stalled and wrecked vehicles.

More of the creatures had collected on the roof of the first rig, milling around aimlessly, scuttling back and forth as if looking for some way off the mountain.

Emily revved the engine and moved toward the space at the back of the first rig, keeping the Cat moving as fast as she safely could. She edged around the back of the first trailer and aimed toward the second larger gap.

As she passed the end of the trailer, something heavy hit the top of the Cat's roof.

Rhiannon squealed as first one, then a stream of the spider-aliens landed on the roof and then jumped down to the snow beside them. A constant stream of the creatures poured off Emily's side, hitting the snow, rolling, and righting themselves, then leaping and jumping as they hit the snow. It was almost as though the snow was burning them. Some of the creatures took off toward the nearest vehicle; others bounced like scalded cats until they either stopped moving or disappeared off the lip of the road.

As Emily finally cleared the first truck, the flow of aliens stopped, but not before one final creature launched itself off the top of the truck. It hit hard on the roof and bounced down onto the extended hood of the cab. It scrabbled around and clacked toward Emily and a screaming Rhiannon, smacking against the reinforced windshield. It clung there for a moment, each of its two eyestalks focusing on one of the humans inside the cab.

Thor's head appeared between the two seats, drool flying from his mouth as he snarled and barked at the unwanted hitchhiker.

The malamute's barking only grew more manic as the alien's bulbous black head reared back and the two cutting appendages that passed for jaws suddenly began to spin furiously. In seconds they were nothing but a blur of motion. The creature's head dropped forward and connected with the windshield. Instantly the inside of the cabin was filled with a high-pitch whine, worse than a hundred sets of fingernails on a blackboard. A plume of pulverized glass flew from the junction of windshield and alien.

Emily's vision, already half-obstructed by the creature's huge corkscrew-like body, was blocked completely, her senses overwhelmed by the piercing screech of pulverizing glass.

She hit the brake rather than risk a collision.

A second later and a circle of glass fell away, crashing onto the dashboard. The reinforced glass of the windshield refused to shatter and fell to the floor. The creature eased its head through the newly opened space, swiveling back and forth as if surveying the cab's interior. Its matte-black skin seemed to brighten as it touched the much warmer air of the Cat's cabin.

Rhiannon was screaming over and over, "Emily! Kill it. Kill it."

Thor was still trying, unsuccessfully, thank God, to push his way between the seats and reach the creature, which was already forcing itself through the portal it had created. Rhiannon had shrunk as far back into her seat as she could, trying to remain out of its reach.

"Thor. Get back," Emily screamed as she twisted around and pushed herself between the dog and the seats, reaching for the shotgun. "Get back, Thor," she yelled again when the dog continued to try to move forward. The dog finally acceded and wriggled free of the space. It was all the room Emily needed, and her fingers found the strap of the shotgun.

She pulled the Mossberg toward her, grabbing it with both hands. Swinging around, she brought the gun down to her side, aiming the barrel at the creature's head.

It was halfway through the hole now, its eyestalks swiveling back and forth. Emily paused, her finger on the trigger. If she fired the gun in here, there was no telling what kind of damage the buckshot might do. It could ricochet around the cabin and maim her, Rhiannon, or Thor. The blast would surely kill the creature, but this close it meant an added danger from flying alien carcass. She couldn't risk it.

Emily flipped the shotgun around and hit the creature between its two eyestalks with the butt of the shotgun.

The eyestalks shrunk back, and the thing's buzz-saw jaws flew wide apart. It was, Emily supposed, the closest the alien could come to expressing surprise. But it didn't back away, so she hit it again, this time aiming for the top eyestalk. It exploded into a mess of black goo.

That seemed to get the message across that it was not welcome, and the thing rapidly pulled back through the hole, skittering off the hood of the Sno-Cat.

With the alien gone, the cabin was now replaced with the rumble of the idling engine flowing in through the hole in the windshield. She was going to have to figure out some way to fix that.

"It's the warmth of the cabin," Emily said with sudden realization, more to herself than Rhiannon. "These things are surrounded by snow and ice. They must be extremely sensitive to changes in temperature. That makes the inside of this cabin the fucking Ritz-Carlton for them."

Whatever weird weather anomaly had caused the sudden warming of the air outside had increased the ambient temperature on this side of the mountain enough to thaw the creatures out. Now they were instinctively looking for a way off the mountain. That meant Jacob's observation was only half-right. The cold only stopped the effects of the red rain. It was going to take prolonged exposure to frigid weather to have the same effect on the creatures as she had seen with the aliens at the playground, back in Fairbanks.

The thought had no sooner entered her mind than Rhiannon screamed a warning, "Look!"

Emily followed the girl's eyes. "Oh! Shit!" she hissed from lips that suddenly felt dry and cracked. Clambering over the sides of the big rig in front of them was another wave of spider-aliens. They leaped from the side of the rig, making a beeline for the stationary Cat, attracted by the plume of escaping warm air of the cabin.

Emily floored the accelerator, sending a spray of melting snow up from the tracks as the Cat began picking up speed. There were at least sixty of the little bastards heading toward them, Emily estimated. There was no turning back now, though; she had to keep plowing forward. Aiming the front of the Cat toward a space between the next two vehicles, Emily pushed the speed up to thirty-five.

"Hold on," she yelled at Rhiannon over the roaring engine just before the Cat hit the leading edge of the onrushing aliens.

There were several resounding thuds as the machine met the monsters. The thuds were quickly followed by a series of satisfying pops and crunches as the tracks of the Cat crushed the carapaces of the first few unlucky creatures.

More tried to leap onto the Cat as it rolled over them, but they either bounced harmlessly off the sides or were caught by the four tracks and crushed to a purple pulp. One did manage to land on the gantry running alongside Emily, but it skidded and slipped along the metal surface, unable to find purchase, before sliding off the opposite end.

And then they were through the creatures. Emily gunned the engine, pushing the Cat up to forty in an attempt to leave the creatures behind. She gained some distance, but the things were persistent little buggers; she could see them streaming down the hill behind her even as the gap between them widened.

There was enough space between the next few vehicles that Emily didn't need to slow down, and the distance between them and their pursuers grew even greater. One hundred, then two hundred, then three hundred feet separated them. But as she slowed the Cat to maneuver around a blind hairpin corner, she was forced to slam on the brakes again.

A truck, towing a thirty-foot flatbed, had come to a halt right at the apex of the turn; its cab took up the entirety of the center portion of the snow-covered road, leaving less than ten feet of space separating it from the right edge. Beyond the edge, an almost sheer drop fell the final sixty feet or so to the plain below.

Emily stared back through the rear window toward the summit. The creatures were still doggedly following her, swarming down the mountainside.

There was no time to lose. She had to risk it.

Emily reversed the Cat back until she was as close to the edge as she dared.

"Rhiannon, I need you to be my eyes," Emily said, trying to keep the panic she felt from her voice. "Look out the window on your side and tell me how much space there is between us and the edge, all right?" Rhiannon stared blankly at Emily for a second, then nodded and scooted over a little until she was pressed tightly against the door.

"How much, honey? Quickly." Emily could see the wave of creatures closing in on them in the side-view mirror.

Rhiannon turned and held her two hands up in the air to illustrate the distance. "This much," she said. About ten inches. That gave Emily a little more room to edge over, just a couple of inches but no more. Rhiannon's face was almost as white as the snow, and Emily could see a vein twitching convulsively in her throat.

As she edged the Cat closer to the lip of the road, Rhiannon reduced the gap between her hands accordingly. "We're getting awfully close," she gulped, glancing down at the drop just inches away from her side of the Cat.

Emily reassessed her angle of approach to the space between the stalled truck and the lip of the road. This was the best she could do without risking one of the tracks slipping off the edge. She wiped away a bead of sweat that had trickled into her left eye, then allowed her foot to caress the accelerator.

Gently, gently does it.

The Cat moved slowly forward, inching its way toward the gap.

The cab of the wrecked big rig loomed large on Emily's left side as she eased the Cat gradually past it, the left rearview mirror scraping noisily against the front edge of the truck's engine cowling. Emily ignored the screeching of metal against metal, focusing entirely on keeping the vehicle as far to the left as was possible.

The front two tracks of the Cat were clear of the cab now, safely on solid ground but with less than two feet of space left between the front of the vehicle and the curving edge of the road. She brought the Cat to a dead stop and turned the wheel as far to the left as she could until she could see the tips of the left track poking out from beneath the gantry. She eased the vehicle forward, ignoring the gasp from Rhiannon as the kid surely saw how close the back of the Cat was to the edge. Pushing down on the accelerator, Emily glanced at the mirror on the right side of the cab; she could see the back right track was hanging over the precipice, spinning in midair above the drop-off.

And then the creatures hit the almost stationary Cat like a tsunami, and Emily felt the vehicle slide farther sideways on the slushy ground. She couldn't see a thing now as the creatures hammered into the vehicle, fighting each other to get to the already open hole in the windshield.

Emily cursed and pushed harder on the accelerator, but it was useless. She couldn't see a thing, and, as more of the creatures joined those already jostling for position, she felt their added weight finally prove too much and gravity take hold.

Emily instinctively threw an arm out across Rhiannon's chest as she felt the front of the Cat begin to slowly tip skyward.

They balanced for a second on the lip of the cliff, and Emily thought that maybe, just maybe, the tracks would find some traction, but that thought quickly disappeared as she felt the Cat begin to slide over the edge. And then it was all too late.

■ ■ ■

It was over in a matter of seconds. But it felt like minutes.

Inside the Cat the cabin was dark, every inch of the exterior covered in the crawling horrors. That was probably a godsend. It meant Rhiannon wouldn't see the fall. But that didn't stop the girl from screaming as the massive vehicle began to pick up speed, sliding backward down the cliff toward the valley floor below.

Emily felt the Cat begin to turn, the weight of the engine compartment dragging the front of the vehicle sideways, and for a moment she thought they were going to tip over and roll the remainder of the way. But the big vehicle remained upright as, now facing forward, they continued their slide.

One by one, the spider-aliens either leaped clear or were thrown from the Cat as it bounced and slid over the escarpment. Emily saw flailing forms of aliens bouncing past her, followed by an avalanche of snow and other debris.

The Cat hit something hard, maybe an outcrop of rock, and the right side lifted off the ground, dislodging more of the aliens into the air. The tracks came down again with a ringing of strained suspension springs that jarred the occupants and snapped Emily's teeth together painfully.

A rush of cold and snow entered through the windshield, filling the cabin with freezing air.

Emily had a clear view of the onrushing valley at the base of the escarpment as they hurtled toward it. Glancing over at Rhiannon, Emily could see the girl was pushed back into the support of her chair, her eyes pinched shut in terror.

"Hold on. It's almost over," she tried to say, but the words were lost in the rumble of the Cat's headlong fall.

Then came a bone-jarring shudder as the Cat thudded deep into a snowbank at the base of the cliff, sending a cascade of white powder high into the air. The Cat rocked three times as it settled back on its four creaking tracks.

All was silent.

■ ■ ■

"Are you okay?" Emily asked Rhiannon as she tried to unlatch the girl's safety harness.

Rhiannon opened her eyes and gave a weak smile, accompanied by two thumbs up.

Thor peeked his head back through the gap between Emily and Rhiannon, whining quietly. He was fine, apparently.

The Mossberg lay at Emily's feet. She picked it up and cradled it to her as she looked around the exterior of the cabin. The front of the Cat was buried almost up to the windshield in the snow-bank that had finally brought them to a stop. But to the left and right of her, she could see an occasional broken limb sticking up from beneath the snow or the shattered carapace of an alien.

The only sound was their breathing. That meant the engine was dead. If it wouldn't start, then they would be as good as dead themselves out there. The temperature could drop to minus thirty in a heartbeat. There was no way they could survive and no hope of rescue.

Emily said a silent prayer to whatever gods might be looking over them and turned the ignition key. The engine fired up instantly, and Emily raised her eyes skyward in an equally silent thank-you.

She moved the gear stick into reverse and began to edge the Cat out of the wall of snow.

They had landed at the base of the ravine. On the right was a wall of rock that might just as well have been Everest; on the left was the final curve of the road. Beyond that was the open plain of snow that would lead them to their next destination.

Emily accelerated the Cat slowly, listening for any noises that might indicate a problem with the engine or a broken track. The only sound was the roar of the engine and the whistle of wind through the hole in the windshield.

"We'll have to do something about that," she said to Rhiannon, nodding toward the hole. "Or we're going to freeze to death in here." There was no way even the powerful heater could keep up with the freezing air that was rushing in.

They had lost the left mirror on the driver's side during the fall, and one of the supply boxes had broken open and spilled its contents over the back row of seats.

They left the ravine behind them, zagged left a few hundred feet across a field of white that seemed to stretch out to eternity, and then bumped up onto the road.

Emily put another five miles behind them before she finally felt safe enough to stop the Cat and jury-rig a repair for the gaping hole. She emptied the remaining cans of food from the spilled cardboard box, then pulled it apart at the seams, taping the cardboard to the windshield with medical tape from the first aid kit.

"It ain't pretty, but it'll have to do," she said to Rhiannon, staring at the repair.

With nothing but clear road ahead of them now, the Cat picked up speed and roared down the road toward Coldfoot.

CHAPTER TWENTY-FIVE

The place looked like a cross between an Old West town from some black-and-white fifties cowboy movie and a POW camp.

"Welcome to Coldfoot," a sign had proclaimed. And you're welcome to it, Emily thought as she steered the Cat into the center of the encampment.

To the south were rows of single-wide billets that Emily assumed must be the "hotel" accommodation a sign a few miles outside of town had hinted at. All she really cared about was following the hand-painted hardwood signs to the gas station.

In front of the farthest wooden building, Emily saw the familiar shape of two gas pumps, conspicuous by their brushed metal bodies and bright-blue tops. Adjacent to the pumps was a chain-linked area, and secured behind the fence were several huge metal cylinders that Emily guessed was where the gasoline for the pumps and heating fuel for the buildings was stored.

It seemed logical to Emily that the farther north they traveled, the less effect the red rain might have had on the people crazy enough to want to live in this godforsaken land, especially after what they had witnessed back on the mountain. That could mean the chances of there being more human survivors rose accordingly, and Emily was well beyond trusting anyone she didn't know at this point.

Emily pulled the Cat to a standstill beside the first gas pump.

The day still had a few hours' worth of daylight left in it, if you could call the weak gray luminescence struggling to make it through the thick layer of nimbostratus cloud light. The utter solitude of this place would drive me crazy within a week, she thought as she left the Cat idling and leaped down to the snow-packed ground. That solitude, such a contrast to her beloved New York, bothered her more now than the aliens. She had already proven she could deal with the invaders. The loneness and solitude of this barren place? That was a whole other matter.

The Cat had a one-hundred-gallon-capacity gas tank, situated outside the cab, behind the rear seats. There was still just under a quarter of a tank left, and they were already a little over halfway to their destination. So a full tank should be more than enough to get them to Deadhorse, barring any more unforeseen excursions.

The two gas pumps were both unlocked, but without any electricity to power them, it made no difference. Emily pulled the lever on the diesel dispenser anyway; it clicked uselessly. When Emily had needed fuel for the Durango, she had simply siphoned it from abandoned vehicles along the route using the hand pump, negating the need to figure out how to access storage tanks at gas stations. But the Cat required a very specific type of treated diesel that could withstand the subfreezing temperatures. And Emily had no idea whether that was something she could just pull from another truck and no way to tell what was in the tank of the vehicle, anyway.

But now she was going to have to work out some way to get the gas from either the pumps or from the large storage containers behind the fenced-off area...assuming that was what they were. If she was wrong and the gas tanks were buried in the frozen ground like a regular gas station, then they were screwed, because she had no idea how she would be able to locate the access port for the ground tank beneath two feet of snow.

Emily crunched through the snow to the fence; there was a padlocked gate at front. She tugged the padlock, hoping it might have been left unlocked, but was rewarded with only a shower of snow falling from the chain-link fence.

She could just make out some kind of nozzle-like protrusion on the one tank closest to her, but she couldn't be sure how useful it would be to her unless she could get in there and inspect it. The key for the lock could be anywhere and was probably hidden away somewhere safe. She would have to find something to cut this lock.

Of the three buildings she could see, the large battleship-gray prefabricated Quonset hut looked the most likely to have what she was looking for.

"Coming?" Emily called to Rhiannon as she walked back to the Cat, but the girl shook her head slowly from behind the cabin's glass. Sure, her look said, I'll leave this nice warm vehicle to come trek through the snow with you...not!

"Smart girl," Emily said and continued crunching through the snow to the building.

■ ■ ■

It was some kind of workshop, she thought, or maybe a mechanics shop? There were a couple of pieces of huge yellow earthmoving machinery, a backhoe, and some kind of excavator stored inside. They loomed out of the darkness like flash-frozen monsters. On one side of the building were three walled-off bays, each lined with workbenches and an assortment of tools and bits and pieces of mechanical doohickeys. Peg-Boards on the wall of each bay held wrenches and screwdrivers and other hand tools.

Even deserted and frozen, the place still smelled of grease and sweat, almost normal. But after the encounter on the mountain, she was not going to rush in unprepared. That little excursion had proven that the red rain was far more resilient than any of them had given it credit for. She kept the shotgun tucked under her arm, just in case of any more close encounters of the holy-fuck kind.

Emily shone her flashlight over the benches, searching for anything that looked like it would be a match for the large padlock on the gate.

"Bingo," she said as she stepped into the third bay, her light falling on a large red bolt cutter resting against the far wall near a stack of oil drums. The frozen steel tool was like picking up an icicle; she could feel the cold seeping through the thick padding of her gloves. She had to move it from one hand to the other periodically so her hand didn't freeze up.

She was heading back to the exit when she spotted a pile of wooden sheets, offcuts from some project, slotted in between two workbenches. Emily looked through them until she found a thin piece she approximated would fit over the hole the alien had left in the Cat's windshield. She would have preferred something transparent, but beggars could not be choosers these days. A few more minutes of rummaging around the work area turned up a roll of gray industrial-strength tape.

Emily followed her own footprints back to the fuel storage area, raising the bolt cutter in mock salute as she passed the idling Cat.

Rhiannon looked unimpressed.

Placing the open jaws of the cutter over the shackle of the lock, Emily squeezed as hard as she could on the long handles of the cutter. The lock slipped from between the jaws before she could apply enough pressure; the chain snapped it back against the gate.

It was going to take a little more finesse than brawn, she thought. She repositioned the cutter's jaws against the lock, this time leaning in slightly, pushing the lock back against the chain link of the gate, using it for leverage. She applied pressure gradually, feeling her muscles tense across her shoulders until the hardened jaws finally severed the shackle with a sharp metallic snap. She dropped the cutters into the snow beside her and wiggled the lock until it came free of the chain, which she pulled through the gate and dumped next to the cutters.

The base of the gate was covered in snow, and it took her several minutes of pushing and pulling until she was able to force it wide enough that she could slip through into the storage area.

Emily moved quickly to the first tank. Stenciled on the side in large black characters were a bunch of symbols and numbers. Next to them was the word UNLEADED.

Okay, that wasn't what she wanted. She moved to the next tank; this one was upright instead of horizontal like the first one. A similar set of black characters had been painted on this one, although the numbers were different. Beneath them was the magic word: DIESEL.

A pipe, about twice as thick as her arm, led from the opposite side of the tank, then made an abrupt right-angle turn and dropped down, disappearing into the snow and, presumably, into the ground, where it would run to the pumps beyond the fence line. Beneath that pipe was a second, smaller pipe that looked more like a water spigot but twice as large. A big metal lever was fixed to the side of the outlet. EMERGENCY SIPHON PORT was stenciled in the same black letters where the smaller pipe met the tank.

She grasped the lever with both hands and pulled. A spurt of noxious-smelling diesel fuel cascaded from the mouth of the port, staining the snow brown. Jesus, it smelled bad. Emily forced the lever back into place, cutting off the flow. Well at least she knew it worked.

The space between the two storage tanks was far too narrow for Emily to have any hope of safely negotiating in the Cat, so she was going to have to transfer the fuel by hand, she supposed.

How, though? She had left the five-gallon gas can back in Fairbanks when they'd abandoned the Durango. She still had the siphon, but that would be useless for this job.

She'd seen a couple of large metal gas cans on the shelf of one of the bays in the Quonset hut where she had found the bolt cutter, and she headed back to the building, quickly located what she was looking for, and carried it back to the Cat. It was smaller than the large plastic can she had used to siphon fuel for the SUV, probably three gallons, she guessed, but that was good, because it meant she could enlist Rhia to help her.

Rhiannon had fallen asleep in the warm cabin of the Cat, and Emily had to nudge her to wake her.

"I need your help," Emily said as she slipped into the driver's seat, revved the engine, and maneuvered the Cat as close to the chain-link gate as she safely could.

"Put on your gloves—it's cold out there."

■ ■ ■

Emily had Rhiannon positioned on the back of the Cat, its engine turned off now, as she passed the gas can to the girl to pour into the open mouth of the vehicle's fuel tank.

The stink from the diesel was terrible, and Emily had taken her scarf and wrapped it around her nose and mouth to make sure she didn't pass out from the fumes as she filled the three-gallon container. That didn't stop the fumes from reaching her eyes, though, and she found herself having to fight rubbing them each time she pulled the handle on the tank's port.

After twenty or so trips back and forth between the Cat and the tank, Emily could feel her back and shoulder muscles begin to complain. They'd managed to transfer about sixty gallons, by her estimation, and when she counted the quarter tank left in the tank, that meant there was only another five trips left before they should be done.

"My feet are cold," moaned Rhiannon, shuffling from side to side to illustrate her displeasure.

"Mine, too," Emily shouted as she trudged back to the fuel tank. "Not much longer now."

The clouds had thinned as they worked, allowing the midday sun to finally put in an appearance. It was a strange experience to be crunching through snow almost up to your knees with the sun so bright overhead and yet be so damn cold.

Emily filled the can one final time and heaved it back to the waiting Cat. She placed it on the gantry and then climbed up herself. When she had poured the last few drops into the Cat, she replaced the metal cap on the tank and screwed it down tight, tossing the empty can out into the snow.

She stood for a moment in the sun, catching her breath and stretching out the kinks in her back. Thank God she didn't have to do that every day; she would be a wreck.

She had left the sheet of wood and tape she'd found earlier resting on the Cat's rear track. Now she picked them up and climbed into the cabin. She stripped away the makeshift repair from the windshield, tossing it out into the snow. While Rhiannon held the board, Emily quickly taped it into place, doubling up the amount of tape just to be sure.

Back in the driver's seat, the board partially obscured the right side of her view, but she could make do.

"Let's make camp," Emily said to Rhiannon as she steered the Cat toward what looked like the reception area for the hotel. A sign above the door read SLATE CREEK INN in large red letters.

She was reticent to leave the warmth of the cab behind them again so soon, but their cramped legs and stiff backs welcomed the promise of an opportunity to rest. "Stay in the Cat with Thor, okay? Until I know it's safe."

Rhiannon clearly wanted out of the claustrophobic cab, but she nodded her acknowledgment.

There were no signs of any other survivors in the camp—no telltale smoke from a fire, no fresh tracks in the snow. Of course that didn't mean that there couldn't be someone inside any of these buildings. The rumble of the Cat's engine would have traveled for miles, arriving long before they had and alerting anyone or anything that they were going to have visitors.

Emily climbed the wooden steps up to the entrance and pushed open the door with her shoulder. Leaning inside, she quickly looked over the room. There was a rickety-looking reception desk and a well-worn but comfortable-looking sofa in one corner. A selection of candy bars on a rack in front of the register sat next to a line of mummified sandwiches. Against the farthest wall was a glass-fronted refrigerator with a selection of still-frozen ice cream on one of the shelves. Several liter-size bottles of soda were lined up like soldiers along a metal rack next to the refrigerator.

Emily made her way down the corridor connecting the reception area to the rooms and checked each room one by one.

She settled on the last room at the farthest end of the building. The beds were still made, each with a thick gray blanket. The room was also the farthest from the entrance, so there was only one direction any possible threat could come from, which meant she would be able to sleep a little more comfortably.

Back at the Cat, Emily collected Rhiannon and Thor, along with their supplies, then led them back through the building to their accommodations.

Rhiannon made a face when she saw the wood-lined walls of the tiny room, but she flopped down on the left bed with a huge sigh as though she had been on her feet all day instead of cruising in the comfort of a heated cab, snoozing her way through the majority of the journey.

The room was far too small for them to use the gas cooker safely, so Emily designated the next room down as their kitchen for the evening and set up the gas stove on the floor between the beds in that room. Despite the relative comfort the Cat had afforded them, they were both looking forward to something hot, Emily thought as she heated the stew. They were both tired of the granola bars and bags of chips they had snacked on for most of the journey since leaving Fairbanks. Emily still had a couple of cans of Dinty Moore beef stew that she had been saving, and her mouth began to water at the thought of it, even though the stuff gave her awful gas. Well, she could always blame Thor.

Back in their room, Emily found Rhiannon sitting on the side of her bed. The girl's head was in her hands and tears rolled down her cheeks, forming a tiny partially frozen pool of spilled emotion between her feet. Thor was sitting next to the girl on the bed, his head in her lap, his eyes fixed on the child.

"Hey?" said Emily, gently setting the bowls of steaming stew on the floor. "What's wrong, kiddo?" It took Rhiannon a few moments to gather herself before she answered.

"What day is it?" she said.

Emily had to pause for a moment and think. Jeez? She hadn't given it much thought, but she was pretty sure it was..."Thursday," she said. "Yeah. It's a Thursday. Why?"

"But what date...What date is it?"

Emily did some quick math in her head. "It's the twenty-fourth," she replied. This apparently was the wrong answer because the girl burst into tears again.

"Hey, hey, hey." Emily slid in next to the girl, their parkas crackling against each other as she placed her arm around Rhiannon's shoulder, pulling her close. "What is it, sweetheart? What's wrong?"

Through a barrage of sniffles and tears Rhiannon turned and looked at Emily. "It's my birthday," she said. "Today's my birthday."

Emily was taken aback, but after a moment, she leaned in and gave Rhiannon a kiss on the crown of her head. "Happy birthday," she said, pulling back and smiling as genuinely as she could. "How old are you?"

"Thirteen."

"Wow! You're a teenager, kiddo. Congratulations. We have to do something special. Hold on here for a moment." Emily grabbed the flashlight and headed out of the room, toward the reception area. Pushing through the doors, she shone her light around the darkening room until she found what she was looking for. She pulled open the door to the refrigerator and grabbed a selection of the ice-cream cartons and a liter of Coke to go with it. The Coke was almost ice, but she figured she could squeeze out a glass or so each; it might be a little slushy, but still…

"Here you go, birthday girl," she said as she reentered the room. "Sorry I don't have any candles." She handed the girl a fork from the backpack. "Or clean spoons," she added with a smile. "You know, the best way to eat ice cream is with a fork anyway. Makes it easier." To illustrate the point, Emily popped the top off the tub of Strawberry Surprise and scooped a forkful into her mouth.

"Mmmmm! Mmmmm! Mmmmm! Here, try some." Rhiannon halfheartedly dug into the tub and pulled out a large chunk of strawberry-laden ice cream and took a bite while Thor watched expectantly.

"Can't leave you out, can we?" said Emily as she tossed Thor a piece of the frozen confectionery. He swallowed it whole and beat his tail against the blanket in appreciation. "Nope. No more for you until you wish Rhiannon a happy birthday," she insisted. This brought a smile to Rhia's face, and Emily seized the moment, popping open the tub of double chocolate fudge. Rhiannon's eyes lit up as she chewed the ice cream, savoring the flavor.

"Owww," she said. "Brain freeze."

For some reason the irony of eating ice cream in a freezing shack just a few miles from the edge of the Arctic Circle and getting brain freeze suddenly became the funniest thing both Rhiannon and Emily had ever heard. It started with a fit of giggles from Rhiannon, as she clasped her hand to her forehead, and quickly spread to Emily, then back to Rhiannon until they were both roaring with laughter. Thor skipped between the two, barking his confusion but happy to join in anyway.

In the midst of the laughter, Emily had an idea. She glanced out the window. There was still enough light left for what she was planning.

"Okay, birthday girl. Why don't you grab those two plastic boxes from inside the backpack for me?"

Rhiannon looked perplexed. "These?" she asked as she pulled the two plastic cases containing the pistols Emily had scavenged from the store back in Fairbanks. Opening the cases, Emily pulled out the Glock and then the smaller Ruger Bearcat revolver.

"Guns?" said Rhiannon, a little awed.

Emily smiled back at her. "One for each of us," she said and winked. She checked both pistols, trying to remember the lessons Nathan had given to her on handling guns so very long ago, then loaded them carefully, adding a handful of extra ammo for each weapon into both her jacket's front pockets. Rhiannon watched her intently as she worked on the pistols.

"All right," Emily said finally, satisfied the pistols were safe. "Eat your stew and then let's go shoot something."

■ ■ ■

They stood just outside the reception building, facing a drift of snow. Emily had placed the empty cans of stew on the top of the drift, then added four bottles of frozen soda.

"The most important thing is to always treat a gun like it's loaded," said Emily as she unpacked the two pistols from their cases. "And never point it at anyone, or anything…unless you intend to shoot it."

Emily popped out the cylinder of the Ruger and checked it was empty, then handed it to Rhiannon. "How's it feel?"

Rhiannon balanced the little pistol in her hand, gauging its weight. "It's lighter than I thought," she said.

"Yeah, well, it's just a beginner's pistol, so it's a good one to start you off with. You want to shoot something?"

Rhia nodded enthusiastically. Emily beckoned for the gun back and proceeded to load it from the box of .22 rounds. "See, you pop open the chamber like this." Emily pressed the release on the side of the pistol and the chamber slipped out. "Then you insert one round into each of the holes," she continued as she loaded the pistol. "And always make sure your finger is off the trigger, okay? Here you go." She handed the loaded weapon back to the girl.

Emily moved behind Rhia and took both her wrists in her hands. "So now you need to stand with your feet a little bit apart." Emily demonstrated the correct shooting stance. "That's it, maybe just a little wider. Perfect. Now, bring the arm with your pistol in it up and point it in the direction of the target. Bring your other hand up and cup it around the gun hand like this…That's right. How's that feel?"

"Okay," said Rhiannon, suppressing a nervous giggle.

"All right, now look through the notch on the rear sight until you see the pokey-up bit at the end of the barrel. Got it? Now make sure they are level with each other. Focus on that front sight again—make sure you keep both sights level—and put it over what you want to shoot."

Emily let go of the girl and allowed her to position the gun herself.

"I'm really nervous."

"That's okay, sweetie. So was I the first time I fired a gun, but there's no need to be. Just relax and concentrate. Now use your thumb to pull back the hammer."

Emily watched as Rhia slipped her thumb over the notched hammer and pulled it back until it clicked into place.

"Perfect. You ready? Okay, put your finger on the trigger, but don't pull it yet. Now breathe just a little bit, and, when you're ready, pull the trigger real slow."

Rhiannon let out a nervous squeak at the crack of the gun firing, completely missing any of the targets they had set up. The squeak quickly flowed into a fit of excited giggles as she brought the gun back up on the next target, cocked it, and squeezed off another round. That one went wide, too. But her third shot clipped a can and sent it spinning into the air.

"Yes!" she yelled, waving both hands in the air.

"Careful, that thing's still loaded. You don't want to accidentally shoot yourself...or me."

"Sorry."

"S'okay. Just remember guns are dangerous. Let's try again."

Emily had been waiting for an appropriate time to teach the kid how to shoot since she had picked up the pistols in Fairbanks. The sooner she learned, the safer she would be. The future was an unknown quantity for all of them now, and Emily would need to pass on as many of her survival skills as possible to the girl.

Emily waited until Rhiannon had fired off all six rounds, then showed her how to pop open the cylinder, dump the spent cartridges, and reload with new ammo. As she watched Rhia carefully aim and fire off each round, she checked her Glock, fed rounds into the magazine, and slammed it home.

"Not bad," she said, "Not bad at all." Actually the kid was pretty damn good, hitting four of the six targets. For a kid who had never fired a gun before, that was quite impressive.

When Rhia had discharged her final round, Emily asked her to empty the gun and set it aside. "Go set up those targets for me, would you?"

Rhia crunched through the snow and set the fallen cans and plastic bottles upright again, then crunched her way back to Emily.

It had been a while since she had fired a handgun, and it had never been her favorite thing to do. She preferred the stopping power of her Mossberg, but the pistol would be a more convenient weapon to carry with her than the shotgun, and it was quite easily concealed, too.

Making sure Rhiannon was behind her, she sighted on the first target and fired, popping the can into the air. She took aim at the next and sent that one cartwheeling away, too. She finished off the rest of the targets with similar efficiency; the boom of the nine-millimeter rounds echoed around the camp.

"Now I know who to call if we're ever attacked by a roving band of canned fruit," laughed Rhiannon.

"You're pretty sassy for a kid who only managed to hit half her targets," mocked Emily, sticking her tongue out at the girl. "Why don't you see if you can do better this time?"

They spent another half hour plinking away at their makeshift targets, which by then were little more than shredded metal and plastic. By the time they packed their weapons away, Rhiannon was able to hit everything she aimed at. She was turning into a regular Katniss...minus the bow.

They made their way back to the bedroom by the light of their flashlights. Emily pulled the blanket back from Rhiannon's bed for her. "Climb in, birthday girl," she said, her own eyes beginning to ache with exhaustion. Rhiannon slipped between the sheets and turned to face Emily; the fur around her parka's hood surrounded her face like a halo.

"Will you sleep next to me?" she asked, the hint of embarrassment in her voice all but hidden by the return of her sadness.

Emily hesitated, then climbed in next to her, pulled the blanket over both of them, and slipped her arm around the girl's chest, pulling her close.

"Emily?" Rhia asked, her voice little more than a whisper.

"Yes, sweetheart?"

"I miss my daddy and Ben."

Emily had to gain control of her own emotions before she answered. "I know, baby. I know."

CHAPTER TWENTY-SIX

Deadhorse was a sprawling town of storage outbuildings, temporary housing, offices, heavy equipment, and other vehicles. There seemed to be acres and acres of it. Calling it a "town" was a bit of a misnomer, though; it looked more like some kind of rapidly assembled military base, with little thought or reason to how it had been laid out. Over the rooftops of a nearby garage, Emily could see several gigantic cranes, their booms reaching across the sky like frozen skeletal fingers.

"We need to let Jacob know we've arrived," Emily said, smiling at Rhiannon.

"Can I call him?" she pleaded.

"Of course. Grab the phone for me." There had been little opportunity to charge the sat-phone over the past few days; once they had hit Fairbanks, they had pretty much said good-bye to the sun, so they had been relying on the battery backup system. That was empty now, and there was very little charge left in the actual sat-phone's battery. There was enough, maybe, for twenty minutes or so of talk time, if she was lucky. Rhiannon pulled the phone from the side pocket of the backpack, unfolded the antenna, and pressed the On button. She waited for it to wake, then hit Redial and the Speakerphone buttons in succession.

The phone rang a few times longer than normal before Jacob picked up. "Emily."

"No, it's Rhia. Emily's driving. She said I could call you. I learned to shoot."

There was a pause on the other end as Jacob considered how and what to reply to first. "Well," he said finally. "That's great, I guess." There was a certain stiffness to his voice that Emily hadn't heard in all the times they had talked, and she wondered if he was feeling okay.

"We're here," Rhiannon continued, as if Jacob had said nothing at all. "We just arrived in Deadhorse."

"That's fantastic. Emily, do you know where you are exactly? Do you see any street signs?" The stiff tone had all but disappeared from Jacob's voice. Emily and Rhiannon's heads swiveled back and forth, searching for some kind of an indication of where they were. She didn't recall having seen any road signs since they had passed the weathered sign announcing they had arrived at Deadhorse. The place was a rabbit warren, and with the road surfaces buried beneath several feet of snow, there were no visual cues to guide them, either.

"There's nothing," Emily answered. "We're outside a building called Red Dragon Construction, if that's of any help."

It wasn't; Jacob had never heard of them. "There are hundreds of businesses in and around Deadhorse," he said. "New ones arrived every week, and it's been a while since I've been over there. You just need to head north until you hit Prudhoe Bay on the coast. You can't miss it—it's all that separates you from the

Arctic. When you reach it, you have to look for the dock. You'll know it when you see it. There'll be a boat there you can use to get to me."

"A boat?" Emily said. No one had said anything about her having to drive—if that's what you did with a boat—a freaking boat anywhere. "I thought one of you would come and pick us up?"

"We would, but we lost our boat in a storm a couple of nights ago. So it's a good job you arrived when you did, otherwise we'd have to swim over."

Nice of him to let her know, Emily thought. But she said, "Well, okay, I guess. If I can learn to drive a car and one of whatever the hell you call this thing we're sitting in, I guess I can drive a boat."

"Pilot," Jacob corrected.

"What?"

"You pilot a boat."

"Really? All right. I guess I can pilot a boat then."

The phone made a beeping sound in her ear that it had never made before. She glanced quickly at the front readout: "Low Battery" flashed repeatedly on the LCD screen.

"Jacob, the phone's about to die. Tell me how we get to you."

■ ■ ■

The storm blew in fifteen minutes later. It started as a swirling white mist wafting low against the ground, sending mini tornadoes of already fallen powder swirling into the air. It quickly gathered momentum, and soon huge flakes of snow fell like petals from the pregnant clouds, dropping a silent white curtain over the land. Emily had the Cat's windshield wipers on full blast, but even they couldn't help keep back the veil of white that had descended. Within a minute visibility had dropped to thirty feet, then twenty, and then Emily could barely see much farther than the end of the engine cowling. The Cat's headlamps did little to help; their powerful beams were dissipated by every falling particle of snow.

A huge gust of wind buffeted the Cat, rattling the cabin.

"Shit," Emily spat, leaning forward in the driver's seat in the hope of gaining a few extra inches of visibility, her nose almost touching the glass of the windshield. There was no way she was going to be able to navigate through this. She could be going around in circles for all she knew, or worse, she could drive off onto one of the frozen lakes that dotted the spaces between buildings. A second gust of wind hit the Cat, this time from behind. The vehicle bucked, and Emily thought she felt the Cat lift slightly off its tracks before dropping down again. It felt like the entire ground beneath them was shifting, like they were in the middle of an earthquake.

Before the world had disappeared, she had passed a two-level office building on the left. It was only a few hundred feet behind them, but as she tried to locate it again, there was no sign of it. The ravenous snowstorm had already devoured all trace of it. She could either choose to sit the storm out or try and find the building, which she thought would at least offer some better shelter than the cab of the Cat. Who knew how long the storm could last? It might be hours or it could be days, and they only had so much gas left.

Rhiannon was doing her best to keep her composure, but Emily could see the girl was spooked. They were completely disorientated by the storm that fizzed and swirled by their windows like static on a TV screen.

"I saw a building a little while back," Emily told her. "I'm going to try and find it again." Rhiannon nodded and slipped into her parka while Emily turned the Cat around until she was pointing in what she thought was the approximate direction of the office building she had spotted.

She eased the Cat forward at a slow crawl, barely four miles an hour. She searched the depthless white ahead, a dull ache already beginning to form at the back of her neck and behind her eyes as she strained for a sign, anything, that would indicate where the building was.

Wind thudded against the side of the Cat. Rhiannon yelped, and Thor gave an agitated bark from the backseat.

The building could be five feet away and she would drive right past it. As if to illustrate the hopelessness of their predicament, an extra strong flurry of snow splattered against the windshield. Momentarily overwhelmed, the windshield wipers strained against the sudden added weight until finally flinging the snow off the side of the Cat and continuing their relentless swish-swish back and forth.

The big machine continued to edge forward as minute after minute passed, and still there was no sign of the building she had seen. Emily was convinced she had passed it. She was going to have to turn around.

"There it is." Rhiannon's excited cry was accompanied by the sound of her knuckles hitting the glass of the window. "There. On the right."

Emily strained to see past the girl, who was still excitedly pointing into the white beyond the cab. There was…something…just…"Yes!" Emily shouted excitedly. She could make out a darker shadow in the swirling snow in front of them and off to the right. It had to be it.

She swung the Cat in that direction and edged forward until she was certain it was the building and not some weird trick of the storm.

Yes! There it was. A two-story box of a building with only the occasional narrow window sitting flush against the weatherworn outer walls to disrupt the absolute utilitarian functionality of the design.

"Hold on," said Emily, finally aware that she had been biting so hard on her bottom lip she could taste blood. "I have to swing this thing around." She needed to maneuver the Cat as close to the entrance on her side as possible, so she could hop out and make sure the doors of the building were unlocked. The Cat's thermometer registered the outside temperature as minus fifteen degrees. If you factored in the windchill, it was probably another ten or fifteen beyond that. She would have only minutes to get them inside before the effects of that kind of low temperature began to affect them.

She pulled the Cat away from the building, then turned the wheel hard, disengaging the right-side tracks while the left continued to move, turning the vehicle while not moving it forward. When she thought she had the right angle of approach, she began to edge forward while slowly turning the wheel to the left a few degrees at a time. The taupe front of the office resolved into view, its narrow windows rattling as another blast of wind rushed past the Cat, hammering at the walls. Emily twisted the wheel a little farther and slid the Cat forward the few remaining feet until she was parallel with the building.

She found the entrance to the building farther along. It was a recessed area covered by a portico; icicles hung like fangs from the edges of the overhang.

Emily put on her jacket, pulled the hood fully over her head, and zipped it up.

"Are you ready?" she asked Rhiannon. The girl nodded affirmatively, a flashlight already cradled in her lap.

She waited for the next blast of wind to pass, then pushed open the door of the cab, leaped out, and slammed the door shut behind her, almost losing her balance as the wind flared up again and pushed her toward the edge of the metal gantry. She steadied herself, then beckoned to Rhiannon to follow her. The kid was out and beside her in a second, Thor close behind. Even he gave a shiver as the wind cut through the group huddling against the side of the big machine.

"Let's go," Emily yelled, her voice muffled by the material of the hood and the roaring of the wind ripping past the building.

They climbed carefully down to the ground and headed into the enclosed entrance area. Emily rattled the big door. It was locked.

"Shit. Stay here. I have to head back to the Cat," she told Rhiannon.

Back at the vehicle, Emily opened the rear passenger door, pulled out the shotgun, and climbed back down again. The wind had gone from the occasional gust to an almost constant force against her now, bashing and pushing her as she staggered through the ever-deepening snow back to where she had left the girl and the dog.

"What are you going to do?" Rhiannon yelled over the wind when she saw the shotgun in Emily's gloved hands.

"Unlock the door," she yelled back. "Now, take Thor and get around the corner for me, okay?"

When she was sure both of her companions were out of harm's way from any ricochets from the shotgun, Emily examined the door, inspecting where she thought the lock mechanism should be. Even with the cover of the portico, it was still almost impossible to see straight; the snow whirled and gushed around the recess of the entrance. When she was certain she knew where the keyhole was, she brought the shotgun to her shoulder and aimed, but her gloved finger could not fit through the trigger guard of the weapon.

Have to take it off, she thought. She leaned the shotgun against the door, unzipped the glove, and pulled off the Velcro flap that secured it around her wrist. Instantly she felt the freezing sting of the wind begin to whip her body heat away. It was like plunging her hand into an icy bowl of water; she could feel the blood in her arm begin to chill all the way up to her elbow already. She picked up the shotgun again and brought it up to the lock, the end of the muzzle just a couple of inches from the door, then slipped her finger onto the trigger. She gave a yell of pain and almost dropped the gun. The metal of the trigger against her finger felt like flame against her exposed skin. Gritting her teeth against the pain, she turned her head away from the door and pulled the trigger.

When she looked back, there was a gaping hole where the lock had been. She quickly fitted the glove back over her throbbing hand, grabbed the door handle, and pulled. It swung toward her.

"Rhiannon!" Emily yelled. "Let's move."

Rhiannon's head appeared around the corner of the portico, closely followed by Thor's. Emily held the door open and beckoned them both into the darkness of the building, then followed them inside.

■ ■ ■

Water fell from the ceiling ahead of them, caught in the beam of the flashlight as it drip-drip-dripped from the acoustic tiles, forming a semifrozen pool of slush on the heavy-duty carpet of the reception area. There were pictures lining the walls of oil rigs, dirty but happy-looking workers, construction crews hard at work, and big pieces of mechanical equipment that Emily had no idea what they did.

Dear God, it was freezing. Even with the thick coats, trousers, and gloves, she could still feel the insidious siphoning away of heat from her body. Is this what they were going to be condemned to? For the rest of her life would she be bundled up like this, always wondering when she would feel warm again? Wondering if she would ever see the sun, feel it against her skin? It was the kind of cold that, once it burrowed into the marrow of your bones, you would need to spend a month on a beach in the Caribbean sun to ever erase the memory of it. Emily pulled off her glove again and moved her trigger finger into the light of her flashlight. A red crescent moon–shaped welt had already formed on the soft pad between the knuckle and the fingertip. It stung like a son of a—

"Emily?" Rhiannon's questioning voice pulled her back into the moment. "Are you okay?"

No. No, she was most certainly not okay. She was probably the furthest away from okay she had ever been. That's what she wanted to say, but instead she said, "Yes, sweetheart. I'm fine. Let's find a room to wait this out, shall we?"

"I wish we'd brought the supply bag with us. I'm starved," the kid continued, as if this was just another day. And, Emily supposed, it was just another day for her now. She would probably forget the majority of her early life, the little luxuries that had made her life so very easy and enjoyable before all this shit fell to earth. Little Rhiannon would adapt, overcome, and move on. Assuming, of course, that she lived through whatever hardships and challenges were still headed their way. I, on the other hand, Emily mused, am too goddamn old for all this.

Emily fished around in one of her parka's many pockets and pulled out a Mars bar she had stashed there at some point. "Here you go," she said, handing it to Rhia.

While the girl snacked on the candy, Emily checked out the rooms they were passing, pushing open doors and peeking inside cabinets. There was little point in looking around, she supposed, but what else were they supposed to do until the storm passed? They had been sitting for most of the past couple of days; a half hour of exercise wandering around this place would not do them any harm. If they had to, they would spend the night there, but there was still plenty of time for them to get to the dock Jacob had mentioned. He had said that the Stockton Islands were about a ten-mile ride northeast of Deadhorse by boat.

"Don't worry," he had told her when she'd said she had never even been on a boat let alone navigated one before. "Just hug the coast as closely as you can, and you won't miss me. You'll do just fine."

Emily absentmindedly pushed open another door with the toe of her boot and was about to step inside but stopped halfway across the threshold, instinctively turning her body to block Rhiannon from seeing any farther into the room, squelching the scream of horror that rose to her throat.

Six...no, seven bodies lay sprawled on the floor in one corner of the room. There were two women and the rest were men. They had died panicked, climbing over each other in a vain attempt to escape the threat that had stood in the room with them.

"Stay outside," Emily almost yelled at Rhiannon, who had bumped into her back and now stood in the corridor perplexed.

"What—"

"Just do as I say, please."

The girl gave a huff and leaned her back against the opposite wall, bouncing the heel of her left boot off the carpet in agitation.

Emily turned back to the bodies. A layer of frost covered the skin of all of the victims, like freezer-burned meat that had been left too long in a refrigerator. They looked totally unaffected by the red rain. No sign of infection at all. But as Emily inched closer, she could see each person had been shot at least once, some several times.

Had they survived the red rain only to be murdered? Or had this all happened in the panic before the effects took hold? It was impossible to tell. But what was certain was that someone had murdered these people in cold blood and she had no way to know if that person was still waiting in the building for them.

Emily backed out of the room, making sure she closed the door behind her. Rhiannon was still sulking against the far wall, but she stopped kicking her heel when she saw the look on Emily's face.

"Is something wrong?" she asked.

"Yes," said Emily. "Something is very wrong."

■ ■ ■

Outside the storm blew with as much ferocity as it had when they'd first entered. The offices no longer seemed silent. Instead, every move, every exhalation, every crackle of material against skin seemed amplified beyond normal, revealing their position to whoever had murdered those people in the room. Every creak above their heads or squeak of some unseen tile or loose window suddenly became the killer, creeping toward them. In a moment, the building had turned from a sanctuary into a potential trap... or a tomb.

Emily pulled Rhiannon close to her. "Don't make a sound," she whispered into her ear. "We have to get out of here now."

They could hole up in the office and hope that the killer of those poor people was gone or dead somewhere out there, but Emily knew there was no way she could be sure of their safety. Especially knowing that at any moment someone could burst in and try to kill them, or worse. And what if there was more than one assailant? What if there were two or three of them? She was confident she could defend Rhia and herself against one person, but more than that? She didn't know if she could do it, especially as they were obviously armed. And what if they found the Cat outside? They could take that and leave her and Rhiannon stranded with no means of escape, condemned to a slow death by freezing or starvation.

She looked down at Thor. He seemed perfectly at ease, but he hadn't strayed very far from them since they had entered the building. And now that she thought about it, he hadn't disappeared for his usual exploration of the offices. Maybe he could sense death in these rooms or maybe he sensed something or someone else.

Her mind was so damn tired. Having to continually think two steps ahead was taking its toll on her mentally. Her head felt as fogged as the snow-swept land beyond their shelter's walls.

They had to get out of there now. And that meant taking their chances in the storm.

Whoever had killed those people could still be in the building, and that was just an unacceptable risk. There was only one place that she knew was safe, and that was with Jacob and his crew. If they left now and pushed hard—and didn't get lost in the blizzard outside or crash or drown in some lake—they could reach the coast by late afternoon and find a boat. If they had to sleep in the Cat with the engine running to wait out the storm, so be it. They could afford to lose the fuel at that point.

Her mind made up, Emily turned her attention to Rhiannon.

"Something very bad happened in that room back there," she said in the same whispered tone. "The person who did it might still be here with us, so I think it's better that we get out of here." Rhiannon's eyes became wide, but she nodded that she understood. "We're going to head back to the Cat and drive out of here. It's only a few miles to the coast, and then, once we find the boat, we'll be safe."

Emily unslung the shotgun from her shoulder and smiled at Rhiannon. "Let's go," she mouthed and began heading back toward the reception area. "Keep the light ahead of us," she told the girl as they crept back through the darkened hallway toward the entrance.

They had just entered the reception area and Emily had begun to relax when the outside door suddenly flew open. Emily instantly brought the shotgun to her shoulder, her finger caressing the trigger, but then the door slammed shut again with a thud that echoed off the walls.

"Just the wind," she told Rhiannon. "It was just the wind." This whole place—scratch that, she thought, and make it the entire world—had turned into a haunted house. Every unexpected noise hid something sinister, every shadow a potential killer.

Emily held the exit door shut against the grip of the wind while she checked outside through the small window at the top of the door. The wind had definitely picked up, but the snow looked to have eased a little. She could make out the shapes of covered vehicles in the parking lot about fifty feet or so away and she could see the hulking outline of the snow-covered Cat parked just off to the left. It was an improvement over their arrival, just over an hour or so earlier.

Emily fished the keys to the Cat from her pocket and pushed open the door, ushering Rhiannon and Thor out first. She followed behind them as they made their way to the parked Cat.

Snow had covered the vehicle's tracks. Emily cleared it quickly, then boosted Rhiannon up, followed by Thor, and finally pulled herself up.

It wasn't until they were all in the cab of the Cat with the engine running and the doors all locked that Emily felt they were safe.

■ ■ ■

Emily eased the Sno-Cat away from the building and out into the storm again.

Jacob had told her to just head north until they hit the coast. Visibility was still not much better than fifty feet, so she would have to rely on the digital compass display on the Cat's computer screen to guide them in the right direction.

She kept her speed down to ten miles an hour while trying to take what looked like the most logical route between each set of buildings and on to the next, so she wouldn't veer off course. The ache behind her eyes had turned into a throbbing headache that felt like knives being plunged into her brain. Even through the fog of pain, she quickly realized she could spot where the actual roads were, even though they were buried under several feet of snow, and she began looking for areas where the top layer of snow was just a little higher than the surrounding areas.

She managed to keep the Cat rolling along on a heading of more or less due north, only occasionally having to adjust her course to avoid a building or vehicle that blocked her path. Once she hit something solid and immovable hidden beneath the snow, but the Cat's tracks and suspension were up and over it before she even had time to react.

The wind still pummeled them, lashing great sheets of snow across the vehicle, but then it would pass them by and their limited but acceptable view of the world would return and they would continue on, edging ever closer to their destination. And it seemed to Emily that with each mile that passed, the ferocity of the wind dropped just a little, the snowfall becoming less and less impenetrable.

She wasn't sure whether the ride to the coast took one hour or four—after the first few minutes the landscape all seemed to merge into one—but as she rounded the corner of a large yellow building, Emily saw the ocean about a quarter mile ahead of them.

They had made it.

CHAPTER TWENTY-SEVEN

Emily was surprised at how still the Arctic Ocean was. It was more like a lake than any of the oceans she had ever seen in real life or on TV. Waves of dirty gray water lapped gently at the snow-covered shoreline, the only movement on an otherwise glasslike surface.

Prudhoe Bay was a horseshoe-shaped concavity about four miles across at its mouth. In the distance Emily could see a set of huge tanks jutting up above the horizon on the opposite side of the bay; ahead of her the bay curved away toward the distant horizon.

She brought the Cat to a halt at what she judged was a safe distance from the shoreline. It was impossible to judge exactly where the land ended and the sand or shale or whatever lay beneath the snow started.

Her view was substantially better than it had been when they first set out; the snow had seemed to almost fade to nothing as they'd neared the coast. Still, low clouds covered the sky from horizon to horizon, making it difficult to see much farther than a mile or so.

"It's beautiful," said Rhiannon.

Emily supposed it was, in its own way. Not exactly her first choice of where she would want to spend the rest of her life, but at least she had a life to look forward to, unlike the majority of humanity.

Her eyes followed the coast as it curved off to her right, then headed north. About a mile off from their location, Emily could see a spit of land jutting off from the coastline. A large blue building sat at the end of it, about five hundred feet out into the bay.

"I think that's where we need to be," she said to Rhiannon, pointing so the girl could see. "That's the dock where Jacob said we would find the boat."

The engine growled back into life as Emily accelerated the Cat toward the distant dock. A relatively clear access road appeared from the snow as they approached the point where the offshoot of land jutted out into the water. It extended up toward the blue building, so Emily turned the Cat onto it, relieved to be on a solid surface for the first time in almost seven hundred miles.

The building was made from huge sheets of corrugated steel with a large gap at the southern end, big enough for the Cat to easily drive through with room to spare. There didn't appear to have ever been doors to the building, or if there had been, they were long gone. She parked the Cat in a space below a set of metal stairs that led up to a second-level office, reached by a gangway that ran around the perimeter of the building.

Rhiannon was out of the Cat before Emily could stop her. She'd jumped down to the ground and had run around to Emily's side of the vehicle, closely followed by Thor, before Emily had even managed to open her own door.

"Careful," Emily yelled, stooping to pick up the Mossberg. The smell of brine and ozone filled her lungs as she stepped off the track of the Cat onto the ground next to Rhiannon.

The seaward side of the building had a large section of its wall cut away, exposing the concrete floor to the sea. Emily assumed that was to allow boats to pull into the building and discharge their cargo and any passengers out of reach of the kind of storm she had just driven through.

There were two boats tied to mooring bollards. One looked like it was a tug boat or a fishing trawler. It bobbed up and down, pulling against the mooring, old automobile tires tied around the body of the boat banging against the concrete dock. There was no way in hell she was going to be able to pilot that thing.

The second boat, moored at the opposite end of the dock, was a lot smaller. Emily judged it to be about twenty or so feet in length; its shape reminded her of some of the fishing boats she would see out on the lakes back in Denison, Iowa, when she was growing up. It had an enclosed cabin, about the same size as the Sno-Cat, with several radio masts and what Emily took to maybe be a radar system of some kind. She wasn't sure. At the back of the boat were two large outboard motors. Printed along the side of the hull in red were the words: UNIVERSITY OF ALASKA FAIRBANKS—CLIMATE RESEARCH.

That was the boat they were looking for.

"Stay away from the edge," Emily warned as Rhiannon took a couple of inquisitive steps closer to the boat.

"Do you know how to drive this?" she asked, looking back over her shoulder at Emily as she ran her hands down the hull of the larger boat.

"You 'pilot' a boat," Emily corrected her. "And I have absolutely no clue."

■ ■ ■

Rhiannon handed Emily the last of the supplies from the pile they had made on the dockside. Emily stowed them in a back corner of the wheelhouse and on one of the six seats the boat sported.

The controls of the boat were similar to the Dodge Durango and the Sno-Cat only in that they all had a steering wheel. That was about where the similarity ended. There were several gauges and indicators on the control console that Emily figured had something to do with the speed, oil pressure, and wind direction. A black box with a dull LCD screen was perched just behind the steering wheel, and Emily again assumed that this was some kind of navigation instrument similar to a GPS, or maybe it was a sonar. She had no idea. There were no brake or accelerator pedals, just a handle to the right of the captain's chair that she thought was probably the throttle for the two big engines at the back of the boat. Next to that was the slot for the ignition; the key had been helpfully sitting on the captain's seat when they'd arrived. To the right of the ignition a large red button read: ENGINE START.

She had no idea what any of the gizmos or other dials actually did, nor did she think that she needed to. "You just need to start the engine and point it north along the coast," Jacob had explained to her. "It's a double hull, so it's really stable. Just don't hit anything, and you'll be fine." She hoped he was right, because she was sure that if she capsized them, they wouldn't last more than two minutes in these frigid ice-strewn waters.

"Is that the last of it?" she asked.

Rhiannon nodded enthusiastically. "That's it, Cap'n," she said, in a pretty good impression of Johnny Depp's character from the *Pirates of the Caribbean* movies. She had been using the same accent and addressing Emily as Cap'n ever since they had started switching the supplies from the Cat to the boat. Rhia was dreadfully impressed with her own mimicry, apparently, because a fit of giggles always followed the sentence.

Emily didn't mind; given the circumstances, it was good to hear the kid laughing. And it helped relieve the tension she felt about taking the boat out.

The SUV and Cat had been one thing: she knew where the brakes were and could always stop and just get out if the need arose. But this was something totally different. The closest she had ever come to a boat was watching a rerun of *Titanic* on TV. If something went wrong out there, she could end up drowning the both of them.

Just stick close to the coastline, and you'll be fine, Jacob's memory reminded her again.

"Okay, you landlubber," Emily said, playing along with her own best pirate voice. "Let's untie that knotty rope thing over there and see what we can do, shall we?"

Rhiannon pulled at the knot of the rope tied to the mooring bollard, tossing it onto the deck of the boat, narrowly missing Thor, who had already made himself comfortable next to the supplies. Emily took Rhiannon's hand and helped her leap into the boat, which was already beginning to bob away from the concrete dock.

She made her way back into the wheelhouse and sat in the captain's chair. "Best sit down," she said to Rhiannon. She turned the key to the "on" position and pressed the big red button next to it.

There was a sound like metal rubbed against metal, then each of the two engines coughed once, billowed a gray puff of smoke, and sparked into life, kicking a fountain of water into the air. The boat immediately began to move forward, heading straight for the tugboat on the opposite side of the dock.

"Oh, shit," said Rhiannon, instantly throwing her hand over her mouth, her eyes betraying her surprise at letting slip a cuss-word in front of Emily. If Emily had noticed, she didn't let on; she was too busy turning the wheel frantically to the right, trying to avoid the slowly but inexorably approaching bigger vessel.

The boat began to turn...sharply. It missed the other boat, but now it was heading toward the metal wall of the shed separating the sea from the inside of the dock. She spun the wheel in the opposite direction, this time not so hard. The pointy end of the boat began to gradually drift away from the wall as it leveled out. When the sides of the boat were parallel with the dock and the opposite wall, Emily moved the wheel back to the center position and, after a couple more minor corrections, managed to get the boat moving in a straight line.

She aimed the front of the boat for the gap that led out to the ocean beyond, her hand hovering over the throttle lever but still too unsure to touch it.

They coasted through the opening and into the open water, bouncing on the rougher waves beyond the dock building. The front of the boat dipped suddenly and rose dramatically before dropping down onto the surface with a splash that rocked the inside of the vessel. Emily dropped her hand to the throttle and pushed slowly, listening to the throb of the engines increase as the boat began to pick up speed. The pointy bit—wasn't it called the prow?—began to cut through the waves, which, contrary to her beachside observation, were a hell of a lot bigger than they had looked from the safety of the Sno-Cat's cabin.

The incoming tide pushed back against the engines, and Emily had the distinct impression that they weren't actually mov-ing. Although how she was supposed to judge whether she was making any kind of headway was kind of beyond her. Everything out there seemed to be moving, and any object that she could use to judge her speed by was either too far away or shrouded by the clouds and falling snow.

"Screw it," she said and pushed the throttle lever forward. This time the engines roared, and there was no doubt that they were moving as the prow lifted slightly off the ocean's surface and pushed Emily and Rhiannon back into their seats.

"Wow!" said Rhiannon as the boat bounced and tilted over the waves, the coast a couple of hundred feet off the right of the boat now as Emily swung parallel to it and followed Jacob's instructions, heading north along its rocky edge.

They were moving fast, water spraying across the glass of the wheelhouse. Emily almost pulled back on the throttle; her hand hovered over it as she considered what she should do next. It would be the safest thing to do, but she was so tired of all this. Tired of the constant stress and worry and driving and eating shitty meals and more driving. Tired of always being afraid and, dear God almighty, she was so very, very tired of traveling. She just wanted to lie in a bed and know that she was going to be sleeping in it the next night and the night after that. To eat a hot meal and have someone who wasn't a teenager to talk to.

She wanted for all of this to finally be over.

That reality was now just forty miles or so away. They were almost there.

Her hand dropped to her side as she let the boat speed on.

CHAPTER TWENTY-EIGHT

Emily was convinced the temperature had dropped at least ten degrees since they'd left the harbor. There was a heater in the cabin, but it was struggling, working overtime just to keep the temperature above freezing. Rhiannon had situated herself next to it, blocking the flow of warm air into the cabin, which didn't really help.

They had left the confines of Prudhoe Bay and entered the open sea beyond. As Emily had banked the boat around the outcrop that marked the entrance to the bay, a stronger crosscurrent caught the boat and slammed them sideways, pushing them rapidly toward the coast. The boat pitched and tossed like a roller coaster as Emily fought the wheel to keep from beaching.

"Oh my God. I'm going to throw up," burped Rhiannon, her face turning green.

Emily ignored her and kept turning the wheel until the boat was facing out to sea again, then she powered up the engines and fought back against the waves that grabbed at the keel of the craft.

She pushed the throttle all the way to 75 percent and felt the propellers push the boat forward, cutting through the waves as they sped back out to sea. Judging they were far enough from the shore to not risk becoming grounded, Emily turned the boat back onto its new eastern heading and looked over at Rhiannon, who was still looking a little green but had managed to keep her food down. Thor was curled up in the corner, fast asleep and apparently oblivious to how close they had come to becoming a shipwreck.

They saw the first iceberg fifteen minutes later; it wasn't very big, not much more than a ten-foot-by-fifteen-foot sheet of ice floating on the surface of the sea. But Emily gave it a wide birth, memories of the movie *Titanic* rising once again to the surface.

An iceberg! It was all a little too surreal.

■ ■ ■

An hour later they spotted the family of polar bears. There were three of them—a mother and two cubs—sauntering along the shoreline, their white coats stained brown with mud as they dipped their heads to examine rock-pools or lifted their noses to the wind, sniffing inquisitively.

Emily slowed the boat and joined Rhiannon in gawking at the sight. Even Thor seemed excited, watching from the back of the boat, his paws resting on a shelf so he could get a better look. It would have been a beautiful sight even before the devastation of the red rain. Seeing this first hint that there was still hope that some life had escaped the rain's effects, well, it was just magical.

"Look how big they are," said Rhiannon. "I never thought they would be so big." The kid was right; the adult had to weigh at least four hundred pounds.

When momma bear stopped and turned to face the boat, taking a couple of tentative steps out into the ocean toward them, Emily decided they might be hungrier than they looked and eased the throttle forward, quickly putting some distance between the bears and the boat as she accelerated east.

Jacob had told them to look for maps when they were on board the boat, and they had found a bunch of them stowed in a drawer. Emily had reassigned Rhiannon her old job as navigator and set her to work finding a map that showed their destination. Rhiannon had quickly found one labeled "McClure and Stockton Islands and Vicinity" and laid it out on the floor where she could get a good look at it.

Glancing down at the map from behind the wheel, Emily thought it didn't look like any kind of map she had ever seen. It gave a detailed outline of the coastline, but the sea was filled with squiggly lines and numbers that she thought probably represented the depth of the sea in those locations.

Emily couldn't afford to take her attention off piloting the boat, so she was relying on Rhiannon to accurately predict their position, which she seemed to be very good at. She had quickly ascertained their position after leaving Prudhoe Bay and was calling out landmarks before they even appeared.

"This is Foggy Island Bay," she had announced at one point. "There's going to be something called a shoal coming up." A few minutes later they had passed the shoal, a collection of elongated sandbars that formed a natural harbor. "Now we need to keep heading east, toward…" She paused as she tried to pronounce the name of the upcoming landmark. "Tig…Tig…Var…Iak. Tigvariak Island!" Rhiannon picked up the map and folded it so it was small enough to carry, staggering over to Emily as the boat bucked and rolled.

"Here's where we are." She tapped a finger against the coast-line. "And here's Tigvariak Island." Her finger traced an imaginary line to a largish island just off the coast of the mainland. "And then," she continued, "we just have to head this way to get to Jacob's island." She unfolded the top of the map to reveal the group of islands collectively known as the Stocktons, sitting about six miles farther out to sea and northeast of the farthest tip of Tigvariak Island.

Jacob was on the largest of the islands: Pole Island, a scythe-shaped mass of land approximately four miles in length and a quarter-mile wide.

It took the little boat another two hours to reach Tigvariak Island, a desolate-looking lump of rock that looked to be nothing more than rolling tundra. As Emily steered the boat along the craggy west coast of the island, she felt her nerves begin to get the better of her. They were about to head out into open ocean, and soon after they would be miles from land, with no navigational equipment other than the large compass on the boat's control panel. As long as she kept the boat heading in a northeast direction, there was little chance that they would miss the little cluster of islands, but the idea of being so far from land made her very uneasy.

She had come this far using Jacob's advice to guide her, and he had not been wrong so far, she reminded herself. If he said she could do it, then she had better believe she could.

There were only a few miles of their journey left. And she'd be damned if she was going to turn back now.

■ ■ ■

The coast of Alaska was a distant shadow on the horizon behind them as the little boat continued to bounce and cleave its way northeast through the swell of the Arctic Ocean. The farther away from land they moved, the more icebergs they saw in the water. While most of them were small clumps of floating white that bobbed harmlessly by, occasionally they would spot a larger sheet of ice that could easily put a hole in the hull of the boat. Emily had stationed Rhiannon up front with her; her younger eyes were better equipped to spot the dangerous bergs well before they got too close. Emily steered around them, hoping that these minor adjustments to their voyage would not throw them too far off from their original course.

The sea had become rougher, too. Huge swells lifted the boat, then dropped them down again, sending waves of water onto the deck outside their enclosed cabin. To the west Emily could see a bank of black clouds that descended from the sky down to sea level. It looked to be heading their way, and Emily hoped to God that they made it to shore before the storm caught up with them.

Rhiannon had spotted the storm, too, and she was in the process of explaining that she thought they were only a few miles offshore of Pole Island when a huge wave struck the boat, sending the prow almost vertical before dropping it again, slamming the hull into the ocean's surface.

Emily screamed and clung on to the wheel as it suddenly seemed to gain a life all its own. Rhiannon and Thor both squealed in unison and slipped across the floor toward the back of the cabin. Rhiannon managed to grab the back of a chair and steady herself, but Thor collided with the rear wall and yelped in pain and fright.

"Hold on," yelled Emily as another wave lifted them sideways, then deposited them unceremoniously down again with a thunderous splash. Thor skidded back toward the front of the cabin, his paws scrambling for grip but finding no purchase on the plastic floor. He collided squarely with the back of Emily's calves, buckling her knees and sending her toppling astern, her hands slipping off the metal of the boat's wheel. She slid backward and collided with the bottom edge of a seat, yelling in pain as, even through the layers of cold-weather gear, the plastic cut painfully across her shoulders.

Rhiannon looked mortified. She clung to her chair like a life preserver as the boat bucked and thrashed, hitting wave after wave, the wheel spinning wildly back and forth.

"Tie yourself down," Emily yelled to Rhiannon, pointing to the black safety belt that hung limply from the seat as she crawled her way back toward the captain's chair. Rhiannon dragged herself into the seat and grabbed the safety belt, clicking it into place as she gripped the base of the chair with both hands as tightly as she could.

Emily reached out for the support that fixed the captain's chair to the deck and grabbed it. She looked back toward the back of the cabin for Thor; he was scrambling toward her. She grabbed the big dog's collar and heaved him toward her, sliding the terrified dog over the floor. When she was sure she had a firm grip, she pulled Thor up to her and then pushed him into the space between the seat support and the flat of the boat's control console, jamming him in as best she could. When he was safe, she pulled herself to her feet and flung herself into the captain's seat. She jammed her feet under Thor's belly so he couldn't move and quickly fastened her own seat belt into place. Then she grabbed the wheel and glanced at the compass; the boat was now heading west.

"Shit!" Emily turned the wheel, fighting the rogue waves as they tried to force the boat in the direction they wanted to take it. She thrust the throttle forward until it would go no farther. The boat instantly swung around, the engines thrusting them up the front of another wave and through it this time, rather than over. She couldn't see anything through the haze of water kicked up by the speeding boat as it sliced the ocean apart.

Emily glanced down at the control panel, located the switch she was looking for, and pushed it. The two large wipers began throwing the water off the glass windshield, and within seconds she could see clearly again.

Ahead of them, not more than a quarter mile away, appearing out of the spray like Avalon from the mist, was the shadowy outline of land.

CHAPTER TWENTY-NINE

Emily could see a fragile-looking wooden dock sticking out from a shale beach that sloped down to meet the crashing waves.

She fought the wheel and used what little strength she still had left to turn it until the prow of the boat was heading toward it. The waves were still roaring in fast and hard, smashing against the side of the boat, and she could feel the current trying to drag them away from the rapidly approaching beach. She was half-tempted to reduce the boat's speed to the minimum needed to make headway and plant the boat, pointy end first, into the shale of the beach. It looked deep enough to slow them.

But Jacob had warned her that this boat was their only way to escape off the island when the time came. If she damaged it, there was no guarantee they had the tools or expertise to fix it. Or worse still, she might plant the boat in the shale and sink the damn thing, or it could even be swept out to sea, and them along with it, with no way to beach it.

No, she was going to have to try to bring it in alongside the jetty and secure it.

Here we go again, she thought as she eased the throttle down and tried to judge the best angle to reach the dock safely.

The boat pitched hard to the left, scraping the front side along the wooden dock, cracking a plank and sending the pieces flying through the air. Emily resisted the urge to turn the wheel all the way to the right, which would just send the back end crashing into the dock, too; this needed finesse.

The swell was not as strong this close to the shore, but the waves were hitting more frequently, so she needed to constantly adjust the boat's attitude. She eased the throttle to just above the "stop" marker and angled the front of the boat slightly away from the side of the dock as the beach drew rapidly closer.

"Slow down, damn you," she hissed through clenched teeth. "Slow. The. Fuck. Down."

Now she was just a passenger.

The boat gave a final lurch forward, then stopped, bobbing like a fishing float on the ocean's surface, a few feet from the edge of the dock.

Close enough, she judged.

Emily unfastened her seat belt and ran to the back of the cabin. Flinging open the door, she grabbed the mooring rope from the deck and launched herself over the side of the boat before it could drift any farther away. She landed on the jetty and ran to the nearby mooring bollard, unreeling the rope behind her.

How the hell was she supposed to tie this thing off so it wouldn't float away?

The cold wind beat against her and spray from the sea soaked her unprotected head with freezing water, sending stinging droplets of salt water into her eyes. If she stood there much longer she was going to either freeze or get blown into the water and drown. Emily strained against the rope, pulling as hard as she could to get the boat closer to the shore. She looped the end of the rope around the metal bollard and then tied it off the only way she knew how, with a bow. It might look weird, but at least she knew it was a secure knot…and it added a little panache, too. A win-win situation if you asked her.

She leaped carefully back onto the deck of the boat, slipping on the wet surface, before opening the door to the cabin. She could hear the engines still idling, barely audible against the crashing of the waves against the shore and the wind that whipped past the cabin.

Inside she pressed the same red button she had to start the engines and felt rather than heard the purr of the engines slowly die away.

Emily turned to Rhiannon and just looked at her. It was as if the whole world had suddenly stopped rotating. Here she was, how many days and how many thousands of miles later?

She was finally here.

It felt as though she had been holding her breath from the moment she had first seen the red rain fall that fateful day.

A sense of peace, almost serenity, washed over her.

"Grab your stuff," Emily said finally. "We're almost home."

■ ■ ■

"Just your backpack for now," Emily told Rhiannon. "We'll come back for the rest of the supplies tomorrow, when we have some extra pairs of hands."

Rhiannon nodded and placed the backpack over her shoulders. "I'll take Thor," she said.

Emily was confident her knot would hold the boat in place, but she was only leaving nonessential food supplies behind just in case she was wrong. From what Jacob had told her, the research team had more than enough to last if the worst should happen and the boat was swept away or the supplies were damaged. Emily grabbed the key from the ignition and secured it in her jacket pocket.

"Ready?" she asked as she swung her backpack up onto her shoulders and slipped the flashlight into the side pocket.

The smile pasted across Rhiannon's face was answer enough. Emily swung open the door and held it open. The cabin was instantly filled with spray driven in by the wind. Rhiannon slipped past Emily and leaped up onto the dock.

Having traveled the majority of the last eight days or so in comparative luxury to the bike ride that had started her journey, Emily was not surprised at how heavy the backpack felt as she made her way to the back of the boat.

"Come on, Thor," the girl called from the dock. The dog followed her obediently, leaping across the space between the dock and the boat as though it were nonexistent. He stood next to Rhiannon, waiting for Emily to join them, the fur of his gray coat ruffling and flying in the wind, his eyes crinkled against the constant ocean spray.

Once Emily was safely on the dock, the three new arrivals to the island began walking the seventy feet or so to land. The wooden dock extended up the beach before abutting up against a roughly constructed concrete path that, judging from the cracks and missing chunks, had seen better days. The concrete path wound up the rising beach and disappeared between two mounds of shale.

As they reached the top of the path, Emily saw a cluster of buildings in the distance. A pole with a blinking red light atop it jutted into the air at the center of the camp.

"Why does only one of them have lights on?" asked Rhiannon, referring to the slivers of orange light they could see seeping from the windows of the largest of the buildings.

"They are probably trying to conserve power," Emily replied, struggling to be heard over the wind that seemed intent on blowing them off the island.

At least they knew in which building they would find Jacob and the team now, she thought as they angled off the path toward the light.

On the eastern side of the building, Emily could see a heavy metal door set slightly back in a recessed alcove. At the door's center was a large metal wheel.

Emily took the wheel in both hands and twisted it. It turned freely, squeaking loudly as it rotated. There was a dull metallic clunk, and the door opened slightly.

"Inside," she said to Rhiannon and Thor, pulling the door wide enough for them all to slip through and then pulling it closed again behind them. There was a second wheel on the inside, and she spun that until the door closed securely.

They found themselves inside a room; it was small, about twelve feet in length with hooks on either wall from which hung cold-weather gear. A dim light set in the ceiling illuminated a set of wooden benches running low along the walls, and beneath those were several pairs of boots.

A second door at the opposite end of the room had a simple lever to open it.

Emily pulled the door open and stepped through into a larger room with scattered tables, seats, and a set of metal lockers on the right. A coffeepot—empty—sat on a desk next to a tray of plastic mugs and condiments. A refrigerator hummed next to it.

The room was deserted, but a corridor, with several thick pipes running along the ceiling, extended off from the room to her left, disappearing in an abrupt right turn farther along.

"Hello," she called out. "Is there anybody here?"

From somewhere along the corridor the sound of a door opening was accompanied by a ringing harmony of voices and music. The Beach Boys, "California Girls," if I'm not mistaken, Emily thought. The music stopped. Either the door had been closed again or someone had switched off the music.

"Hello?" she called again. "It's Emily and Rhiannon. We're... here."

"And Thor," said Rhiannon as she stroked the dog's head. "Don't forget Thor."

Another sound reached them now: a high-pitched squeak, then a slight pause followed by another squeak, slowly getting louder as it approached them. Thor's head tilted slightly, his ears perking up as an unsure growl bubbled up from his throat.

"Shush," Emily chided him. "It's okay, boy."

A man, roughly thirty Emily guessed, with a neatly trimmed dark-brown beard and a pair of glasses perched on his nose appeared from around the corner of the corridor.

He stopped for a moment and stared at the three visitors.

Thor gave another uncertain growl but quieted at the touch of Emily's hand on his head.

"Hello, Emily. Hello, Rhiannon," said the stranger, a smile breaking across his pale face as he rolled his wheelchair into the room. "I'm Jacob, and it is so very nice to finally meet you both in person."

CHAPTER THIRTY

The wheelchair was a surprise to Emily.

Jacob had never mentioned anything about being disabled. But then why would he? It was hardly relevant.

Emily had imagined how this moment would be, this first meeting between them. She had a little speech ready, but she found herself unable to speak a word of it. Instead she walked over to him, placed her arms gently around his neck, and whispered into his ear, "Thank you," soaking the collar of his shirt with the tears that had begun to flow even before she had taken a step.

Rhiannon joined them for the group hug; even Thor came over and gave Jacob an exploratory sniff.

"Let's get you out of that gear," he said after Emily and Rhia finally broke away. "Maybe you'd like a shower or something to eat?"

"I'd love to meet the rest of your team," Emily replied.

"Of course, but why don't I get you to your room first? You can freshen up and then we'll deal with that. Okay?"

"Sure," Emily replied with a smile. He was politely letting them know that they smelled worse than a week-old dead cat, she realized. "Lead the way."

Jacob accompanied them from the first room, Emily on one side of the wheelchair and Rhiannon on the other. "This is my room," he said, indicating a door on the right of the corridor. "And these two are yours. I assumed you wouldn't mind having a room apiece?"

Emily welcomed the idea of some privacy, but she worried about Rhiannon. The two of them had been sharing the same space for so long now, she wasn't sure whether the girl would be reticent about being alone. That concern disappeared as she watched Rhia disappear inside the room with her bag. "See you later," she said, smiling from the doorway.

"When you're done, just head down the corridor to your right. The first big room on your left is the meeting room."

Rhiannon nodded to Jacob and disappeared inside, leaving the two adults alone in the corridor.

"I'd better get freshened up."

"And I'll go rustle up some dinner for you guys. You must be starving."

■ ■ ■

Thirty minutes later there was a quiet knock on Emily's door.

"Can I come in?" asked Rhiannon.

Emily pulled the sweater she had just removed from the backpack over her head and reached for the door handle. She had forgotten just how pretty Rhiannon was; the girl had been hidden under layers of clothes and grime for so long now. Standing in the doorway was a girl transformed. Her long blonde hair fell freely over her shoulder, newly washed and shiny. She had on a pair of loose blue jogging pants and a turtleneck sweater and the biggest smile she had ever seen from the kid.

"They have a hair dryer," she whispered, as though it was the greatest discovery of her young life. Emily understood. After stepping out of the shower, she had luxuriated in the feeling of the hot air of her own dryer.

"You look beautiful," she told the girl. Rhia blushed at the compliment.

"Well, I think it's time we went and introduced ourselves to everyone, don't you?"

Rhiannon nodded in excitement.

Thor was laying on the bed, his head over the edge, tail thumping against the sheets.

"Come on," she told the malamute. "Let's go do this."

■ ■ ■

Jacob was waiting in the meeting room for the new arrivals. On the table in the center of the room were two plates with metal warming covers to keep the food hot. A pitcher of water and another of orange juice rested nearby, with a complement of glasses and cutlery.

"I saved something special for Thor," said Jacob, and he reached for a bowl of what looked like chopped beef roast, placing it on the floor for the dog, who began devouring the food with his usual gusto.

"Quite the appetite," remarked Jacob.

Emily lifted the cover off her plate and revealed a burger between two buns. There was a side of lettuce and onions, along with a couple of packets of ketchup and mayonnaise.

"I didn't know if you liked lettuce on your burger or not, but I did assume you wanted cheese," he continued, beckoning to Rhiannon to join him at the table. "Enjoy."

"Oh my God," Rhiannon said after taking her first bite of the burger. A look of utter bliss swept across her face. Here was a girl who had found nirvana.

Emily couldn't help herself, she laughed, spraying a fine mist of her own burger—which was as delicious as she had imagined it would be—over the table.

Rhiannon choked down her own bite of the burger and coughed. "Sorry," she said, snickering.

"Wow! What a great first impression we've made," laughed Emily after she swallowed her food. "Sorry about that, it's just the tension…This is just all such a relief."

Jacob joined them in their laughter, raising both hands in a gesture of détente. "Not a problem at all, ladies."

They ate the rest of the food in silence, savoring the flavors and the full feeling as their stomachs began to process the burgers. It was the first real food they had eaten since leaving Stuyvesant.

"That was delicious," said Emily after finishing. "Thank you."

"You're more than welcome. There's dessert. Parfaits, if you would like one?" Rhiannon nodded her head enthusiastically; Emily declined. Jacob wheeled himself over to a small refrigerator and pulled out a plastic container of parfait, complete with a disposable plastic spoon attached to the lid. "Sure I can't tempt you?" he asked Emily.

"No. Thanks. I think I'll pass."

Rhiannon eagerly dug into the plastic cup of fruit and cream. She devoured it with the same look of bliss she had while eating the burger. The two adults sat back and watched, enjoying the child's pure joy.

Finally, Emily spoke. "Thank you so much for that. I honestly don't know what either of us would have done without you, Jacob. We would have…well…I guess we would have been lost without you."

"I'm just glad you're here, safe and sound," he replied.

"So, do you think we can meet the rest of your team?" she asked, smiling in anticipation.

Jacob bit his bottom lip for a second, dropping his eyes to his immobile feet. When he raised them again, it was to meet Emily's expectant gaze.

"There is nobody else," he said finally.

"What? I'm sorry. What did you say?"

"There is nobody else," he repeated. "It's just me."

CHAPTER THIRTY-ONE

There. Is. Nobody. Else.

Even when she sounded them out individually, the words just did not fit together as a sentence. They didn't seem to want to stay still in Emily's brain long enough for her to rationalize what Jacob really meant by them. They kept sliding around, bouncing off of each other, refusing to form any recognizable meaning.

"What?" she repeated for the third or fourth time.

"I know you're probably confused, and I know you're probably very upset, but I just need you to hear me out, okay? I need you to understand why I had to do what I did."

Emily couldn't quite fathom what he was saying. "But you said you had a team. What about your team?"

"They left, not long after the rain began. They wanted to head back to Fairbanks and check it out. I volunteered to stay to keep the place running. They said they would be back. They never came back."

Emily thought about the convoy full of dead people on the road to Fairbanks and the murdered men and women she had found in Deadhorse. Could any of them have been a part of Jacob's team? she wondered.

She glanced over at Rhiannon. Her mouth was agape as she stared hard at Jacob. "Emily?" she asked. "What does he mean?" Her voice cracked with uncertainty.

"I don't know, sweetheart. But why don't you come on over here beside me while we figure this out?" She patted the seat next to her. The sound of the chair scraping across the floor as Rhiannon jumped to her feet and ran to Emily's side was grating in the suddenly painful silence filling the room. "Good girl," she said, placing a reassuring hand on the kid's knee as she took the chair next to Emily.

Jacob began to wheel his chair over to where the two women sat. "I really can expl—"

Emily jumped to her feet. "Stay right where you are," she bellowed. "Do not fucking come anywhere near us."

Jacob froze, a look of utter horror crossing his face.

Thor, who had been dozing quietly under the table, was suddenly at Emily's side. He sat down next to her, his eyes focused on Jacob.

Jacob swallowed hard and backed up from the trio, very aware of Thor's silent lupine gaze. "I had no choice," he said after a pause, his voice as calm and soothing as it had been during their countless telephone conversations. "If I had told you I was here alone, would you have come?"

Emily didn't answer.

"No, of course you wouldn't. You would have thought I was some kind of nut job, and you wouldn't have come here. You would have just stayed in your apartment and waited. And you would have died."

Rhiannon began to quietly cry, fat tears trickling over her cheeks and staining the front of her jogging pants. Emily switched her arm from the child's knee and wrapped it around her shoulder, never taking her eyes off Jacob.

"I told the team not to leave," he continued. "I warned them that they should stay. But they had families, wives, mothers, kids. Someone had to stay. Someone had to. But I knew. I knew that they wouldn't be coming back." His voice had taken on a tone of sadness, maybe even mixed with frustration. "When I found you, Emily, I knew I couldn't tell you I was here alone, so I lied. I'm sorry, but I had to try to save you."

"And what about your wife? Sandra, wasn't it? She was supposed to be back at Fairbanks University. Was any of that true?"

Jacob could not meet her gaze. He chose to stare at his feet and shake his head in answer.

"You risked mine and Rhiannon's life to try to save your own skin? Is what you did?" she yelled, suddenly on her feet, her voice livid with anger. "You brought us all the way here to rescue you? You fucking piece of shit." Emily's words hit Jacob like hammer blows; she could see him physically reeling as each word struck home.

Good!

"You were stranded here, and you needed us to come and rescue you? All that…that sanctimonious posturing about wanting to save me, it's just bullshit you use to convince yourself that you were doing the right thing, isn't it? Answer me, goddamn you!"

Emily had to admit, the look of hurt on his face was good. *He actually believes what he said,* she thought. She shook her head at him in complete disbelief.

"Wow! Just wow."

Rhiannon threw her arms around Emily's waist, sinking her head deeper into her shoulder as she sobbed. Emily could feel the dampness of Rhia's tears seeping through the material of her sweater.

Jacob took a deep breath, composing himself, then spoke. His voice was level and clear, free of any hint of anger. "Yes, you're somewhat right. I did want you to come and rescue me, but it was an added benefit. I have enough food here to last me a year, probably a lot longer. But most of all I wanted to help you, Emily. You were the only person I knew for certain was still alive, and I wanted to save you. I didn't make anything else up. Everything I told you about traveling north was true. You've seen that for yourself. I did not lie to you about any of that."

Emily bent in and kissed the crying girl on the forehead. "It's okay. It's okay," she said, not sure if she was trying to convince Rhiannon or herself. What was she supposed to believe? There was no doubt that he was not lying about the cold holding back the spread of the alien infestation, but everything else had the thin veneer of pretense to it. How was she supposed to trust him? Where was she supposed to go? Where could she go? God! She thought she had left all the pain and stress behind her when they'd stepped onto the island. Instead, she was handed a whole new package of BS.

"You had me riding a fucking bike here, Jacob," she whispered, her voice heavy with disappointment as the anger began to seep away, replaced by a feeling of emptiness.

Jacob pushed his wheelchair closer to the two girls. "Look," he said, keeping his voice low. "I know I screwed up by not telling you, and I am truly sorry. But you're here now. You are safe, and I know we can make a go of this. We can figure it all out. I promise you."

Emily had, at least until today, always considered herself a good judge of character. It was something she had honed over the course of her career as a journalist, an essential tool that had served her well. She looked up from Rhiannon and met Jacob's eyes. There was no cruelty there. No deceit. Fear? Yes. Regret? Maybe.

"I'm sorry," he said finally.

From somewhere else in the building a buzzing hissing sound filtered through the still air. It sounded like the static that flowed between AM radio stations. The buzzing became louder, then dropped away, then returned a little stronger as the static finally resolved into a garbled human voice.

"This is ZzzZZZzz HM ZzzzzzZZzzzz ZzzzZZZzzzz. Do yo zzZzzZZzz me?"

All three occupants of the room looked up. A look of stunned disbelief crossed over Jacob's face, and Emily was sure her own face had the same look of astonishment.

It was a man's voice but Emily could only make out the occasional word through the buzz of the interference.

"Who's that?" asked Rhiannon, wiping away the tears and snot from her face with the back of her hands. As if in answer to her question, there was another burst of static, then the man's voice boomed loud and clear down the hallway.

"This is Captain Edward Constantine of her Majesty's Royal Navy submarine HMS *Vengeance*. Do you read me?"

Emily continued to stare at Jacob, unsure of whether she should trust him or just shoot him. Finally, she took a deep breath and spoke.

"Show me where your radio room is."

EPILOGUE

From her perch, high above the world, Commander Mulligan watched as the blanket of red closed over all but the tiniest sliver of North America.

The warning she had issued to the survivors on the planet's surface regarding the storm's destructive potential had been greatly underestimated, she had come to realize. That storm had been only the forerunner of something much larger. Something far more awesome.

Over the past six days she had witnessed more and more storms form over the earth's major landmasses, seething pools of blood that swirled and flowed across continents and seas. She had watched them gestate; growing from tiny spots of red before gradually expanding, reaching out with crimson feelers to find and merge with other systems, each growing in size and ferocity with every orbit the ISS made around the earth.

She had managed to count eight of these massive storms, each one at least a thousand miles across, before, like their earlier incarnations, they, too, had begun searching out and connecting with each other. A continual barrage of lightning, each bolt hundreds of miles in length, exploded silently across the anvil of the planet, illuminating the storms from within like some grand light show.

Over the course of days, each storm found the other, and when they touched they fused into a single, massive superstorm, which in turn gradually expanded to blanket the world in a swirling pall of vermilion cloud.

That storm had grown exponentially in ferocity and size until it blotted out everything but two small cones of blue over each of the planet's poles.

And what would emerge from that chaos below her? she wondered. Who could say? She was certain, though, that if the red curtain was ever lifted, the world it revealed would be a very different place from what any of them had known. A small part of her welcomed the fact that she would never set foot on her planet again.

Fiona wondered how Emily had fared. Had they made it? She would never meet the woman, but she had sounded strong, had struck her as a more than capable individual. If anyone could have made that incredible journey, she believed it would have been Emily. Still, the silence she had met with each time she tried to reestablish contact with Jacob had been disconcerting.

It did not bode well for the tiny group of survivors.

"God help them," she whispered to the invisible world beneath her.

Far, far below the station, a dark-red cataract within the storm raged over what had once been Alberta, Canada.

"God help them all."

ACKNOWLEDGMENTS

My thanks to everyone involved in helping to make this second book a reality. In no particular order, they are: David Pomerico and his 47North team members who do such a fine job of finding and eliminating my spelling and grammatical errors (of which there are a lot!), promoting my books, and catering to my every whim and desire.

A very special mention goes to my developmental editor Jeff VanderMeer, whose patience in the face of my frustration was inexhaustible(ish). Much appreciated.

I would also like to thank the Tucker Sno-Cat Corporation for sending me photos of the interior of the Sno-Cat vehicle featured in this book. I really want to try one of those things out someday.

And the good people of Coldfoot, Alaska who gave me guidance on the layout of their camp, despite the fact that I killed them all off in the book. That's going above and beyond the call, in my opinion.

To my wife, and biggest fan, Karen. Thank you, love.

And last, but most definitely not least, I would like to thank you, my readers. I cannot tell you how amazing it is to receive your emails and tweets telling me how much you enjoy reading Emily's story. Keep 'em coming.

Thank you.

ABOUT THE AUTHOR

A native of Cardiff, Wales, Paul Antony Jones now resides in Las Vegas, Nevada. He has worked as a newspaper reporter and commercial copywriter, but his passion is penning fiction. A self-described science geek, he's a voracious reader of scientific periodicals, as well as a fan of things mysterious, unknown, and fringe-related. That fascination inspired his first novel, *Extinction Point*, and its first sequel, *Extinction Point: Exodus*. Emily Baxter's adventures will continue in future installments of the series. Join the author's mailing list at DisturbedUniverse.com.